PERMACULTURE

PERMACULTURE

FIONA CAMERON

Flying Swan Press

www.flyingswanpress.com

This edition first published in the UK 2018 by Flying Swan Press, Apt 3657, Chynoweth House, Trevisomme Park, Truro, TR4 8UN

ISBN 978-0-9933314-5-9 mobi

ISBN 978-0-9933314-6-6 paperback

The main action of this book takes place in the space between one waxing gibbous moon and the next, at the year-end of 2012 and the beginning of 2013, in and around the small fishing town of Kirkcudbright, on the Solway Firth coast in SW Scotland.

ONE

It was the surreal colour of the carrots that convinced Fergus Learmonth he had to rescue his wife, Belle.

Perfect, gleaming, sinuous, vermillion cylinders and whorls, topped by feathery leaves that were almost impossibly green for the time of year. They merited a place in a glamorous veg calendar. Carrots grown by Belle's friend Remi in her permaculture plots. Allegedly. Beautiful, but sinister (the vegetables; Fergus found their grower merely sinister).

It had been the first crisp, bright day after a run of dreich ones where you needed the lights on from late morning. All four Learmonths had taken a brisk walk across to the far side of the Dee estuary; the fresh air had put some of the roses back in Belle's cheeks.

Fergus had been contemplating, as he did regularly, how fortunate he was. At the age of fifty-four, he'd become a father for the first time in his life, and the twins (due to turn five in

March) were as clever, good-looking and healthy as anyone could hope for. He had a comely, talented, agreeable wife, and a successful career he not only loved, but one that paid handsomely, now that the crime novels he wrote were selling well in the States. *Fergus Learmonth, the man who has everything.* That single thought brought a frisson of anxiety. He gave himself a mental slap. *Too much of the Puritan upbringing, young man. As if there is a God, never mind one who'd big you up just to slap you down.*

He noticed the stoop in his wife's shoulders as she picked up the Day-Glo vegetables and started to rinse them under the tap. His spirits plummeted.

'What's wrong, Belle?'

She turned those limpid, amber-coloured eyes on him. 'Nothing.' But the smile she gave was wan.

And she looked so *weary*. The twins were exhausting (he'd never harboured any illusions that having exceptionally bright kids is an easier gig than the opposite; having a child at all at forty-five is bound to be a handful, never mind two at once). As they'd grown, she had simply found fresh things to worry about. He'd offered over and over to get help in the house – after all, she'd had that before they met. But she was so touchy these days, he knew better than to suggest it again. Indeed, he'd been choosing his words carefully for years, ever since Belle had that wee wobble after the twins were born. And on top of everything, he knew she was depressed by the fact that the picture gallery she'd owned since she was twenty-five was making no money.

He slid his arms around her waist and rested his cheek against her sleek, fragrant hair. 'Tired?'

'Maybe a little.'

He reached round and gently prised the vegetables from her fingers. He laid them on the draining board. 'Let's go out for supper.'

'It's a shame to waste these, they're so fresh.'

'How does she manage to get freshly-lifted carrots at this time of year? She must be buying them in from someplace like Kenya, same as the supermarkets.'

'Nonsense. She grows them inside the polytunnels, with all that organic compost. It's the same as the way the Victorians used to be able to grow pineapples in the Highlands. The permaculture beds are like an electric blanket. And she has the hot-water pipes from the solar panels. Anyway, see? They're all strange shapes and sizes. You don't get *that* in Tesco, because the EU won't allow it.'

He refused to rise to the bait and get into another argument about the tyranny of Brussels. Belle had been as much of a Europhile as he was until she met Remi. 'I must go and see this set-up of hers sometime,' he said, by way of a peace-offering. He imagined the whole thing would put Heath Robinson to shame.

'You should too. You'll be impressed. Why do you dislike her so much, after all she's done for us?'

'I don't dislike her. I've never felt you had much in common.' That was a downright lie. He detested and mistrusted Remi.

'Well, we do.'

'Fine.'

Belle snorted. 'You don't sound as if you mean it.'

'What's wrong? I don't want to fight with you.' He tightened his arms around her, and his heart flooded with relief as she sighed and relaxed against his chest.

'I'm sorry. You're right – I'm tired.'

'Tell you what, sweetheart. I'll summon the brats and we'll eat at the Roseberry.'

'We haven't booked. And on a Sunday, this close to Christmas.'

'You know they'll always find a space for us. Come on – you don't need to change, do you? That dress looks fine.'

He strode to the bottom of the stairs and called to his children. Two eager faces peered over the landing bannister. Edmund and Esmée. He gazed fondly up at them. They were growing tall. The best kids in the world.

He'd imagined they'd all be settled in Edinburgh by now; in a lofty classical terrace somewhere in the delectable liminal zone between Stockbridge and Dean and the New Town, with a safe walled garden for all of them, animals included. But here they were, still living in the small seaside town of Kirkcudbright, in Ashers, the gracious old mansion Belle had inherited from her adoptive father. It wasn't so bad. Fergus had spent a small fortune on the place over the past five years, but it had been worth it. At least the roof didn't leak now, and the heating worked.

He hoped they weren't stymying the twins' social skills by not having little pals in to play often enough. But no: they were just fine.

'Faces and hands washed please, you two. And Esmée, brush your hair. We're going out for supper.'

'To Aunt Briony's?' asked Edmund hopefully. 'Hurrah!'

The twins loved eating out at the Roseberry Arms. Briony Hall, the owner, had been their mother's friend for more than twenty years, and was the twins' godmother. Spoilt them horribly – but since neither he nor Belle had siblings, maybe it didn't do much harm.

A moment later, the twins were beside him, faces shining, hair brushed, jackets buttoned.

'Scampi!' said Edmund, jumping up and down. 'Scrummy scampi.'

'Or burger!' sang Esmée, pirouetting so that her hair flew out around her like a cloak. 'And *chips*.'

Fergus sighed. Such pedestrian tastes! He'd have preferred his children to be more sophisticated, but they *were* children, for God's sake. Time enough to educate their palettes once the family moved to the capital.

'Maybe those aren't on the menu tonight,' said Belle sternly, emerging into the hallway.

But nothing was ever too much trouble for Briony's chef as far as the twins were concerned. They could have asked for roast swan with white truffle sauce, and he'd have produced it.

At least there was no nonsense about being vegetarian, like those dreadful kids who'd come to their fourth birthday party. Imagine allowing children that age to decide they were vegetarian! Downright irresponsible. That was something they should make up their own minds about once they were old enough to vote.

He chuckled. Another good thing about the Roseberry: no point in inviting Remi to share a meal with them there, since her only tipple was wine made from grapes trampled by virgins under the light of the full moon, or some such tosh. *Biodynamic*. They didn't hold with stuff like that in Briony's establishment.

Fergus lifted his wife's camelhair coat from the hallstand. 'Ready, Belle?'

'I need to get Archie in from the garden. Where's Gorby?'

'Asleep on the sofa,' announced Esmée.

Fergus peered into the sitting room, where the cat was

curled in a ball among his favourite cushions. His throat tightened. The animal seemed to spend more and more of his time asleep, and didn't go outdoors much. He was old; he was nineteen. Fergus tiptoed into the room and smoothed Gorby's still-silky fur; you could feel his bones these days.

Belle's pug, Archie, bounded in, shaking dead leaves from his nose. She rubbed his ears and murmured to him, 'Go and sit with your mogg. We won't be long. I daresay there may be a doggy bag.'

On an impulse, Fergus gathered his wife into his arms again and kissed her. The twins made sick-bucket noises, but he merely laughed. No harm in kids knowing that their parents loved each other – and after all, he and Belle were both experts, having been raised by mothers short on love for anyone but themselves. They'd vowed, when they realised they were to be parents, that they'd never subject their children to the frozen tundra of a loveless marriage.

'Stop it, you'll mess my face!' Belle's voice was suddenly sharp again.

He smiled to himself. She'd always been a nippy sweetie – it was one of the things that had made him fall in love with her. He preferred women with spirit.

Of course, a table was found for them, and the meal was an unqualified success. Fergus loved the Roseberry Arms – the type of solid, respectable, well-maintained hotel that had become so rare in Scotland. Kirkcudbright wouldn't be the same without it. Stability was what counted. The same with Valvona & Crolla, that venerable Edinburgh institution, established in 1934. Every time he entered it, Fergus was transported back to the days when he'd accompany his grandmother on shopping trips there. *Continuity* matters. *Like the observance of ritual, it has a steadying effect in a fast-moving world.*

As they started the short walk home, Fergus slid his arm around Belle's waist, and she rested her head against his shoulder.

The twins charged down the street and vanished into the dark tunnel of the close that led to Ashers.

'See?' said Belle sleepily. 'They couldn't do *that* if we lived in Edinburgh. They're safe here. There's no real crime. No murders, no kidnappings, no street fights or innocent people getting stabbed. Although, I forgot to tell you, when I was swimming yesterday, there were police working their way along the beach, and poking among the bushes, as if they were looking for something. I thought that was a bit odd?'

'Mmmm.' Fergus wasn't listening fully. He was revelling in the way she snuggled against him. Thank God, Remi hadn't managed to drive a wedge between them in *that*.

The twins could be put to bed in short order once they got in. None of the palaver of baths tonight. For God's sake, when he was young you didn't have a bath every night, and civilisation didn't founder. A quick shower and into their rooms, so that he could take his wife to bed.

He supervised his children as they fooled around in the warm spray like otters, struck by how incredibly good-looking they were, with his dark hair and Belle's topaz eyes. Another dozen years and the boys would be round his daughter like bears at a salmon-run. Amazing to think he was responsible for the existence of such superlative human beings.

They'd been the making of him. Without them, he'd not have been the New Fergus. He'd still have been the old one: rootless, arid, miserable, drinking too much whisky and smoking himself towards a slow death. Without them, he and Belle would probably not have married – might not have stayed together, in fact. He'd certainly never have been able to settle to novel-writing as a career.

He'd kill anyone who ever tried to harm his kids in any way. Kill without compunction. The surge of pride and affection was replaced by fear.

Who'd look after them if anything happened to him? *Pushing sixty is pushing sixty, and there are no guarantees.* Belle would cope, but she shouldn't have to do it on her own. And if some catastrophe befell her too, with both his parents and hers long gone, and no aunts or uncles? It'd leave them so exposed. *Childhood is short nowadays. And the Jimmy Savile scandal shows the world's full of people who damage children without a second thought.*

He gave himself a mental shake. 'Right, kids, you're clean now. Out, dried and into bed before I count ten. One... two...'

Esmée tossed her head. 'Don't be *silly*, Daddy.'

He frowned at her. 'And don't you be so cheeky, young lady.'

She was turning into a real little madam, already with the imperious air of her paternal grandmother, the redoubtable Esmée Fairbairn of Inveresk, after whom she was named. Belle tended to spoil her. In fact, he'd only seen her lose her temper with her daughter on a handful of occasions. Most recently when Esmée threw down a miniature watering can, and broke the spout off it. Belle had flown into a rage, and slapped the child. He'd been taken aback – he knew the thing had belonged to his wife for a long time, but it was hardly a valuable antique; it had been falling apart with rust before the child damaged it.

But Esmée *did* need discipline. Fergus felt a pang of sympathy for Eddie, already a little in his sister's shadow.

Fergus wakened early, Belle snuggled under the crook of his arm.

He'd read somewhere that the white heat of passion rarely lasts for more than eighteen months. Then the brain chemistry reverts back to what it was before. And indeed, that was how his previous relationships had been. What he felt for Belle was the slow steady burn of a peat fire rather than the blaze of kiln-dried logs. The sort of heat that keeps you warm for a lifetime.

He laughed softly to himself. If anyone six years earlier had told him the story of a couple who had met when she was forty-five and he was fifty-three, and that their first days of passion had got her with child, and led to the birth of twins nine months later, without a doubt he'd have sniggered and said, 'Shit happens', and poured himself another whisky to toast the fact he had managed to avoid fathering children.

But that was before. That was the old Fergus.

He smiled to himself once more. After the twins were safely born, and obviously in good health, he'd taken himself quietly off to Dumfries and had the snip, because Belle was obviously still fertile. Indeed, she was nowhere near the menopause, as far as he could tell – though it's not something they ever discussed. And although he adored his children, two was enough. The twins had been a happy accident. One he had never regretted, after that first moment of blind panic.

There was no sound from their room. He lay awake, daydreaming, thinking about how grateful he was to Briony Hall, and what a good friend she had been to him as well as to

Belle. She'd introduced them, after all, back in 2007, when Belle's former partner, Roddy McCulloch, had disappeared with no warning. Briony had a friend of a friend who knew that Fergus had set himself up as a private investigator, putting to use the skills in tracing people he'd developed during his TV career. Finding scammers and dishonest businessmen who didn't want to be found. So she'd got his contact details and passed them on to Belle. And the tale had unfolded from there. They'd been man and wife within six months from that first meeting.

They'd wed with what his grandmother would have called 'unseemly haste' – she'd have pursed her lips and raised her eyebrows – in Kirkcudbright registry office. Belle had seemed a little upset by that, once the day grew close, and he'd been daft enough to suggest that if she felt so strongly about it, there was time to arrange a church wedding (though he wasn't at all sure if he'd find a minister willing to remarry a man who'd already been through two other church weddings as well as a further civil one. He'd have to find one who believed in 'third time lucky'.)

But Belle had simply hissed, 'Shut *up*, Fergus.'

And he'd shut up.

Briony had taken it upon herself to arrange their wedding, as if she were Belle's mother rather than her friend. She'd helped draw up the guest list; about sixty people, all the bride's friends. He'd thought about inviting Anita Forrest, the TV producer and former colleague who'd been such a stalwart friend over the years. After all, Belle had met her, and they'd seemed to get on well. In the end, he'd decided that might not be tactful, since he knew Belle had subsequently twigged that he and Anita had been an item, years back.

Briony had closed the entire hotel to other guests the day before the wedding, so that he could spend the night away from the bride, in the traditional fashion (and they were nothing if not traditional in Kirkcudbright). 'I want you to feel you're at home, not in a hotel,' she'd said.

The reception had been held in the Roseberry's elegant function room. He couldn't remember what he'd eaten; his brain was fully occupied with the fact that he was married for the fourth time, to a woman he truly loved, and he was about to become a father.

There had been a three-tier wedding-cake, complete with fancy icing (God knows what strings Briony pulled to get *that* made so quickly) and a local dance band.

They'd played one of those slow songs you can only shuffle to (*Closer to You*, went the repetitive chorus). He'd drawn Belle tight against him, and shuffled, his cheek against her hair, her head resting against his shoulder.

She was wearing heels, in honour of the formal occasion, and a silky number in a pale peachy colour that made her skin and hair glow. She'd made her own wedding dress, and it looked every bit as good as anything you could buy. When he'd admired it, she'd said with some asperity that there was no way she was going into a shop and asking for a maternity wedding dress. 'Though I'm sure you can get such things these days,' she'd added. 'Probably get the full fig: white lace, train, veil, tiara of lily of the valley, and enough stretch at the stomach to accommodate the full nine months.'

And, just for a moment, he'd thought she was going to weep. Because she'd been brought up by an adoptive father who was so set in his ways, and so old-fashioned, she was unworldly in a way he found delectable.

'It doesn't *matter*, Belle,' he'd said.

She'd been exaggerating wildly, in any case. Holding her close, he could feel the swell of her belly, he could *tell* by then, though no one who didn't know would have noticed; they'd wasted no time once she'd realised she was expecting.

Then the band had switched to a waltz, a tune he recognised; the band's vocalist launched into the lyrics and he caught the word 'Leith'. Briony had smiled at him and called across the room, 'It's about Leith.' Belle grinned broadly and told him, 'It's 'Sunshine on Leith'. The Proclaimers. You know.'

He loathed the Proclaimers, with their thick, gallus Falkirk accents, but he was waltzing with his *wife*. This wasn't merely a different life; he was a different person. It wasn't the life he'd envisioned for himself at this age. It was better; infinitely better. He felt *complete*. And he'd realised that he was happy, uncomplicatedly happy, down to his toes, for the first time in his existence. So happy that perhaps he could learn to like the Proclaimers. He knew that neither their hostess nor the band would have had the faintest idea that this was the anthem sung at Easter Road, and if he'd had the least interest in football, he'd have been a Hearts, not a Hibs, supporter.

This is what I was *born* for, he told himself.

He'd listened properly to the words, and they brought home to him that not so long ago his heart *had* been broken – for the father he'd never known (because he was killed in Korea before Fergus was a year old), and the mother who'd been happy to leave his care and upbringing to her parents, through two failed marriages, then the ghastly third marriage, to Serena MacKenzie.

But now his heart was mended. He was a hundred, no a million, years away from being the man who'd wept, openly and in private, over Serena. He was done with the feeling that he was going through the motions of living with nothing to live for.

He thought back to the first time he'd seen Belle – *really* seen her, as a woman rather than an irascible and impatient client. She'd been pruning the roses in Ashers' garden, with immense concentration and care, and she'd tied her hair back, so that it wouldn't get caught on the thorns. He had realised since what it was she'd reminded him of: Waterhouse's painting, *My Sweet Rose*.

'Thanks, Briony,' he whispered, his lips against his wife's hair.

And something further he appreciated about the owner of the Roseberry: he knew she was as worried as he was about Remi's baleful influence on Belle, although she was too loyal ever to admit it. The one time he'd tried to raise the subject with her, being as tactful as he could, she'd pursed her lips and said, 'I think Belle's old enough to choose her own friends, Fergus. She seems to get a lot out of the friendship.' She'd sighed and turned away, but not before Fergus had read the expression in her eyes.

Belle stirred in his arms, yawned and stretched.

'Mornin'.'

'Morning, gorgeous. You're not meaning to go swimming today, are you? It's Christmas Eve.'

She smiled sleepily. 'I'll maybe give it a miss today and tomorrow. Need to go on Boxing Day, though. That's the one nobody ever misses.'

He laughed softly. 'Shall I make the breakfast, Belle?'

'That'd be lovely.'

She snuggled down again. Belle. No one called her anything

except that now. The name Fergus had invented for her almost the same day he arrived in her life in 2007. So the name she'd loathed from childhood onwards – Mabel, which most of her friends had shortened to 'Mabs' – had become a distant memory.

It felt both decadent and delicious to take a day off from her swimming. She chuckled to herself. The last five years had been a steep learning curve for Fergus – probably even steeper than for her. She'd fallen in love with the blustering, hard-drinking, tweedy, sweary Fergus. But she preferred the new one. That made her serious again. She had changed too. Which of them had got the raw deal?

The twins barrelled out of their room and thundered down the stairs, Esmée shushing Edmund loudly, and telling him not to wake Mummy.

The next excitement would be moving the twins into separate rooms, before they had their New Year holiday.

Belle's heart sank a little at the thought. How short childhood was these days. And how vulnerable children were, with all the things one heard about the dangers awaiting them out in the world. So some days, she worried over how fast they were growing up. Others, she breathed a sigh of relief that she'd got them successfully to almost five years old. She had vague memories of reading that five was the magic age even in the early twentieth century: if they survived till their fifth birthday, children had a reasonable chance of making it to adulthood. And they'd be five in three months.

Eddie was to stay on in the room he and Esmée shared up until then. Belle had spent the past month decorating what had been the spare-spare bedroom for her daughter. It had been repapered (not with anything produced by Disney, but with an expensive Swedish design featuring songbirds). New furniture had also been bought – a proper grown-up dressing table and matching chest of drawers.

When Fergus had tried to protest that Edmund was getting nothing new, Belle tossed her head and said, 'But he's being left with the *much* bigger room. That's the room I had when I was a girl. He can have some new furniture in due course. We couldn't have put Esmée in there as it was. It hadn't been decorated since before I was born, I should think.'

She lay awake, listening to the rumble of Fergus's voice, as he negotiated breakfast arrangements with them.

When she'd told him about the five-year-old safety point, he'd struggled not to laugh, because she was utterly serious. 'Belle, that book would be talking about years and years ago. It's not like that nowadays. The twins are absolutely fine.'

'I know that. But it stuck in my mind. They're so vulnerable.'

'And we make sure no harm can come to them.'

She'd smiled at last. 'I know that too. In my *head*.'

'It's all worked out perfectly. They're happy and strong and healthy. You've made a wonderful job of bringing them up. I wish I'd had a mother as competent as you.'

She'd stroked his hair. 'Poor wee Fergus.'

Fergus. Her entire life had changed since she'd met him, but she knew that he still worried about her. That was why he'd seemed relieved that she'd skip the swim in the Solway for a day or two.

In the early days, he'd sometimes follow her surreptitiously; there was nothing wrong with her long-distance vision – she'd seen the sun glint off his binoculars, up on the roadway high above the sea, and she'd seen the XC90's distinctive silver nose only half-hidden by the gorse bushes.

At first, she was quietly furious, but when she thought about it, she was touched by his concern. He'd been handling her like spun glass since that emotional wobble four years before. By a year later, it had turned to anger again; he was treating her as if she were unstable, not to be trusted as a responsible adult. As if she'd have allowed herself to get into real danger now she had children to look after!

'By the way,' she'd said casually to her fellow-swimmers, 'that character up on the road with binoculars isn't a peeping Tom. It's my husband. He's afraid I'll drown.'

They'd chortled. 'And he's going to save you from *there*?'

Only Remi didn't laugh when Belle told her; one of the few times her friend let a chance to mock him go by.

Nowadays, she knew he didn't follow her. Not every day anyhow.

But she was continually worried that she'd mess up with raising the twins, scar them emotionally. She didn't know how to do it; she had no memory of a maternal role-model.

Fergus was useless as a sounding-board. As bad as Briony. Just platitudes about 'doing fine'. 'You're not scarred,' he'd point out. 'And there's no way *you're* going to abandon your kids.'

It had been no use; she couldn't stop worrying about every detail, spending days in a fug of anxiety over accidents that *could* happen. Once she'd almost reached the stage of being confident that both twins would still be breathing come morning, she'd started worrying about things like the laburnum tree outside the front door, when the children learned to walk.

'They need to be *taught*, Belle!' Fergus had said. 'That tree was there when you were a child. There was one in my grandparents' garden. Neither of us poisoned ourselves eating the seeds.'

But there had always been something else to worry about. It made Fergus short-tempered with her.

'But they're so helpless,' she'd say. 'It's such a responsibility!'

And she'd get up once more to check they were both alive. There had been nights, quite recently, when she still did that.

Usually, when she was having a panic session over how she'd cope with two children, Fergus calmly pointed out the advantages: they would be there for each other; playmates – and able to continue to share, as their parents aged.

'How many times I used to long to have someone else to share the burdens,' he said. 'You must have too, surely? Look at the situation Briony's in, having to cope alone with her mother.'

Belle always had to think about that. She bit her lip. 'Maybe if there had been two of us, Rose might not have left. It must be more difficult to abandon *two* children. On the other hand, she might have left even earlier.'

Rose was her adoptive mother, who had run off with a man when Belle was four. She was aware that Fergus was keen to trace her – after all, she'd been more than twenty years younger than Father. There was every chance she was still alive. Belle was equally aware that she never wanted to hear of the woman, or set eyes on her again.

Sounds of pots and pans from the kitchen. He'd bring her breakfast in bed; something to compound her guilt over skipping today's swim. She giggled. Even now, she worried about the fact that she didn't see herself as an enthusiastic cook, whereas Fergus was a bit of a foodie. From the start of their relationship, in fact from the day he'd moved in with her, he had done most of the cooking.

'Well, sounds as if no one ever taught you,' he'd said soothingly. 'My grandmother saw it as her duty to make sure I could cook for myself and iron my own shirts. I wasn't let off the hook because I was a boy. A woman well before her time, Esmée Fairbairn.'

Belle had always felt that the woman sounded like a managing cow of the worst sort. She could visualise her: a tweedy dame, with a voice like a foghorn. But she also knew that was unfair. There were photographs. Fergus's grandmother had been a tall, elegant person, very like her daughter, Maud, in looks – the mother who had been happy to pack her son off to the Fairbairns' establishment at Inveresk in the school holidays.

'We always had someone come in to do the cooking,' she'd confessed. 'Father couldn't boil an egg, and had no intention of learning.'

And she'd be off to that place in her mind she'd retreat to when she was trying to remember the time before Rose left.

She was aware that Fergus recognised this. Always, there was an urgent need to change the subject.

'What was your favourite dish when you were the twins' age?'

'Chicken curry. My grandmother made a mean curry. How about you?'

'I don't remember liking anything specially much.'

She pulled the bedclothes to her chin, reluctant to leave her warm nest. Perhaps later that day she'd fetch home a painting from the gallery to hang in the space opposite the bed. The nude portrait of her (aged twenty) by Roddy McCulloch which used to hang there, before being moved to Fergus's study in 2007, had finally been banished to the attic. 'Until the twins are older,' she'd told Fergus – though in fact, she wouldn't have minded getting rid of it. The young woman in it, with her pert, high breasts and smooth belly, was not just from a different era; she was a different person. He'd read her mind. 'Don't you dare dispose of it,' Fergus had said. 'It can go back in my study eventually, if you don't want it in the bedroom.' And he had shrugged and carried it carefully upstairs for safekeeping.

TWO

DI Tom Ellis gazed dejectedly at the screen of his computer, and ran his fingers through his hair.

He loathed missing person cases. Tedious, and no chance to get your name noticed when you cracked them. Dumfries and Galloway seemed to get more than its fair share – only three of the other forces in Scotland had more per thousand of population. As often as not, it'd be some old person who'd got confused and wandered off. Either that, or a stroppy teenager who'd had a barney with the parents. He sighed, thinking of his own two daughters. *There, but for the grace of God...* They were well past that age now. Not that it didn't bring other problems. But at least *his* mother was sound in mind and body at seventy-seven.

Why was CID getting involved at this stage anyway? Uniforms could surely deal with it. Because, damn it, it was Christmas. His team should be at home with their families. There were more than seven hundred people on the long-term missing list in Scotland.

He read the next paragraph of the notes, and perked up a

little. This case was different, because Angus McPhedrie was *famous*, even though he'd never made it past the first team of a fairly obscure English football club (and that was thirteen years ago).

At least a week with no trace, and some peculiar contextual details. Tom mentally up-scaled it to a more exciting category. He couldn't remember a kidnapping on his patch, in all his years in the job. McPhedrie owned a holiday chalet at Colvend, and that was the last place he'd been seen (there were conflicting reports on exactly when). Brownie points on offer for solving this one quickly. The kind that could provide a shove up to the next rung. Detective *Chief* Inspector Ellis.

Time was running out. The Dumfries and Galloway force was due to be subsumed into Police Scotland on the first of April next year (there had been plenty of jokes about the date), along with every other force north of the border. And everyone knew what happened when mergers took place: all the dead wood cut out, top jobs gone and not replaced. A freeze on promotion. The word was that some parts of the new structure would be in place even sooner.

By the end of March, he'd heard, the Specialist Crime Division would be up and running; nearly two thousand detectives, mostly from the old Strathclyde force no doubt, would be handed responsibility for every case that was remotely interesting. He desperately wanted to be one of them – not that he'd applied. In such a small force everyone would have known, and what if he'd been rejected, maybe not even interviewed? No way he could have sashayed back into the office next day as if nothing had happened.

Onwards and upwards, Tom. He straightened his tie and headed out to rally the troops.

He regarded his team with some distaste. Need to crack this one before that cow the Chief Super was breathing down his neck (Tom had never quite settled to having a woman as his boss). No chance of promotion to DCI, ever, if he couldn't nail a simple case like this. Prospects of a decent pension down the sodding drain.

It didn't help that the first person he set eyes on was the newest smart-arse on the block, DC David Giles, with his degree in criminology and his hair that looked as if it had been permed. Arrived at work on a BMW motorbike that would have cost as much as most cops could afford to spend on a car. Obviously reckoned he was going to make it to Chief Constable by the time he was thirty. Less than a year in the job, and thought he knew the bloody works. *The type that gets fast-tracked these days.*

Tom clapped his hands. 'Right, you sorry crew. Where are we with this Misper at Colvend? Can't be beyond us to get it cleared up by lunchtime.'

DS Rachel Field looked up eagerly. He liked Rach. She'd been on his team for six years, and he hoped that getting bumped up to sergeant meant she felt settled in the job, wasn't looking to move on. Giles could move on as soon as he fucking well liked.

Rachel strode across the office to stand in front of the whiteboard plastered with pictures, maps and scribbles.

She consulted her notes. 'Angus McPhedrie. Age forty-three. Born on the outskirts of Dumfries, at Georgetown, but left to become a professional footballer when he was eighteen.' Hadn't remarried since his second divorce, two years ago, but was reputed to have a string of girlfriends. He'd ended his career with Plymouth United, but he'd made money, the way footballers do, and from what they'd been able to learn, he'd always been one to splash the cash. 'Reported missing by the fish van owner on the 18th.'

Tom raised his eyebrows.

'Apparently McPhedrie is one of his best customers. Eats lots of fish. Keep-fit fanatic.'

'He's been interviewed?' asked Giles. 'The fish seller, I mean.'

That earned him a withering look. 'Naturally. When he stopped at the chalet he gave it a few minutes, and when there was no sign of your man, he went to the door. It was ajar, so he went inside and called out. No answer, so he looked in all the rooms. Nada. The bedclothes were pulled up neatly, so he thought McPhedrie had maybe gone out for a jog. His car was still there. The guy thought it was weird that he'd have gone out and left the door open, so when he'd finished his round he went back. That'd have been about half-ten on the 16th. That's when he called it in. Local uniforms were in attendance before one. The fish guy had hung around waiting for them. He said he hadn't touched anything. They searched the premises, but found no trace of McPhedrie, or indication of a struggle or a break-in. They did a brief house to house, but no one had seen the Misper since a couple of days before. A lot of the chalets are empty, this time of year.' Rachel glanced at her notes again. 'There seem to be several versions of when the last sighting was, but the latest would have been around lunchtime on the 15th.'

'Number-plate not picked up on ANPR?' asked Tom. 'I take it we *know* his number?'

Rachel cleared her throat. 'As I said, his car's parked there. Tidy two-year-old Beamer. Locked. The keys are in the house.'

'So, what exactly are we looking for here? Some bozo who's

gone out for a walk and fallen, a week ago, and bloody uniforms can't find him?'

'Or gone for a swim and drowned?' added Giles. 'Where would a body wash up if it went in there?'

'If the tide was going out, could be Cumbria. Anyway, who swims at this time of year?'

'People do, Rach,' said Tom, turning morose. A bunch of idiotic women swam in the Solway every day, even in winter. There had been a pic in the *Galloway News* last year. The cutting was secreted in his desk drawer. The Sulwath Sisters, or some such stupid name. Mabs Mountjoy was one of them. *Must stop thinking of her as that. Mabel* Learmonth. *Belle, her man calls her. She should have been Mabs Ellis, twenty-seven years ago.* He sighed again. The case was sounding less and less like a kidnapping. Accidental deaths were even more tedious than missing persons.

'Someone must have an idea if he goes swimming, or jogging, or fucking well paragliding?'

'There's his cleaning woman,' said Rachel.

'A cleaning woman for a holiday chalet?'

'He's had the place for years – she looks after it when he's not there too.'

'Interviewed?'

'Of course.'

'And?'

'She hasn't seen him since the 14th. She should have been there last week, on the 21st, but she missed it because her daughter had a fever.'

'You been to have a dekko at this chalet, Rach?' asked Tom.

She nodded. 'It's a real high-spec one. Nothing suspicious that I could see.'

'And forensics turned up nothing?'

'They've not been. There's no sign of anything being disturbed. McPhedrie's wallet is there in the bedside drawer – around three hundred in it, in cash. Passport's there too. His Apple laptop and a hi-fi system are sitting out in the open, and an expensive TV.'

Tom snapped his fingers. 'There must be *some* clues. Right – I'm off there. Rach, you can come with me. Giles, get a few bloody SOCOs out of their beds. We need to get this one tied up pronto. Oh, and Giles – find out where this guy lives when he's not up with us, and get the local boys to check it out.'

'Already done. *Sir*.' Giles was smirking. 'He owns a property in Warrington.'

'For God's sake! Well, *they* won't have time to bother with it. Triple murder there two days ago.' Tom thumped the desk he was sitting on, hard enough to hurt his hand. 'Look, this bugger's probably a bit absent-minded. Headed the ball too many times when he was a player. He'll have taken off to spend Christmas in one of these fancy hotels.' His wife, Jackie, was forever nagging him to do that, now the kids were away. Cost a bloody mint.

'What – without his car?' said Rachel.

'He could have got a lift. That'll be it. Someone picked him up. Some dolly bird.'

'And he forgot to lock the door or lift his wallet?'

'Told you. His brain's probably addled. Check out the places that do Festive Break specials, Giles.'

'Within what radius?'

'Within the whole fucking country if necessary. We need to find this character. I have no intention of missing my Christmas dinner. Right, DS Field, we're out of here.'

Tom felt a chill run across his shoulders as he stood in the main living room of the log-built chalet. It wasn't only the cold – and it was *bloody* cold, even although the Solway coast seldom got its worst weather until after New Year. He laid his hand on the wood-stove; icy. He opened its glass door; just a bed of dead, grey wood-ash. No sign of documents being burned, or anything like that.

Jackie had demanded a wood-burner once they'd finished redecorating. Not like this one, he decided; it was ugly, though he quite fancied the polished slate hearth.

No, it wasn't the cold: there was a sense of – what? – *Evil*: though it wasn't the sort of thing he'd ever say out loud, to his colleagues or his wife or his pals. When you were a DI, you didn't allow your thoughts to wander in such ridiculous directions. In any case, Tom had no time for all the guff you saw on the telly about detectives using their *intuition*. OK, you needed to have a feel for it, but good, solid police work was what got results, not intu-sodding-ition.

All the same, there was *something*.

He remembered a film he'd seen as a child. Something about a ship called the *Mary Celeste*. And there was a poem at school about the Flannan Lighthouse. *Everything laid out for a meal, everything normal, so you expect the people to walk back in any moment; except, there isn't a soul anywhere to be found. Never traced. Never any answers, to this day.*

Uniforms had been there already, after the alarm had been raised. They'd got a locksmith in to make the place secure, just in case. The SOCOs had arrived too, white-suited and masked.

He looked up at Rachel, to see if she was feeling the vibe

too. She was standing, hands in pockets, humming under her breath. She looked bored.

'Looks as if we missed the Golden Hour, guv.'

'The golden *hour*? We missed the golden bloody week by the looks of it, sergeant. Right, we're both going over this place a centimetre at a time. We don't want another of these balls-ups like the one in Fife, where the guy's lying dead in his airing cupboard and we're fannying about leaving him on the Misper register until the maggots start crawling down the garden path.' He glared at the senior SOCO, a woman called Gibson. 'You hear that?'

She shrugged. 'Uniforms have already been over it with a dog.'

Tom swore under his breath. He'd heard all the apocryphal tales of plods who were first on the scene washing a knife that was the most likely murder weapon 'because it was dirty', and putting it back in a drawer. Things were better these days – but far from perfect. 'Then we need to get them back to turn over every fucking stone near this gaff. *Comprenez*?'

Gibson shrugged again as if to say, 'Nothing to do with me. *Sir*.'

Tom took in the expensive curved-screen TV, the opulent furniture, the paintings on the walls. All this, in what was a holiday home. Fuck it! Jackie would think this was bloody marvellous. He shook his shoulders free of the jealousy, and entered detective mode.

The far end of the room was laid out as a swanky kitchen. Lot of built-in appliances. He opened the larder fridge. A half-empty litre container of milk, best before 23rd December. One and a half packs of Normandy butter, unsalted. An unopened pack of Edam cheese, and a half-used pack of Cheddar. A full punnet of green seedless grapes, starting to discolour. Half a melon wrapped in clingfilm, but turning brown around the cut surface. An unopened pack of unsmoked bacon (Danish). Four eggs. The door-shelves were completely filled with bottles of white wine: Italian Pinot Grigio, Premieres Côtes de Bordeaux, Gewurtztraminer.

'Strange diet he had,' observed Tom. 'Come on, Rach, look lively. Have you checked the other rooms?'

She glared at him. 'Empty. There are two bedrooms, just one with a bed in it.'

'And the other?'

'Not a sausage. No furniture, no boxes, nothing.'

'There must be some hints as to where this guy has vanished to? Folk don't disappear off the face of the earth. There are *always* clues.'

He strode into the larger bedroom, pulled open the wardrobe. A multi-layered hanger of ties. Tom ran his fingers over them. Silk. You could tell, even gloved-up. He'd fancy one or two like these himself, even if he was almost the only one in CID who bothered with a tie these days.

Expensive-looking suits and white shirts. Not at all what you'd expect anyone to wear on holiday. 'Snappy dresser, by the looks of it. Why would anyone wear gear like this in Colvend, Rach?'

She pulled a face. 'Search me.' She opened a drawer. 'Likes his bling too.' In a gloved hand she held up a leather box fitted out for cufflinks. 'One set missing. Maybe that's a bit of a clue. You wouldn't put on cufflinks to go jogging.'

'What the hell are we *doing* here, Rach? There's no evidence at all of a crime.'

One of the SOCOs was crawling around the floor of the main room. He looked up, and stretched his shoulders.

Tom sighed. 'You getting anything?' The man shrugged and shook his head. 'It's as if it's been professionally cleaned, by someone who knew what they were doing. No dabs, no hairs. No blood, so far. No sign of forced entry. Nothing to indicate a struggle, or an unplanned departure. The only place we've found fingermarks was on the bottles in the fridge.' He prodded the screen of an iPad and held it out to Tom.

'Any match on the Ident1 database?'

The SOCO shrugged again.

'So, from this stuff in the fridge, how long would you say he's been gone?'

'I'd say the 15th or 16th sounds about right.'

A seventeen-inch MacBook Pro laptop was lying open in plain sight, on the dining table, its screen blank.

'You taking that with you for the IT boys?' asked the SOCO.

Tom gestured to Rachel. 'Bag it up.'

'There's a wallet with several hundred in cash in assorted used notes in the bedside drawer.'

'Bag that up too, Rach. Not a robbery then?'

'Doesn't look like it.'

'Like the *Mary Celeste*.'

'That's about it.'

Tom gestured to encompass the room. 'Does this look to you like someone who's done a runner? Why would he leave all this kit?'

The SOCO rolled his eyes.

'And these prints on the bottles?' asked Tom.

'They'll need to be examined by an expert, but I'm ninety-nine per cent certain they're from one person. The guy who raised the alarm said he was careful not to touch anything inside.'

'Thought this footballer was supposed to be a womaniser? Surely there should be signs of visitors? Suspiciously clean?'

'Yep.'

'And you said there's no sign of blood?'

'None.'

Tom looked hopelessly at the floors. All solid wood in the living area, with a few scatter rugs. Tiles in the kitchen.

'Bedrooms solid floors too?'

'Yup.'

Shit!

'And no sign of blood between the boards?'

'Not a drop.'

'DNA?'

'What looks like semen on the bed-sheets. We're swabbing and taping everything that can be swabbed or taped.'

'Bugger!'

It'd take weeks to get results on that anyway. No chance of madam the Chief Super signing the chitty for a rushed job when they weren't even sure there had been a crime, and with Christmas and New Year coming up...

He gazed around the room, and his eye lit on a photo of a flabby middle-aged man. 'Who's that – do we know?'

'The Misper himself, according to the fish seller,' said Rachel.

'Fuck's sake! That's a footballer?'

'Ex-footballer. It's years since he played.'

'I thought you said he liked to keep himself fit?'

'I suppose a lot of them go that way once they stop playing.'

Tom pulled in his stomach and stood up tall. 'I look more like a professional sportsman than that slob. What age is he again?'

'A few years younger than you.'

He threw Rachel a look. 'A few years younger than you, *sir*.' She ducked away from him.

'I'd never let myself go like that.' Tom caught sight of himself in the mirror over the sofa. Yes. He still had it. His mind drifted off once more to whether he should think about going back into uniform to get that next step up.

'So what's happening in the great outdoors? I suppose there isn't an attic for the plods to have missed in here. Have they given up?' he asked no one in particular.

'They pulled in uniforms from all over the area for fingertip searches of the ground around the chalet. Volunteers from elsewhere on the holiday site, plus the adjacent village too. Quite a number helping comb local woodland now. The coastguard has men out searching the local beaches,' said Rachel.

Tom knew in his bones they'd all come up blank. This was no simple case of someone dropping dead while out for a stroll, or stringing himself up from a tree.

'Find anything like a passport?'

'Yep. Like I said, in the bedside drawer. It's McPhedrie's.'

'Don't know about you, but if I wanted to make a quick getaway for any reason – woman trouble, whatever – I'd take my money and my passport, wouldn't you, Sergeant Field? Not to mention putting my laptop away somewhere out of sight, and locking the bloody door.'

A uniformed PC hove into view and Tom assumed his SIO tone. 'Anything from the door-to-doors, constable?'

'Nothing useful. Last time people remember seeing him was

"a few days back". No one remembered any unusual sounds, or seeing strange vehicles, or taxis or whatever.'

'People? There are actually more than this guy living in holiday chalets at this time of year?'

'About a third of them are occupied.'

'So what's the word on this guy – living alone?'

'Apparently. They weren't aware of any women – or men – visiting. Said he kept himself to himself. Didn't mix, didn't seem to come and go to any sort of timetable.'

'Who the hell would come here in winter? Folk who didn't know any better,' he answered his own question. 'What you looking at me like that for, Rach? It's miserable, and everything's shut. Who'd come to a sodding shed in the arse-end of Scotland for Christmas?' He grinned to himself. He knew full well that DC Giles' posh parents lived in a Colt house, not unlike this one in build, outside Newton Stewart.

Rachel bridled a little. She clearly had a soft spot for her gormless colleague.

'These chalets are mega-expensive,' she said crossly. 'This probably cost the thick end of two hundred k. They're built to a high standard. Well-insulated. Probably better insulated than – most ordinary houses.'

He knew she'd been about to say, 'than your house'.

'I bet this is fine and cosy with the heating on and the stove lit,' she added.

Tom clicked his fingers. 'That's it! The heating. Why would he have turned off the heating if he wasn't going far? What does it run on?'

Rachel peered out at the kitchen window. 'Bottled gas, I'd say. Must cost a fortune to run.'

'Check if it's run out then, or if it's been switched off.'

She tutted and opened kitchen cupboard doors until she found the control unit. 'It should be on,' she said. 'Bet the bottle has run out.'

Not much of a clue there. They should be able to find out when he last bought gas, but that wasn't going to tell them anything.

'You guys got any idea how long it might be since this place was heated?' he asked the nearest SOCO.

The man guffawed. 'Not an inkling. With the outside temperatures nearly zero at night, it wouldn't take long to cool down with no heating.' He stood up, hitched his face-mask down and stretched his back. 'We'll be off soon,' he said. 'Not a lot more we can do here.'

'How long before you see if you've got anything useful in the way of DNA?'

Another shrug. 'Weeks. Since we've nothing to match it to, not a lot of help anyway.'

Bugger! Tom was interested in forensics. He'd used all of his CPD courses to improve his knowledge of that side. In fact, he'd often felt that he'd have been well-advised to try to move across early in his career.

'Finding anything else in the bedroom, Rach?' he called.

'Nothing. All the drawers are full of clean clothes. He's a tidy guy, I'll say that for him.'

'Who reported him missing again?'

'Guy who drives the fish van. Apparently McPhedrie always buys fish, lots of it – always at least two pieces of haddie and a salmon fillet and...'

'I don't want his shopping list, Rach. Get on with it.'

She flounced a little, and muttered under her breath about getting out of bed on the wrong side. 'He came in, had a dekko, got the wind up a bit and called it in on his mobile, once he reached a place with signal.'

'The uniforms got a statement from him?'

'Yep.'

Tom stared morosely at the beige ceramic tiles on the kitchen floor. 'Hey, come here – what's that?'

She appeared at his shoulder. 'Footwear mark, I'd say. But it's very faint.'

'Does that mean some bugger's been in here without over-shoes then? SOCO getting careless?'

'They looked at it. Didn't seem to think it was of any interest.'

'A plod, you reckon? Or this fish van man? Or a nosey neighbour?'

'Search me.'

'But look, Rach, it's not an ordinary scuff mark. It's a straight line, and it goes on for at least half a metre. No sign at all of tread on it.'

'I suppose not.' She dropped to her knees and studied it. She touched the end of the black smear with a gloved finger. 'Pretty thoroughly ground in.'

Tom crouched beside her. 'I wonder...'

Rachel scuffed her own foot against the floor. 'Might not be footmarks. Maybe he was dragging something heavy outside.'

'But what, and to where? His car's sitting there, for God's sake. There was nothing heavy lying anywhere near the house. SOCO *did* search the wheelie bin?'

'Eventually. Said there was sod all in it.'

Tom slammed his fist on the table. 'So – tyre marks in the vicinity?'

'Dozens. It's a narrow roadway, and everyone going to the

chalets beyond this one passes along it. Not to mention delivery vans, the post. This fish man.'

'Who comes at what time?'

'Quarter past eight every Tuesday. Like clockwork, according to the neighbours.'

'You wouldn't park on a road like that and drag a body out?'

'Maybe at night you would. No lighting of any sort, remember.'

DC Giles breezed in. 'Hope I'm not interrupting anything.'

They both glared at him.

'Thought you were checking on hotels?' said Tom.

'I checked all of them in a hundred-mile radius, then set Shona onto checking further afield. Whatcha found, Rach?' added Giles. He stood over her. For a moment, Tom thought he was about to ruffle her hair. His throat tightened with fury.

'Tom noticed this mark. Just wondering about it.'

'Shoe scuff,' said Giles. 'My mum's got these same tiles. Devil for picking up marks. She's always bawling at me to lift my feet.'

'We know what it *is*,' snapped Tom. 'We're wondering what it *means*.' He walked towards the door, peering carefully at the floor. 'Look, there's another even fainter one on the wood here. Same thing, no tread. I'd lay money on it someone wearing dark-soled shoes has been dragged across.'

The trio looked at one another.

Tom became aware of a woman standing awkwardly in the doorway. 'You can't come in here,' he said swiftly. Bugger! Had the place not been taped off yet? He glared towards the gateway. She had dodged under the tape unchallenged, by the looks of it. Not a single solitary plod watching it. He remembered from his own days as a rookie what a bastard it was to be set to stand for hours on end, in the freezing cold, in pelting rain, guarding a crime scene. But still! 'Didn't you see "Do not cross"?' he snapped.

'It's all right, DI Ellis,' said Rachel swiftly. 'This is Mr McPhedrie's cleaner. I asked her to come and have a thorough look, so she can tell us if she spots anything missing or disturbed.'

Tom grunted. 'Right, Mrs...?'

'Blair.' She glared at him. 'So can I come in or not?'

'Hang on a mo.' He turned to the more senior SOCO. 'You guys finished here?'

'I'd say so.'

'So someone can come in?'

'I suppose. Maybe put shoe protectors and gloves on them though.'

He beckoned the stranger over, pulling fresh overshoes and gloves from the packages on the hall table. She was lingering inside the doorway.

'Can you put these on before you come in, Mrs Blair. Where are you from, by the way? That's not a local accent I hear.'

'Beeswing.' She glared again. Defiantly.

'Oh, right. But you weren't born there?'

'My, so you *are* a detective. I was born in Warsaw.'

Tom quickly ascertained that she'd last seen McPhedrie on Thursday, the 13th. 'I missed last week, because my wee girl wasn't well. What's happened to him?'

'That's what we're trying to find out. Sounds as if you could have been one of the last people to see him.'

The woman turned pale. 'So has something bad happened?'

'We have no idea, at the moment. Mr McPhedrie appears to

be missing. He hadn't mentioned anything to you about going away on a trip?'

She shook her head.

'You have a mobile number for him?'

The cleaner read out a string of figures; Rachel punched them into her phone, listened for a moment, then shrugged. 'Straight to voicemail.'

'So what was Mr McPhedrie doing for Christmas?' asked Tom.

'Staying here.'

'Not much sign of him stocking up with food for that,' said Rachel.

'He'd never have bought a turkey. But there should be plenty of food in the fridge.' The older woman crossed to open the door of the appliance, and shook her head. 'There should be much more here.'

'He didn't mention any friends he was seeing?'

'He kept himself to himself.'

'No women friends?'

Agneta Blair looked quite shocked. 'Never!'

'He'd been married twice – did either of his ex-wives ever come here?'

'I never saw them. I don't think he kept in touch.'

'Is he usually as tidy as this?'

'He's very particular.'

'But if you haven't been here for ten days or so, would you expect it to be as clean as it is?'

Mrs Blair scanned the room carefully. 'No,' she said slowly. 'If he kept it so well there would be no work for me to do.'

'So, on a normal day that you're here, you'd do what, exactly?' asked Rachel.

'Hoover the floors. Clean the bathroom and kitchen. Clean the cooker.'

'How about washing – did you do that?'

'He did his own laundry. Sometimes I'd iron shirts, if he hadn't got round to it. I'd take his suits to the cleaner for him.'

Tom motioned to the nearest SOCO. 'Can you make sure to check the hoover bag?'

'It's a bagless one. We swabbed for fibres or skin flakes.'

'You check the filter? Might be fibres in that?'

The man rolled his eyes, and Tom clenched his fists. Straws, that's what he was clutching at.

'We'd like you to take a look around and see if you can spot anything that doesn't look right, Mrs Blair,' Rachel was saying. 'We can see he didn't take a lot with him. Please, take your time and see if there's anything that should be here but isn't.'

Agneta Blair scanned the living area, then shook her head and shuffled through to the bathroom. 'His shaving stuff's here. And his electric toothbrush. He'd have taken that if he was going away.' She opened a linen basket. 'Empty. He must have done a wash recently.'

She headed through to the main bedroom, and opened the wardrobe, sliding hangers along the rail. 'His best suit's not here. I suppose he might have taken it to the cleaners – but that's the sort of thing I'd normally deal with for him. One of his pale blue shirts is missing too. He must have been going out somewhere.'

'Flashy dresser, is he?' asked Tom. He saw Rachel smirk slightly. Well, sod it, he wasn't going to apologise for liking to look smart himself.

'Flashy?'

'Smart.'

'He dresses well.' She held up a finger. 'All his shirts are the kind that need cufflinks. Just let me check.'

She slid open one of the wardrobe drawers, and lifted out the brown leather box Rachel had looked at earlier. 'Yes, his best ones aren't here. He must have been going somewhere *special*.'

'Can you describe the clothes that are missing? And these cufflinks?'

'The suit was the same as the ones there. Dark blue. Only it was an Armani one.'

'And the cufflinks?'

'Little gold footballs, with his initials on them. He got them as a present when he was leaving his club. He was very proud of them.'

'Maybe he hadn't brought them with him?'

'He *always* brought them.'

'So – his initials. AM or AMcP, or what?'

'AMcP. I think.'

She continued to open drawers. 'I can't see anything else missing.'

'How was his memory?'

She looked at Tom in incomprehension.

'Did he often forget things?'

'Forget? Not Mr McPhedrie. He's sharp, he is. He always remembers my daughter's birthday, even though he's never here in April. He sends a present for her, every year.'

'That's nice,' said Rachel. 'What age is your daughter?'

'Seven.'

'OK – so forgetful's the wrong word. Is he careless?'

'Careless? How?'

'If I told you he'd left the house unlocked and his wallet inside, you'd be surprised?'

'Very surprised. He's afraid of being robbed. Not here, but at his house in England. He told me he has a burglar alarm there, and safety cameras. He didn't think anyone would rob a chalet. But he's always careful about locking up.'

Tom scratched his neck. 'Shoes? What kind of shoes would he have worn if he was going out for a walk?'

She led the way through to a rack near the front door, scanned through the ones that were there. 'Black leather ones. Quite heavy.'

'He was one of these "no outdoor shoes in the house" types?'

She looked at him sharply. 'He is.'

'Overcoat?'

She gestured to the row of brass hooks behind the door. 'They're all there.'

'Right – so he was dressed to go out somewhere special, but he didn't take a coat, although he left his car here.' He turned aside to Rachel. 'Get Giles to check the taxi firms again. And tell him I mean *all*. The ones in Carlisle too. Maybe he was going there for a train.'

'Did he wear a watch?'

'A fancy one. Tag something.'

'Tag Heuer?'

'That's it. He kept it in the bedside drawer when he didn't have it on.' She strode back to the bedroom. 'Not here. He must be wearing it. Did you know his wallet's here? And his passport?'

Tom nodded.

'Will I do some cleaning anyway?'

'You will not. This might be a crime scene.'

'Should I not empty the bin?'

The two detectives looked guiltily at the stainless steel bin in the corner of the kitchen. 'SOCO will have been through that?' said Tom.

'No idea. Guys,' Rach called after the vanishing white-suited figures, 'you been through this bin?'

The senior one shambled over. 'Er – I'll check it now.'

As she opened it, a whiff of chemical smell hit Tom. It was vaguely familiar. 'What the hell's that?'

The SOCO blushed. 'Dental anaesthetic, I'd say.' She stretched a nitrile-gloved hand into the bin and drew out a syringe.

'Fucking hell!' said Tom. 'Which of the dentists here do home visits?'

'It can be used to stop – or reduce – bleeding. Sir,' the SOCO added as an afterthought.

A sobbing intake of air behind him reminded Tom that the cleaner was standing close by. 'DC Giles, can you show this lady out over the approved path, please. One of the uniformed officers will drive you to the station in Dumfries to make a statement, Mrs Blair.'

He turned to the SOCO again. 'Who the hell would have that, other than dentists?'

'You can get anything online.'

'And enough of this could knock someone out?'

The SOCO was sniffing a cotton pad he'd unearthed from a ziplock bag lower down the bin. 'This could. It's chloroform.'

'Who uses chloroform these days? I didn't know you could even get hold of it. Surely it's a restricted substance?'

'I'm pretty sure you can buy it on eBay. I read about that in a recent case in England.'

'So we're *not* looking for someone who's done a bunk?' said Rachel. 'Abduction?'

Tom shrugged. He struggled to maintain a solemn expression. A fine, juicy kidnapping after all. So much more satisfactory than a Misper enquiry. What you got taught at police college was right enough. The ABC of the job. Accept nothing, believe no one, challenge everything.

Their eyes met, and they moved as one person towards the chalet's door. Outside, there was a wide area of gravel, with McPhedrie's car parked on the left. There were tyre-grooves alongside, but there was no chance of getting decent tyre-*marks* on gravel. Both detectives crouched and examined the silver-grey stones carefully. No sign of a body being dragged here. No sign of blood-spotting.

'I'll make sure the SOCOs take a dekko at this too,' said Tom, straightening up as his mobile pinged.

It was his oppo in Warrington. They'd found time to send uniforms round to McPhedrie's house there after all – posh, by the looks of it; he'd already eyeballed it on Google Street View. Not your normal footballer's pad like the ones you see elsewhere in Cheshire, with stables and swimming pools and security lighting better than the Queen's. A classier house than he could ever afford all the same, and the bugger had only played in the first team in a godforsaken club, then done a bit of training work, apparently. The house had been empty when they'd called, no sign of forced entry (they'd discovered that his cleaner was a keyholder, so they got in no trouble at all). No sign of disturbance. Fridge and freezer empty and switched off. Beds stripped. Neighbours said they hadn't seen him since well before Christmas, and that wasn't unusual; he normally went to Tenerife or to his place in Scotland at that time of year. Neither of his ex-wives had heard from him.

'Did you get a mobile number for him?' asked Tom. That

was the one thing they hadn't found in the chalet, a mobile. The officer in Cheshire read out a number. Same one Mrs Blair had given him. 'We tried it. Straight to voicemail, didn't ring at all. Battery dead, perhaps, or it's turned off.'

'What about these ex-wives?' Once you saw there was some cash and you knew there were exes, there was always a motive somewhere.

'We interviewed both of them. Cast-iron alibis. They were nowhere near his Scottish place. One of them didn't even seem to have a clue it existed.'

Tom muttered his thanks and rang off. 'Fat lot of good *they* are.'

'So you reckon this guy's been offed?' Rachel asked.

'What?'

'Hovis.'

'What the hell are you talking about, sergeant?'

'Brown bread. Dead. Just practising the jargon.' She raised her eyebrows (beautifully thick, well-defined eyebrows; he found himself wondering if she spent hours with tweezers, the way Jackie did. He doubted it, somehow).

The recently-announced Chief Constable of Police Scotland had already been round all the HQs, on his triumphal tour, like a new tom-cat pissing on every bush. He drove an MG sports car. The word was that he wouldn't stay long.

Used a lot of jargon from the Met, to rub it in that he'd not worked all his life within thirty miles of where he was born. Falkirk, that's where he'd been born. Like the Proclaimers. Between the argot and the thick accent, most of them hadn't a clue what he'd been on about. Tom had hated him on sight. The one good thing: it wasn't another bloody woman. They all knew that the Chief Super had flung her hat into the ring to get kicked further upstairs in the free-for-all, and been knocked back. Talk about dual emotions! Tom had been torn between delight at seeing the bitch slapped down and misery that it probably meant none of them would go out in a blaze of glory.

'Right,' said Tom. 'CCTV cameras in the vicinity?'

Rachel grimaced. 'You must be joking. The closest is probably in Dalbeattie. But I suppose there could be private ones.'

Tom shook his head. 'We need to be twice as careful about these nowadays, because of the bloody courts. Still, worth seeing if any of the hotels in the area have a legit, registered one. There's at least one place that's close enough to the road to possibly pick up passing cars. We only need to look at the night of the 14th through to the 18th for now, I'd say. Dalbeattie would have the nearest filling station to here. Worth checking the video from there too, to see if there's anything that catches the eye. Buck up, Rach. We can't afford to dick about on this one.'

THREE

The Learmonth twins had each been given their own pair of field glasses. Proper adult ones that had cost a good deal of money. Belle had been a little dubious at first, but Fergus had convinced her that it'd be an insult to their intelligence to buy 'children's' ones.

The day seemed to be going smoothly. She didn't think of it as 'Christmas' any more. The Winter Solstice, Remi called it. That was much more pragmatic, as well as traditional. There had been no way of avoiding the twins' involvement in the school nativity play; Eddie was the tallest of the early stage children, so he'd been a natural for Joseph. Esmée had thrown a hissy fit because she couldn't be Mary, but in the age of equal opportunities, the Three Wise Men had become One Wise Man and Two Wise Women. Esmée had declared herself the leader, after a long debate with her father over which was the most valuable commodity between gold and frankincense and myrrh.

As she started to prepare the vegetables – Fergus had already got the joint of lamb in hand; they were none of them turkey fans – she thought about how different her children were from most of their schoolmates. Their favourite jaunt – other than to the sea at Sandgreen – was to the bird reserve at Caerlaverock. They both took it seriously. Two earnest students, peering through the binoculars available in the observatory. They'd take it in turns to read the numbers from the leg-rings on the whooper and Bewick's swans (the right leg for males, left for females) and identify the bird from the wallchart in the main hide. After a generous donation from Fergus, there were now whooper swans named Edmund and Esmée – though Belle hadn't been sure that was a good idea either: 'What if one of them doesn't come back next year?' she'd asked. And Fergus had replied that it was never too early for children to recognise that the world is not always a benevolent place.

You could see people thinking, 'Pushy parents.' But she and Fergus had never tried to bring the twins on. There had been no need. They were packed to the eyeballs with natural curiosity, and they were exceptionally quick to learn.

They were gregarious children too, though more at home in the company of adults than their own age-group. However, they seemed to be popular at school.

Ever since the twins were born, Fergus and Belle had walked the fine line between being grateful that the children had each other to play with, and ensuring that they didn't become too interdependent; the books they had read on raising twins warned about this – the secret world, even a secret language, in some cases. But Edmund and Esmée had never seemed to be at any risk of that. They were developing compatible but contrasting personalities.

In fact, now they were almost five Fergus said he found the twins much more interesting than when they were babies. You could hold a conversation with them.

Boxing Day

Fergus tried not to look anxious as he watched at his wife consulting the Solway tide tables one more time, then gathering towels, an extra sweater and a flask of hot coffee into her sports bag. When she had that bout of postnatal depression, Remi had told her that swimming in ultra-cold water could be a cure. He'd said that sounded like complete rubbish, but Belle had shown him the articles and learned papers she'd found online, squared her shoulders and said, 'Well, that's one thing Scotland's never short of, cold water.'

Remi apparently called the sea 'Mother Earth's amniotic sac'. Fergus earnestly hoped Belle would forget most of the dafter stuff once he could get her safely to Edinburgh, away from that bitch's influence.

So for the past four and a half years, she had set off almost every single morning of the year, with a group of equally intrepid women, to swim in the freezing waters of the Solway Firth. They usually swam from the sheltered beach at Carrick Shore, at high tide (it was too shallow to swim otherwise), and at this time of year they all wore sensible wetsuits.

He felt suddenly depressed. *I'm the one who paddles at the edge of life, writing my books; Belle's the swimmer.*

Although he adored his wife, this was one experience

Fergus didn't intend to share with her. In fact, he believed that the swimmers were slightly unbalanced.

But he had to admit, it had done her the world of good. Her skin was glowing, her figure was more slender than when they'd met. She looked the picture of health – and as far as he could gauge, she had shaken off the depression completely, apart from the odd blue day when she'd been overdoing it, and become stressed.

She had even made new friends through her hobby, although one or two of them were (in his eyes) somewhere to the north of weird.

He knew he had to be careful how he approached the subject of her sorties. Nothing riled her more than being fussed over. She'd chided him more than once for treating her as if she were made of eggshell.

As she finally zipped the sports bag, he dug his fingernails into his palms to prevent himself from leaping into the car and driving to the road above Carrick so that he could watch her through field glasses, as he had done several times before, terrified that he'd see her head disappear under the waves and not resurface. She'd be furious if she found out. But he'd only done it to make sure she looked as if she was coping. If he'd seen her get into difficulties, or start to swim too far out, he could have gone after her. He allowed himself a wry smile at the thought of plunging over the dunes and rocks, shedding clothes as he went, and trying to catch up with her, because Belle didn't swim with a mumsy breaststroke, but a crawl as powerful and fast as any man.

One of the first times he had watched her, she'd struck out beyond Ardwall, the little island that sealed the bay safely, into the open sea. He'd been paralysed with fear. Surely she wasn't going to...?

He'd started to run back along the road to where he could get down the cliff and over the dunes. He could swim, he was more than competent; but if he went into the water, he'd lose sight of where he'd last seen her.

He needed to call the coastguard. At least if he stayed where he was, he could direct them to the spot. He drew his phone from his pocket. Fuck! No signal.

He'd peered again, trying to pick out some landmark on the Whithorn peninsula to line up with where he'd last seen her. Then he saw her fluorescent pink bathing cap bobbing above the waves as she turned for the shore again. By the time his heart had regained its regular beat, she was almost on dry land.

The relief had made him weak at the knees. And he'd laughed at himself. *Fergus, what the hell's it going to look like if the cops happen by and see you watching a bunch of scantily-clad women through binoculars?* Or if a caravan-dweller from one of the sites dotted along the coast reported him?

In any case, Belle's companions kept an eye on her too. They wouldn't allow her to come to harm. They looked out for one another. He had headed home, trying to laugh at himself.

That day, he knew he wouldn't relax until he heard Belle arrive safely back in the house.

'Why don't you and the twins come and watch?' She was smiling at him. 'They could bring their new binoculars and get in some practice. Plenty of seabirds around, as well as swimming women.'

So the three of them ended up stationed on the top part of the road, above the dunes, wrapped up in hats and scarves and mufflers against a biting wind. Esmée was kicking up because she wanted to swim with her mother.

Eddie joined in. 'I do too.'

'You're not a good enough swimmer,' said his sister dismissively. 'Mummy says.' Fergus flashed her a warning look. 'Anyway, you're a boy, and the Sulwath Sisters is only for women.'

'And you're a little girl,' said Fergus. 'Not a chance you can go with them until you're much, much older.'

'I see a shelduck,' yelled Edmund, cheerfully.

Esmée raised her binoculars, determined not to be outdone.

Belle had spotted them. She waved; all the other women waved; they did a sort of synchronised swimming act, fooling around in the shallow water for the kids' benefit.

Then she struck out for the open water beyond the island. The swimming group was female-only. She had never been able to ascertain whether this was by design or coincidence. For some reason, she had been reluctant to ask.

But she appreciated the feeling of sisterhood and almost cloistered calm that it brought. Starting cold-water swimming had changed her life. And, of course, it had been Remi who suggested it, when she'd had that spell of the baby blues after the twins were born.

'Cold-water swimming,' Remi had announced, in that businesslike way of hers. 'Nothing like it for curing all types of depression, even the baby blues.'

'You'll come with me?'

Remi had laughed. 'Not on your life. I'm a land-girl. It's you that's the mermaid.'

She'd been terrified, the first few times. She'd never been a fan of artificial pools; the thought of bathing in water that had trapped other people's sweat and dead skin cells, and God knows what else, had always disgusted her. But the open sea, even in sheltered spots like Brighouse Bay and Carrick Shore, had seemed a step too far. It was late spring when she started joining the Sulwath Sisters almost every morning, and even by that first summer, when it was occasionally possible to venture into Scottish seawater without a wetsuit, she'd had to wear tankinis for a while. With a one-piece, either it had been flapping around her arse, or the top made her look as if she should change her name to June, because she was busting out all over.

Fergus had waffled on about being happy to pay for her to have a tummy-tuck, but that it wasn't a procedure entirely without risk. Then he'd added that he found the slack skin on her stomach comely. 'It's a proud badge of motherhood,' he'd said, so understandingly that she'd wanted to kill him. She had slapped him, hard, and stalked off, leaving him looking puzzled and hurt.

Nowadays, her confidence in her relationship with the sea was almost boundless. She hankered after the chance to swim by moonlight, but that would have to be for another year, another lifetime, perhaps. She didn't want to drive her husband to a nervous breakdown.

Belle rolled onto her back to float, remembering to gesture reassuringly first to the watchers up on the roadway. The waves rocked her into calm. The weightlessness lightened her mind.

She relished this time on her own, no Fergus, no kids, no one she had to make conversation with or worry about. No responsibilities, except to remain afloat. The time when she could let her mind drift to the important questions, such as which specific strand of heredity had made her who she was, and could shed a tear or two without seeing the look of concern in her husband's eyes. It helped her keep her temper with him on those days when he was over-solicitous. The stillness. The zen.

That time when I had a week or two when I couldn't get out of bed, and cried a lot. It was years ago. But he still watches me, I know he does. And he must know how I hate it.

I'm tough; if I weren't, I'd have gone under with the worry of being responsible for two children.

But in the end, I have no idea why I'm so prone to worry. If it's hereditary. Why I always seem to need someone as a crutch. First Father, then Roddy. Now Remi, maybe, because I can't afford to let Fergus see what I'm really like. Where does my love of art come from? And my fear of commitment? And why is it I don't just enjoy sex, I need it, I crave it, because until the last few years it filled the gap people refer to as 'love'. Presumably I take after my birth-mother, who was no doubt a slut who got knocked up by mistake then couldn't face the consequences.

In another ten days, when school restarted, she'd be in the water for a second time twice a week. A chlorinated pool instead of the sea, as she helped out with the primary school swimming class. She could see that it was necessary for learners to be in a pool. The twins had been competent swimmers since before they could walk.

She pictured herself, trim in her navy blue swimsuit, whistle on a lanyard around her neck, with a class of five- and six-year-olds eating out of her hand. One hundred per cent in control. She smiled: this was the same Belle who had believed she'd never be able to learn to raise kids, because she didn't know how to relate to them, and had no paradigm for how to be a good mother; that a leopard over forty-five can't alter her spots, not one.

Because she had never accepted what everyone in the town said about her now: that she was good with kids, who'd have thought it, Mabel Mountjoy the confirmed spinster, a model parent?

She had turned out to be a natural with the twins' age-group (though teenagers still terrified her). She didn't talk down to them, just as she didn't talk down to her own children. But she left them in no doubt who was boss. Kids who were notorious for devilment in the classroom behaved for her. Thank God. If there was one thing that drove her to distraction, it was the sheer level of *noise* children that age could make.

The twins were not noisy. In fact, she sometimes wondered if she and Fergus had made them too quiet. It didn't do, in the twenty-first century, to raise kids who were seen and not heard.

Perhaps they didn't play with them enough. They watched nature documentaries on TV with them, in preference to silly children's programmes. They didn't allow them to play violent computer games, the way so many did. They played board games with them instead. But they didn't go in for the rough and tumble games the other nursery parents played with their kids (she knew: she'd seen them in action at various birthday parties. Fathers who didn't mind playing at horses for hours on end, or playing football with the boys). She swam with her children at least once a week. They both took them for long, healthy walks. Fergus taught them and helped them do puzzles. But they didn't *play* with them.

Belle realised with a pang that she didn't know how to play. No one had ever played with her when she was young. She suspected it was the same for Fergus.

At the first opportunity, she'd ask him.

She rolled onto her front, and swam swiftly back to shore. Once there, she dashed out of the sea, peeled off the wetsuit and neoprene bootees, and donned the neat, Velcro-fastened towelling tent she had made for herself. Within minutes, she was dressed and up the road to her family.

Fergus had promised a short New Year's holiday to a secret destination. She knew it wasn't abroad, because there had been no palaver of looking out passports and changing money.

On the way home, she sneezed three times. Fergus gave her an anxious glance. 'I hope you're not coming down with a chill to spoil your surprise holiday.'

'Don't fuss. I'm as strong as a bison.'

What did it matter anyway? The one and only place she ever caught infections was from the air conditioned interior of planes.

She slid her arms round his waist as he stood at the cooker, heating soup to warm her up.

'Fergus – did your mother play with you when you were the twins' age?'

He wriggled round to look at her, eyebrows raised. 'Play with me?'

'You know – games and so on.'

He shook his head. 'She let me help her in the garden. I had a swing and a climbing frame – long before other kids got them. It wasn't metal. I think possibly she got the gardener to make it.'

'So you played on your own?'

She remembered how that felt. Wheeling her doll's pram up and down the garden paths. Helping her mother, with the child's gardening set she was given for her third birthday. She didn't remember feeling lonely or deprived. But then again, she didn't remember being happy. It was all a bit of a blur.

She smiled at Fergus. 'Maybe it's an only-child thing. I didn't mind playing by myself.'

He moved the soup pan off the heat and drew her into his arms. 'What's this about, sweetheart?'

'I worry if we play with the twins enough.'

'Of course we do! And they have each other.'

He walked her across to the window that overlooked the garden. Edmund and Esmée were charging around like dervishes.

'Look at that. These are *not* children who lack attention!'

FOUR

Tom loathed Chief Superintendent Maggie McInnes. Hell, he'd have loathed her even if she'd been a man. Typical of the ones who'd climbed the ladder by digging her heels into other people's backs. He despised her, from her expensive haircut (she didn't get *that* done locally, Jackie assured him, and she should know) to her bloody stiletto shoes. Bitch.

Another with a fucking law degree. In his father's day, if a woman got promotion, there would have been plenty of snide remarks about who she was sleeping with. He smiled grimly to himself as he approached McInnes's door. A summons to her office was never a welcome event.

She didn't invite him to sit down.

'No further forward with this, Ellis?'

'Well, it's been Christmas, ma'am.' As if that'd mean anything to her. Probably worshipped pagan gods who demanded blood sacrifice of male children.

'So? Do you imagine the public expect us to put our feet up because it's Christmas?'

'I think the public realise that even detectives need some time off. To recharge the batteries.'

'Well, let's hope your battery's fully recharged, Ellis, because I need this topped and tailed before the year's out, do you understand? I won't have this force made to look like fools who can't solve a simple missing person enquiry.'

'Begging your pardon, ma'am, but there are hundreds of unsolved Misper cases all over the country. Hundreds. And some that have been unsolved for more than ten years.'

'This isn't one of them. I know it in my bones. Get it sorted, Ellis. Get it sorted today. Get a Misper message out on TV.'

'What time is it?' asked Jackie Ellis's sleepy voice, as Tom got out of bed as quietly as he could.

'God knows. Three or something.'

'Can you not sleep?'

'Of course I can't sleep.'

'This missing person thing?'

He grunted as he headed for the kitchen to make himself a cup of tea. The memory of the dressing-down from McInnes had struck a raw spot.

He chewed the nail of his left index finger. He had to have a plan, because he hadn't spoken to Fergus Learmonth since he had him on the wrong side of a table in Dumfries police station six years earlier, and was more or less accusing him of doing away with Mabs's former lover, Roddy McCulloch.

But the man was clever, no doubt about it. It had been Fergus Learmonth who found the clue that solved *that* case. And yet, and yet: there had also been the mystery of what had happened to Learmonth's ex-wife's Russian gigolo. Another found dead in suspicious circumstances, and Fergus had been the one able to provide the vital information that time too, without a smidgin of evidence to link him to the death.

But there was nothing else for it, because he'd hit a brick wall with the missing person case.

He wanted with all his heart to loathe Fergus Learmonth – if only because he'd succeeded in winning the heart of Mabel Mountjoy and fathering twins on her. But he couldn't help admiring the man.

The word had gone round Scotland that over the past four years Learmonth had helped solve half a dozen missing person cases that'd had other forces stumped – as well as writing the books that had his silly, bearded face grinning out from posters in every Waterstone's in the land. Tom had even noticed one of them at Haymarket Station the last time he'd been in Edinburgh. You couldn't get away from the man, and Kirkcudbright was right up its own backside with glee; the 'Artists' Town' revelling in having one of the world's most successful crime writers in its midst. A celebrity, all of its own.

As he sat in his office next morning, pondering the statements they'd assembled, and his lengthy notes from phone conversations with colleagues in Cheshire Police, one thing struck Tom forcibly: no one seemed to miss Angus McPhedrie, or to be unduly perturbed that he'd disappeared. No one except the fish man and the cleaner. He suspected that in both cases there was a pecuniary reason for the concern. The fish seller, Danny Jack, appeared to be as close to a friend as McPhedrie had in the Galloway area.

Something wasn't right. Why would a man with that much money choose to spend Christmas in a place like Colvend?

He was jolted back to the present by a shout from the open-plan office beside his lair.

'I'm in!'

Tom and his team gathered around Stuart Pirie's desk, which was clear and clean except for McPhedrie's MacBook.

Because so many staff had been due leave over Christmas, it had taken the IT people until that day to install the forensic software that ensured nothing on the hard drive could be altered. It had taken Stuart another day to break the password.

'Every file was password protected, but he was using a sequence of numbers. I've cracked it.'

'And?' asked Tom.

Stuart's lips were pursed. He pressed a key, and there was a collective intake of breath. Tom felt that itch between his shoulder blades he always got when they were onto something *big*. He moved a little to the doorway, where he could surreptitiously scratch his back against the jamb.

As Stuart scrolled through the files the room held a stunned, sinister silence. Not the sort of material Tom had ever grown accustomed to, because they didn't see much of it in Dumfries and Galloway, to tell the truth.

There were no documents of any great interest, and no sign of internet banking activity. But there were seven thousand two hundred photos. Child porn, all of it. Some of the children looked to be extremely young. Toddlers, up to the age of perhaps twelve. Both boys and girls.

Tom's mouth was dry. It was less than three months since the Met had launched Operation Yewtree. Maybe, just maybe, this was his chance to make his mark, get noticed by the people who mattered. But even more than that, there was nothing on the planet he loathed so much as a nonce.

'We need to get this guy,' Rachel said, leaning over Stuart's shoulder. 'You know what happens to paedos inside. We won't even need to hang the bastard ourselves.'

'So that'd be a reason for him to scarper,' said DC Giles. 'Maybe he knew someone was going to spill the beans. He could be anywhere by now. Off in a small boat, even. Ireland. The Continent.'

'He wouldn't have left his passport behind in that case,' said Rachel. 'Not to mention the laptop with all the incriminating evidence on it.'

'Anyone thought to check if any boats are missing from local moorings?' asked Stuart.

Giles consulted his notes. 'Not that I know of.'

But Tom had lost interest. He was thinking back to those scuff marks on the pale cream tiles of the kitchen floor. 'Goddamn it,' he muttered. He relished the mental picture of that scummy fucker being abducted and tortured and killed. Some people asked for it. Best keep that precise thought to himself though. Had to watch what you said the whole bloody time these days. Treat a kiddie-fiddler as equal to any other scumbag. Call him 'Sir'.

So there it was. Paedophile, missing, possibly to be presumed abducted. And not one single clue as to exactly when he'd vanished, or where he – or whatever was left of him – was now. Fucking hopeless. But one thing he found he was sure of: McPhedrie had not left that house willingly. Unless the scuff-marks meant that he had dragged someone else outside. But where? Not to his car.

They'd already ascertained that McPhedrie had paid for his

phone on a direct debit contract, and got a list of his calls. Absolutely nothing there that gave any clues whatsoever.

'Can you get any handle on where he was sourcing these pics, Stuart?' he asked.

'I can try. But these creatures use the dark net.'

Tom cracked his knuckles, and smiled grimly as he saw DS Field wince. 'Right, we all need to remember: we're here to act in the interests of justice, not personal values. At the moment, our main task is to find McPhedrie, see if he's come to harm.'

Tom remembered the reason for his conviction that Cheshire CID would have no time or inclination to help with a Misper case.

'Rach, check again with our colleagues in Cheshire. See if there's any possibility these guys they found in the Bridgewater Canal are flinging up any connections to paedos. You never know. The murders down there certainly sound as if they're linked. And these types don't operate alone. Now, listen up, troops. We don't know yet if this guy's part of a ring, and we don't know how far that ring might stretch.' *Can a ring stretch?* 'Extend,' he added. 'So not a word about this gets out meantime – OK? *Comprenez?* And I mean not a *word*. I know we all detest a nonce. But if this one leads us to the bigger fish, we're doing our job. So no leaks, no careless talk, or I'll have your bollocks to hang on my driving mirror. And that applies to the women too. *No* tip-offs to any of your pals in the media, no matter how many beers they buy you. OK?' He glared at Giles. 'You listening?'

Giles shrugged. Tom didn't see his lips move. 'OK, Giles?'

'OK. *Sir*.

Sullen oaf!

Tom was pretty sure no one in his nick ever took a bung for

passing on juicy info – Dumfries and Galloway wasn't important enough to have many meaty tip-offs. But you never could
tell; and he was well aware that most people in the job detest
child molesters above all criminals. The temptation to spill the
beans would be high.

He had already written the script for that afternoon's press
conference. No need to alter it. No need to mention
McPhedrie's predilection for jerking off over pics of toddlers.

Tom's throat was dry as he turned from Kirkcudbright's High
Street onto the neat cobbled surface of Crosskeys Close. One of
the posh ones. No wheelie bins in evidence. Flower-planters
that'd be burgeoning with colour come spring. And crowning it
at the end, behind the improbably large laburnum tree in its
granite-block circle, Ashers, Mabel Mountjoy's home.

He slowed his steps. It was the most magnificent house in
the town, with its porticoed front door and the elegant propor-
tion of window to wall. And the Learmonth guy had spent a
packet on renovations; it had been the speak of the town for the
past five years. A few weeks after Mabel had married, the whole
edifice had been covered in scaffolding, and builders from
Carlisle (from *Carlisle!*) moved in to replace the roof. Then the
biggest plumbing firm from Dumfries was there for a fortnight
upgrading the heating, God knows what all else.

The newly-painted external walls were the same muted
poached salmon shade; the colour Ashers had always been, as
long as anyone could remember. And it was the hot rumour that
an obscene amount had been spent on the inside too. New
kitchen and bathrooms, an additional bathroom added for the
children, no expense spared. Mabel Mountjoy had played her

cards right, and no mistake, netting a man with money like that to spend, and her knocking at the door of fifty. And now her husband was earning more than ever, if you could believe the *Scotsman*, writing crime novels. What justice was there in a world where those who solved the crimes got paid peanuts, and the fool who sat at a desk making up stories about them got paid a king's ransom? Right from the first one he wrote, Learmonth's books seemed to have flown off the shelves, and now they'd been made into a TV series, and his name was mentioned with the same reverence as Ian Rankin's.

His mother had been furious when Mabel turned him down, all these years ago. 'Who does she think she is? Her own mother was no better than a whore.' She'd pronounced it hoo-er, in the Scots way. Tom's father was dead by then, but he'd hated old Mountjoy too. Hated all lawyers, and imagined that they spent their entire lives trying to get villains off scot-free. Protecting scum. Almost as bad as the criminals themselves. Tom smirked to himself when he thought about that. How would his old man have coped with the situation these days, when all the solicitor had to do was whisper in his client's ear that he didn't have to answer a question, and you ended up with a 'no comment' interview, the bugger not even saying 'Yes' to his own name?

He'd spent the next twenty years trying to hate Mabel. And yet, and yet – when he'd seen her again more than five years ago, when her so-called 'lodger' had vanished off the face of the earth, the old tenderness had resurfaced. *Admit it, Tom Ellis. You're still in love with her, even now you're both middle-aged.*

He couldn't put it off any longer. He was almost at the door, resplendent with its polished brass knocker. He noticed that there was no sign of a doorbell; that had been missed off the list of modernisations. *Either knock or turn and run, man.* Not that he hadn't nipped through the close for a look many times over the past five years. He glanced up at the house once more. It looked like an illustration from one of these magazines Jackie was always reading. The windows appeared to be new too. None of your plastic. New wooden sash and case. That would have cost a good few thou per window. The place looked as good as it would have in its heyday, when the wealthy merchant William Asher had had it built, in 1780-something. Better. William Asher didn't have an extra bathroom put in for his kids.

The house was in darkness, except for what looked to be a lamp in the hallway. Bugger! Maybe they were out?

He knocked and waited; no sound of Mabel's damn dog yapping. He knocked again, then gave up. It was the middle of the holidays. No doubt they'd gone to Edinburgh. He'd heard they had a house there too.

His phone pinged as he stepped back onto the High Street. Missed call from the office. He rang back. 'DI Ellis? The Chief Super wants to see you.'

'What – now? I'm not even in Dumfries. I'm nearly home.'

'I've been told it's urgent.'

'In her office is she?'

'She is.'

He groaned. 'I'm on my way then.'

Fuck! What had he done now?

He could feel sweat on the back of his neck as he entered Margaret McInnes's office. An urgent summons was always particularly bad news. But this time, she almost smiled as she looked up at him (after spending seconds too long studying papers on her desk). A crocodile's smile.

'There's another disappearance, Tom. From Thornhill this time – or just outside it anyway. Sounds a bit similar to the one you're working on. A couple this time, man and wife. Same sort of scenario – house lying open, car still there, no sign of forced entry or burglary. Uniforms have been over it, and can't find any clues. I need you there as soon as possible, to see if you reckon the cases are connected.' She pressed a key on her computer. 'That's the file sent to you. Take a look, then head off, please.'

'You heard what we've found on McPhedrie's laptop?'

She nodded.

'Should I not concentrate on following that up?'

'You should concentrate on what I've asked you to do, DI Ellis.'

FIVE

Belle leaned against the deck rail, face pressed into air that was like wet cotton wool. This was the surprise then. They were on the Calmac ferry from Ardrossan, taking the twins to the Isle of Arran, for a New Year break.

Not strictly fair: the break had been meant for her, Belle, alone. No cooking, no housekeeping, for six precious days. She was tired, right enough. They had spent the time since Christmas moving Esmée into her new room.

They'd brought Archie with them, but left Gorby at home with a sitter. The cat was getting stiff. For the past couple of years, she'd watched him start to measure the jump in a way he never used to. 'I know how you feel, old chap,' Fergus would say, and her heart would be wrung for a moment, because she knew how much he loved the cat. The cat he had owned with Serena, his ex-wife. She prayed the animal wouldn't die while they were away.

Fergus had enthused about the bracing summer holidays spent on Arran with his grandparents. His grandmother in particular was keen on Scottish holidays, apparently. Just as Father had been.

Belle had always taken her holidays, by preference, in places where she could satiate herself with paintings. Fergus's main interest was in architecture. He'd complain that in cities like Florence nowadays you couldn't see the buildings for people. Over the last five years, it seemed his passion for the Moorish architecture of El Andalus had grown. He claimed always to have preferred Spain to Italy.

He'd taken her to the Parador set in the grounds of Granada's Alhambra for their honeymoon. And indeed, the rose-gardens had been wonderful, even in autumn; but *so* crowded! She'd barely been able to appreciate them because of claustrophobia. In fact, she'd probably been a pain in the neck the whole time, because she'd developed morning sickness at last, in the fourth month of her pregnancy.

Bloody Arran!

It was flat calm. Through breaks in the cloud, the tops of the mountains at the island's north end – the ones that formed the head and shoulders of the shape known as the Sleeping Warrior – thrust skywards, then disappeared again after a few minutes.

Fergus was disappointed in the transport. He claimed to have dim recollections of one of the ferries on this route having interesting engines, which you could see from an open doorway in the bowels of the ship. His grandmother was always deputed to take him to see the engines. When they rejoined his grandfather, he knew that the old man had been drinking whisky. 'You could smell it on his breath, even above the fug of diesel and tobacco fumes.' he'd said.

He had already taken Edmund and Esmée on a sortie below

decks, searching for a point where you could see the engines. So everyone was disappointed.

Belle was silent as they disembarked. They drove through Brodick, heading south. Fergus had announced that they'd take the coast road to their destination, instead of cutting across Glen Scorrodale.

As they approached the village of Whiting Bay, she knew she was paler than ever. So pale, in fact, that Fergus suggested stopping at the first available hotel, to get her a brandy.

She tried not to snap at him. A brandy snap. She giggled instead. She heard the sound inside her own head; like a lunatic laughing. From the corner of her eye, she could see the twins staring at her in puzzlement.

'Whiting Bay,' she said. 'This is where we stayed. In a boarding house, with palm trees at both corners of the front garden. It had a huge rock in the back garden too – probably twenty feet high, though that's a child's impression.'

Fergus seemed a little miffed. 'You didn't say you'd been here before?'

'Everyone's been to Arran.'

'When, roughly?'

'Before I went to school.'

'So would you recognise the place where you stayed?'

As they drove through the village, she stared intently at each house, then cried out: 'I'm sure that's it.' There were no palm trees in the garden.

Fergus stopped the car, crossed the road and peered over the fence. Such a literal man. She composed her face into a smile. He was only trying to be kind. He came back to the car, grinning. 'You could be right. There are two tree stumps that look about right for palms. And I can see the big rock you were talking about. So, what a memory! You said you were no more than five when you were here?'

She was shivering. 'Less. I certainly wasn't at primary school.'

'You came with your father?'

She was vague again. 'I suppose so.'

The rest of the surprise was the Lagg Hotel. Family-run, homely and comfortable. The staff couldn't do enough for the kids, and complimented Belle more than once on how well-behaved they were.

Despite an excellent dinner and two whiskies, Belle spent a sleepless night, and barely touched her breakfast. She tried to ignore the increasingly anxious expression on Fergus's face. *Just lose your temper with me for once, why don't you.* But he never did that. That's why her entire world felt as if it were made of eggshells.

The morning had dawned cold and clear and sunny. They all wrapped up in coats, scarves and gloves, and drove up the coast, heading for Catacol. Belle was sure there was nothing of interest there, but the twins had heard Fergus say that the place-name meant 'the gully of the wild cat'. Both children had their new binoculars carefully slung around their necks. They were desperate to see a wild cat.

Belle was given charge of the map. Fergus was in one of his anti-sat-nav phases – not that you'd need it on an island; *keep going long enough and you're back where you started. As with life.*

The island looked different from her memory of it. She began to doubt that she'd visited after all.

'Farmers used to be paid to keep the bracken down,' observed Fergus. 'Look at it now!'

There were stands of it beside the road, dull in its winter bronze, and almost as tall as the wind-sculpted hazel trees.

A couple of miles south of Pirnmill, they found themselves above a wide, sandy bay, sheltered by a headland. There were no houses nearby except what looked like a croft house, with the obligatory palm tree.

'That seems like a pleasant beach, and we'll have it to ourselves. Let me find a better place to park, and we can go down. It looks like the perfect place to paddle.'

'*Paddle*? Fergus, it's December!'

'Says the woman who swims in the sea in December. Come on, Belle, look at the sunshine. We'll top up our vitamin D and get some ozone in our lungs. You know as well as I do, children are impervious to cold.'

The twins were already wending their way over the pale grey lava-rocks to the sand.

Belle stood at the water's edge, feeling her head start to ache with the brilliance of sun reflected off water. She was suddenly aware that the twins had shed their boots and socks and were indeed paddling. She loved that feeling, the way you could curl your toes into the firm sand. She looked across Kilbrannan Sound to the dark hump of Kintyre.

Fergus was shouting at the twins not to go any further out, although they were barely past their ankles.

'But it's not all that cold, Daddy,' Esmée was shouting back, petulant as ever.

'It's safe,' murmured Belle. She felt as if she was in a dream. 'It's shallow for a long way out.'

He looked at her sharply, caught up short by the rapt expression on her face. 'Are you OK?'

She was almost startled by his voice. 'Yes. I'm remembering being here.'

He was keeping a close eye on the kids, who were now splashing cheerfully back towards them. Eddie was brandishing the plastic beaker he must have secreted in his pocket. 'We've got a starfish,' he shouted. 'We're going to find another one so it won't be lonely. A mummy starfish and a daddy one.'

I remember this too. The way voices carried across the water, so that when the Loch Fyne boats passed slowly by, hundreds of yards offshore, you could hear the fishermen talking to one another.

She'd had a vision of herself, aged four, wading across this same bay, the water to the tops of her chubby legs, the hem of her dress soaked and dragging and slowing her down, following two older local boys. It must have been summer.

The water was warm, almost balmy. The boys both had shallow metal buckets, and nets on sticks. They were after crabs. The sand was firm and ridged, and crumbled under my toes. I remember, I remember...

I remember my mother laughing, pointing the camera at me, before I waded out. I remember Rose splashing after me then, making heavy weather of trying to run in the ankle-deep water, calling my name angrily. 'Come here, you wee bisom! Look at the state of your good dress.' A slap on my bare arm. The same arm seized roughly as my mother hauls me back towards the beach. I shriek.

I remember I was less afraid of the skelping I knew I was in for than of losing face in front of the village boys. They turned to stare at me, shrugged, waded on.

There was a man on the beach. Father? But I have no memory of him being on Arran with us.

The adult Belle had an epiphany. It wasn't Father. That was why Rose wasn't paying attention.

'Stupid wee brat,' her mother is saying. 'You could have got stung by a jelly.'

And right enough, on the sand where the tide has been, there are dozens of clear glistening mounds, with purple insides that look like the coloured middles of glass marbles. Jellies. Like a party meal abandoned before the dessert course.

'Make the kids come out, Fergus. There were always jellyfish here, and they can give you a nasty sting. I think there are better beaches further up the coast anyway.'

'There aren't jellyfish in the winter, Belle. They only come in the summer. They come up on the warm currents. The Gulf Stream.'

Edmund was beside them, jumping up and down impatiently. 'Look, look!'

They both admired the single starfish, which Eddie pronounced a mummy one, and a tiny russet-coloured crab, before supervising the careful decanting of both back into the sea.

Esmée stood further up the beach, scanning the horizon with her field glasses.

Catacol was as dull as Belle remembered. A row of houses. Not a wild cat in sight, not even a domesticated one.

Once the twins were in bed, Fergus plied Belle with cocktails, then asked tentatively, 'You were remembering being at that beach with your father?'

'No,' she said slowly. 'I don't think he ever came here. It was Rose.'

He slid an arm round her. 'You were remembering her?'

'I've no memory of her face. But it *was* her. I remembered the place.'

She avoided his eyes. She couldn't stand hearing him banging on again about the therapeutic value of retrieving memories of Rose. *It is* not *conducive to feeling better.*

She was aware that the shell she always felt around her heart was still firmly in place. Even with Fergus, even with her children, there was always the carapace, the distance between them. It would hurt too much to let people inside.

She didn't mention the fact that she had realised Rose was at the beach with another man. She had no clear picture of him anyway, other than dark hair and merry brown eyes. There was also a vague recollection that he was more fun than Father, and made her laugh, but that Rose was always snapping at him, so he'd wink at Belle and roll his eyes. Eyes the colour of amber.

Fergus realised instinctively what was happening, as soon as he asked if it was her father she was remembering. He knew her better than she'd ever admit.

He sensed it was beneficial. Cathartic. A psychiatrist would agree, he was sure. In his heart he despised such people. His mind (but not his heart) flipped back to Serena. He'd wasted a shedload of money on sending her to a shrink, to deal with her frigidity problem, and the experience had made her worse, not better. Not one single bloody bit of good had come of it. Merely another weapon for her to attack him with.

But then, the person being 'analysed' has to be a cooperative and willing partner. Serena had never been that. It's the opposite of the way it is with forensic evidence. You can take a sample of DNA and analyse it whether it wants to be analysed or not. People are different.

In the final analysis (if she had consented to stick with it that far. Ha!), Serena had been unbalanced. Barking mad. He'd known that when he married her. But he had been so bewitched by her looks, her icy refusal to be loved, her fey ways, that he'd believed he could cure her.

Belle was an infinitely more intelligent and complex human being than Serena ever was. She simply baulked at unearthing her past. He was more convinced than ever that Rose was Belle's biological mother. The reasons why this had been hidden, and both Rose and her husband had adopted the child – that he'd probably never know. Belle didn't even like to hear her mother's name mentioned. Every incipient conversation had been closed down abruptly. Although she knew perfectly well that she had the right to access her original birth certificate, she had steadfastly refused to do so.

Once or twice, he had tried to persuade her to at least see if Rose Mountjoy was still around. 'After all,' he'd say, 'if she was in her early twenties when you were adopted, she'd not be eighty yet. No age at all these days.'

Always the same answer: 'No!'

'But wouldn't it be fine for Esmée and Edmund to have at least one grandparent?' Belle knew perfectly well that he missed his own grandparents, who had raised him, more than his mother. She knew that he recalled them with a fondness verging on painful, although it was more than twenty years since they'd died.

'Briony's like a grandmother to them. And far better at it than Rose ever would be. Rose was not the nurturing kind, Fergus.'

'But...'

'I had no grandparents, and I've done fine.'

Her eyes would flash with steel amid the amber. Each time, he'd let it lie.

He had, naturally, done what research he could. He was certain he had found the marriage record for Arthur Mountjoy, but wanted to be sure he had the right one. He had asked Belle casually what Rose's maiden name was.

'Why?'

'I'm interested. The twins may be keen to know more about the family history one day.'

'But she's not a blood relative – why would they be interested?'

Fergus had shrugged helplessly.

'Balquhidder,' she'd mumbled.

'As in "Braes of"? That's an unusual name.'

It had been her turn to shrug. Fergus shuddered inwardly. So his research had been spot-on (not that he'd ever doubted it; he was good at what he did). And that meant the birth certificate he'd found was also the correct one. Rose Balquhidder had been born in Back Wynd, Kirkcudbright, in 1938. A local lass. He'd asked casually in town where Back Wynd was, only to find it had been pulled down in the late 1950s. 'A real slum that was,' said his informant. 'Where the council houses beside the church are now.'

So Rose was not only local, but from a poor family. That explained a lot about why she'd married a wealthy man so much older than her, and then tripped the light fantastic with whoever Belle's father was. But he was getting ahead of himself with that part of the story.

He knew the importance of treading carefully. But what kind of woman would abandon her own child?

He thought back to when he had first met Serena. It had been like a conflagration in a petrol store. Whoomf! Uncontrollable. If he'd been married to someone else then, he might well have abandoned a wife. Because the thing with Serena (he had recognised this since marrying Belle) wasn't love: it was obsession. Once he'd allowed himself to fall under the spell, he had no more power over his own reactions than the worst of drug addicts.

He'd recovered from the obsession as soon as he discovered Belle was pregnant. And once he held the twins, he knew there was nothing on earth that could tempt him to abandon them.

But maybe that's how it was for Rose; an obsession she couldn't resist?

He had dug deeper and found that children of the same surname – Balquhidder – used to model for the local artist, Hornel. Best keep *that* from his wife anyway. Belle even hated the gloomy interior of the famous man's house, run now by the National Trust, although she loved the garden, and a visit to it always left her feeling cheated because Ashers' garden faced inland rather than to the shore. The little girls Hornel painted all seemed to have black or auburn hair, and there was one he had always found tremendously like Belle physically.

On a whim, he had traced the family tree of the girls who were Hornel's models. One of them was called Rose, and right enough, that Rose had married and had a daughter also called Rose, in 1938. Then he found something that jolted his heart into his mouth. The name of the grandmother of the Balquhidder girls who used to model for Hornel: Mabel.

But if she was Belle's biological mother, why hadn't she

passed off the child as her husband's? Unless... He recalled his wife mentioning once, in an insouciant tone, that she was sure her parents didn't share a bedroom.

Belle feigned sleepiness, to get Fergus off the subject of memories of her mother. Had Father missed Rose? She didn't think so. He never spoke her name once after she left, and he mutilated every photo she'd appeared in, so that in most depictions of scenes from Belle's childhood, there was a disembodied stray hand on the grass, or a glimpse of a supernumerary shoulder. But in fact, there were relatively few where both she and Rose were in them, because she was sure it had always been Rose who was the photographer.

When they were first married, and beginning to think of names for the children, Fergus had asked her why she was called Mabel; they'd been laughing about his great-grandmother being called Grizel.

'Is it a family name?' he'd asked.

And she'd shrugged and reminded him she'd originally been landed with the handle 'Maybelle'. 'Maybe Rose saw it on a lipstick,' she'd said casually, singing the Maybelline advertising jingle.

He'd pussy-footed round the topic of whether Father had been cruel to her, beaten her. He hadn't. Nothing more than the occasional slap on the hand when she'd been naughty. He hadn't been sufficiently interested in anything she'd said or done.

Although Belle never spoke about it, Fergus knew that her

father simply erased all memory of Rose after she'd left. Her prior and present existence was whitewashed out, just as her image had been excised from all the photographs, leaving Belle with a childhood of mutilated pictures, although the old man had been careful not to damage any of the photos of Belle herself. Where Rose had been cut out, you could tell that the instrument of excision was a sharp knife, not scissors. The edges were flat and smooth.

So Belle had grown up with no inkling of whether Rose was still alive, whether she remarried, whether there might be half-siblings. She had grown up believing it would be treacherous to even attempt to find out. It would be to betray Father.

'What does it *matter?*' she'd say when Fergus tried to raise the subject. 'It's not as if she was my real mother. Not a blood relative.'

Next morning, the family walked up the glen behind the hotel, through hazel plantations. The leaves crunched underfoot. The weather and the scenery were autumnal, rather than wintry, the same as at home. One of the few advantages of the west coast: the worst of the weather often didn't arrive until January, when the days were starting to get longer again. Belle was uncommunicative. Fergus tried hard not to show he was worried. *We're not out of the woods yet.*

SIX

'Shall we have a quick jaunt to the flat before the kids go back to school?' Fergus asked as he drove carefully off the ferry. He hated the cavalier way the crewmen directed vehicles hither and thither, without paying attention to what they were doing. As if no one cared about their car getting scratched or dented.

'What, straight away?'

'Well, we'd need to go home first and organise the sitter to stay on for Gorby.' They took the pug to the flat with them these days. Carrying the plump, squirming animal up and down four flights of slippery stone stairs was almost worse than having had to carry the twins up and down when they were small.

'We should probably have gone there for New Year, to let them see the fireworks at Hogmanay.'

'They've seen them before, and you always say you hate the crowds.' Belle was, he suspected, subject to claustrophobia in any press of people.

'I don't think there's time to go now. They're back in school on Monday.'

Fergus sighed. Belle hadn't grown to love the city the way he did. Apart from a few miserable and lonely years in London, he had always been more than happy to live in Scotland's capital.

He'd been at school there. He'd been a student there – he had been sufficiently loyal to take both his degree and his PhD at the university which had been his mother's alma mater, and his grandfather's. And he had always lived close to the centre, either in the New Town or on its western periphery, although he also loved to wander the streets of Old Edinburgh, for the frisson it brought, particularly on a winter's evening, even in its sanitised, modern incarnation.

When Belle agreed to marry him he'd decided, on the spur of the moment, to sell the elegant flat in Learmonth Terrace that he'd owned for a tad over six years. The cash from the sale had come in handy, since Ashers was in a sorry state at that point (and in that particular he was Peter Fairbairn's grandson: although he'd sold quickly, he'd sold for top whack). But he had quickly regretted not having a base in Edinburgh.

For he loved the city almost as much as he loved any human being. So once the twins were born, and obviously healthy, he had insisted on shopping for a flat that could be a pied-à-terre as the children grew. In Fergus's heart, any child deprived of Edinburgh during its formative years was an underprivileged child.

When they first went to view the flat in Bruntsfield, he'd dismissed it out of hand, cursing himself for not reading the details carefully enough beforehand. Four flights up, with two babies under a year, and all their paraphernalia? Not a chance.

But Belle had scampered upstairs eagerly in the estate agent's wake, Esmée in the sling on her front, and he'd followed reluctantly with Edmund in a similar contraption.

As soon as they'd entered the flat, Belle had gravitated to the tall kitchen window with its view clear across the Forth to Fife. She'd stood transfixed, gazing out, and sighed. 'You don't feel shut in here,' she'd murmured. 'You can see out.'

She'd barely glanced at the rest of the flat, before pronouncing it perfect. In any case, although he'd paid particular attention to everything else about the building, even climbing perilously onto the wall of the communal back garden so that he could try to see the state of the roof, he could find nothing to fault. The tenement was well-maintained, and the flat had been modernised by the last owners, exactly to his taste.

He'd had one final attempt at persuading Belle to be reasonable.

'It's not practical. How do you get the kids up that stair if you're on your own with them? You can't leave one parked in the buggy at the bottom while you carry the other one up.'

'But I won't *be* here on my own with the children,' she'd said, her voice unusually calm. 'We'll always be here as a family, for our weekend breaks.'

'You're proposing to carry that buggy up four flights every time too?'

Belle rolled her eyes. 'I'm sure there's a solution to that.'

'Each flat has its own cellar, off the passage through to the back green,' said the estate agent helpfully. 'I don't have the key for your one, but I'm sure it's big enough to hold a buggy. Probably hold a lot of their toys too. The back garden's beautifully kept, isn't it Mrs Learmonth? A great place for your little ones to play. Safe.'

Fergus saw a chink of opportunity to object. 'Who looks after it?'

'I believe a man comes in to cut the grass and keep it tidy.'

Fergus guffawed. 'And how much does that cost?'

The estate agent consulted his notes. 'Each flat pays £10 per month.'

'And maybe the other owners won't want children playing there, if they're paying for its upkeep? I don't see any others there just now.'

'Don't be silly, Fergus. No one objects to well-behaved children.' Esmée smiled gummily into her mother's face, as if agreeing. 'It's perfect. I couldn't live in a lower flat, even for weekends. I'd feel as if I couldn't breathe.'

'But Belle...'

'I love it. This is the one. It's not as if we'll be here all the time, Fergus. A weekend a month if we're lucky. And the children are always growing.'

She had that look in her eye. Fergus had realised there was no point in looking at other, more practical solutions. He'd known in that moment it was time to get his cheque book out.

He'd spent much of the next two years waking in a cold sweat, after dreaming that one or other of the twins had taken a tumble on the steep stairs.

But once the children could climb under their own steam, he had to admit it had been the right choice, with its cavernous kitchen – large enough for his grandparents' venerable pine table – cosy sitting room and two capacious bedrooms.

He had built a window seat for Belle in the kitchen, though she'd complained that she didn't want to have her back to the view. She'd either kneel on it or sit with her feet drawn up, for hours on end at twilight, looking across to the lights of Fife.

She had happily taken on the task of restoring the flower beds at either side of the well-kept communal back green, and on their visits in summer she was happy to allow the twins and

Archie to play there all day, while she kept an eye on them from the kitchen window.

It hadn't all been plain sailing though. Bruntsfield was Bruntsfield, after all, not the Grange.

One Saturday night during their second year of ownership, they'd both been wakened by ear-splitting screams from the street.

'You need to go and see what's happened, Fergus. It sounded like a girl screaming.'

And Belle had fussed until he got dressed to go outside and see what was afoot – at which point, she began to fuss that he might get hurt.

There had been no sign of anything or anyone out of the ordinary.

'It's only been students larking about,' he'd pronounced, out of breath from the climb.

'Students!'

'Well, I'm sure you had the odd rowdy night when you were a student. I know I did.'

'I didn't in fact.'

Fergus could have bitten his tongue. He knew, from what she had told him, that she had moved into the artist Roddy McCulloch's West End flat in Glasgow while she was a teenager. Since McCulloch had been much older, presumably she was kept under the thumb.

'So *you* behaved like that when you were a student?' she'd asked, coldly.

'I thought everyone did. You know what rugger players are like when they're celebrating a win.'

She'd snorted, her eyes flashing sparks. 'And you want Eddie to play rugger!'

'Not when he's under three, I don't.'

'Good, because there was another story in the paper last week about the injuries boys pick up. Brain damage, broken limbs. There was that boy who died from concussion the year before last. He wasn't even fourteen.' She shuddered. 'I don't want Eddie going in for dangerous sports, the way you did.'

Fergus had been unwise enough to admit that he'd boxed a little at university too. Not that he'd ever thought to suggest *that* as a future pastime for his son. But he'd been proficient; he had the weight and the height for it, and it had stood him in good stead over the years. He'd been in some tricky situations, but always felt he'd be able to defend himself.

Nowadays, it was martial arts. All the same, he wanted his children to learn to stand up for themselves, so they'd never get bullied at school (when he'd raised that with Belle, she'd said waspishly that there *was* no bullying in the Kirkcudbright schools).

'For fuck's sake, Belle, this is a ridiculous argument to be having!'

'Don't swear when the children might hear you.'

'The children are sensible. They're sound asleep. They can't hear me, so I'll fucking well swear all I like.'

Although he had promised to moderate his language once the twins began to talk, he'd had limited success with that resolve. All his life as a journalist had been spent in an environment where everyone swore like squaddies. The characters in his books swore too, of course they did; and although he'd have hesitated to tell Belle this, when he was on a roll, in the zone, whatever, the characters in the books often felt more real to him than those he lived among. He was pretty confident, from what he had read, that didn't make him a bad husband or father; simply a typical writer.

So although they visited the flat more or less every month, Fergus didn't feel he had made much headway with persuading his wife to move permanently to the capital.

In fact, she had invented so many reasons not to move that his heart sank, merely enumerating them to himself. She claimed to dislike the east coast. 'It's always so cold and grey. And the North Sea – there's no *horizon*. I like to be able to see something across the water.' Fergus gazed at the leaden Galloway sky ahead of them, and sighed.

Apparently, being up in town even created problems with the laundry, particularly now that the twins were at school. Belle always hung their clothes and bedding outdoors to dry, even when anyone could see it was about to start raining. 'I like it to smell of sun and sea and fresh air,' she'd say triumphantly. 'You won't get *that* in Edinburgh. And besides, the people in the rest of the flats are so perjink they'd have forty fits if I started hanging washing in the back green.'

'Nonsense. And you probably get more sun in Edinburgh than you do here!' So everything wouldn't be clammy with moist salt air once it was brought indoors.

'Well, there's the pollution. Look at how dirty the flat's windows get.'

She brandished a copy of the *Scotsman*, with a report of the capital's bad air quality. 'Listen – it says lots of the streets in your precious Edinburgh have failed air quality tests. I don't want my children to be poisoned.'

Fergus tried hard to concentrate on the road. 'Which streets?'

She started to read out a list, and he guffawed. 'Slateford Road? Nicholson Street? We're not going to live anywhere near those. The children wouldn't ever have to be in those areas.' Until they went to university. And perhaps they'd aim higher, and not follow in his footsteps.

In vain he had assured her that when they moved, they wouldn't be living in a place like Bruntsfield.

He knew in his heart that Belle had no deep-seated antipathy to the capital. It was all down to the subject they had skirted around since before the twins were born: if they were to afford the type of house they'd want in Edinburgh, then Ashers would have to be sold.

'It's all very well for you,' Belle would say. 'This is the only home I've ever known. It had been in Father's family for six generations. I don't feel it's mine to sell. You've never had a house you were deeply attached to, from what you've said.'

She was correct. He'd sold his mother's house in Lauder with little compunction after she died. If he could have bought back his grandparents' house at Inveresk, he would have (he had tried more than once, over the years; the current owners had no intention of selling). To the other houses he had owned over the years, he had no great attachment.

And he had no great antipathy to Kirkcudbright. It was a pretty enough place. But when they walked (as they often did) round to the other side of the estuary, and looked back, he was always struck by how tiny it was, despite its castle and its harbour. A village, not a *town*. A territory, a terroir; but not *his*.

Though he had to admit, there was one advantage to living there: although everyone knew who he was, no one gawped.

The townspeople actually appeared to be quite protective of his privacy. And he fully appreciated what a boon that was, after years of being recognised everywhere he went, in his days as a TV presenter. But even in Edinburgh these days, he found he rarely got a second glance. His appearance had changed a lot since he had lost weight, and stopped dressing like a PG Wodehouse character.

He frequently whiled away an hour or so trying to visualise which of the furniture from Ashers would need to go with them when they moved. He was paying a hefty annual fee to hoard some of his grandparents' furniture in the handsome brick building that used to be Jenners' Depository and had transmogrified into upmarket self-storage units. Their rosewood dining table and Hepplewhite chairs. Several mahogany chests of drawers, and sundry occasional tables. His grandmother's Tiffany 'Wisteria' lamp; her pride and joy. The dining furniture in Ashers was good quality Victorian, but not nearly so valuable nor so fine.

He had grown attached to the enormous oak partners' desk in what had been Belle's father's study and was now his writing den. That had to accompany them, wherever they went. He smiled to himself – it'd need to go in a downstairs room, unless he used his carpentry skills to take it apart.

The crux of it: he loved cafes, and he hankered for Edinburgh ones. Belle maintained that was because he was a snob; there were perfectly pleasant cafes in Kirkcudbright, and Castle Douglas, and Dumfries.

'Dumfries?' he'd reply. 'Please!'

'There's nothing wrong with the cafes there,' Belle would say, jutting her chin.

On one such occasion, Eddie had piped up. 'I don't like

them either. Sometimes there are people in them with smelly clothes.'

'Edmund!' Fergus and Belle had gazed at each other, horrified. They knew that this was not a good way for a child to look at the world in 2013, but they also recognised it was probably how both of them looked at the world. The way they'd been brought up was discredited now. It belonged to an era that was past and unlamented.

Fergus recognised that he'd never been never noted for political correctness, but whereas Belle used to laugh at his peccadillos most of the time, these days she lost it with him big-time.

But it was difficult. He didn't want a world where everything was subservient to people who weren't happy with the gender they were born in. He'd tried to curb his racism too, but it was there, under a thin veneer. On the other hand, he loved Europe, and dreamt of having a house in Granada one day (other things being equal, he'd have preferred a holiday house there instead of in Kirkcudbright – what was the point of having two houses in the same country with the same climate, the same culture, the same food?).

Belle, on the other hand, had become more and more leftie-green under Remi's influence. She didn't disapprove of things like spending thousands of pounds on drugs for people who had AIDS.

They'd argued about that more than once. He'd say that if you spent on people who were ill through lifestyle choices, then there was none left to spend on people who were ill through no fault of their own. The trouble was, in his own ears these arguments made him sound like his own grandfather, or worse.

You'd start off defending a view that was a little right-of-centre, and you'd end up coming over as a bloody fascist.

Belle's leftie, socks-and-sandals views irked him because he was sure they weren't *her* views, but Remi's.

'We can't blame Eddie,' said Fergus. 'It's how I was raised – and how you were raised too, I daresay.'

The last time they'd been up in town, he'd taken Belle and the kids to the Royal Commonwealth Pool, newly reopened after a major refurbishment. He could see her softening, as she put Esmée through her paces. He knew she didn't mean to favour their daughter; she couldn't help it. And to be fair, the girl was turning out to be something of a star swimmer, even although she wasn't five yet. As he and Edmund watched, Fergus took his son's hand and squeezed it.

The boy smiled up at him, without rancour. 'Esmée's good, isn't she?' he observed.

It was one of those times Fergus could have sworn his son almost winked at him, and said, 'Women, eh?' Sometimes Eddie was *so* like his great-grandfather, Peter Fairbairn.

But, unlike old Peter, Eddie's skills lay in diplomacy – though he also seemed to be grasping mathematical ideas quickly, giving both his parents some concerns that he'd have left them behind long before he finished primary school.

'Wouldn't you like to go in next time, Eddie?'

'Will you come in with me?' asked the child, and Fergus had to blink away a tear. His exasperation over the way Belle spoiled Esmée evaporated. He needed to work harder at spoiling his son, that was all.

'Of course I will. We'll show them it's not only girls who can swim, won't we?'

When the girls were out and dried and changed, Fergus took them to one of the pleasanter cafes over in Stockbridge.

'There are plenty of other places to swim safely in town too,' he said to Belle. 'There's Warrender Baths, and Drumsheugh – they've been beautifully restored.'

But Belle said stubbornly that she needed to swim in the sea. They'd been through *that* many times before.

He was on firmer ground there. 'Joppa. Or Portobello. I'm sure there are groups who swim there every day of the year.' He wanted to say 'nutters'. Anita Forrest went through a phase of 365 swimming when they both worked at Albion. She'd know. He'd ask her on the quiet, at the first opportunity.

He'd looked online, found there was a sea swimming group at North Berwick, and decided not to mention it to Belle. Too far. He wanted to know she'd always be closer than that.

At least the water at Joppa lay over pure, clean sand. He found the North Sea more pleasing than the Solway coast too, in its own stark way. The pearlescent meld of sea and sky, the liminal spot where you couldn't tell the difference, and the horizon disappeared.

He couldn't imagine why anyone would want to swim at beaches on the Solway when there had been heavy rain, or strong tides running; the water would be the colour of burnt earth with mud-wash.

Belle was still in an awkward mood. 'So why don't you want to live in Joppa?'

'Because it's so easy to drive to it – we don't need to live there.'

Fergus's own principal gripe about the Bruntsfield flat was

that there was nowhere to park the damn car safely. As often as not you'd end up having to walk half a mile in the rain.

No, he must see about buying a family home in town *soon*. The local primary school in Kirkcudbright was far from unsatisfactory. But once the twins were a year or so older – well, it had to be a school like James Gillespie's. There was no other sensible solution.

He had a list of requirements for wherever they *did* fetch up; partly his list, but also Belle's. There would need to be a substantial garden, for the kids and the animals and Belle's laundry.

A central position and plenty of indoor space and a garden in Edinburgh added up to a hefty price tag.

But his first novel was on the point of being released as a TV serial, and he (and his agent) had ensured he was heavily involved, so that he'd make money out of the production. More than that, the publishers knew it'd serve to send the sales of his subsequent books sky-rocketing.

In fact, his finances were at the stage where they wouldn't absolutely *have* to sell Ashers to fund the move to a decent part of Edinburgh. But it'd be a damned expensive place to retain as a holiday home.

As soon as they were home, Fergus closeted himself in his study, on the pretext of needing to catch up with work.

For almost five years, he had put off doing this for Belle's sake. Now he felt he had to, for his children's sake.

Rose was a young woman when she abandoned Belle. If she did indeed go off with another man, Belle may have had younger half-siblings. The twins would have aunts and uncles, and possibly cousins. A safety-net. And a source of certainty, if both they and Belle could be persuaded to have DNA tests.

He searched for another marriage after old Mountjoy divorced Rose, because although he had searched for her death, under both her maiden and married names, he'd never found it.

He widened the search, and found the marriage – in Italy, to Salvatore Albigoni. And he couldn't find a death record there either. He broke into a cold sweat. He found the birth of a son and a daughter to Rose and her new husband. He wondered, not for the first time, about his own children's exotic looks. The twins could easily pass for Italian.

The family members all seemed to be in Tuscany. He found Rose's son's address. Belle's half-brother, in all probability. Perhaps even her full brother.

But in the end, he knew he had to face it: Belle didn't want to know if Rose was her biological mother.

He had broached the subject privately with Briony Hall. She was offhand, but admitted she remembered Rose Mountjoy, vaguely. She'd been sixteen when Rose upped and left; old enough to understand what the older women were talking about – and talk they did. No one had any sympathy for Rose (except Briony herself, by the sound of it: Fergus suspected she'd been sorry for anyone so bonnie and lively, condemned to be hitched for life to that wizened old stick Arthur Mountjoy).

'She was from here, before she married?'

'So I believe.'

He had also tracked down two other people in Kirkcudbright who remembered Rose. He had asked discreet questions to fill in the gaps. What did she look like? One replied that she'd looked like Maureen Swanson. The other stared at him as if he'd uttered an obscenity, and said, 'Not unlike Mabel, only her hair was more a dark brown, not as red as Mabel's. And she had green eyes.'

So he had quizzed Briony again. 'Someone told me she was quite like Belle?'

'I suppose. I remember her as being extremely pretty.'

He'd swallowed hard and put forth his thesis. 'You don't think she could have been Belle's real mother, her biological one?'

Briony's eyes had rolled like those of a startled horse. 'You've been on about this for years, Fergus. Leave it alone. Do you think it wouldn't be more painful to her than anything to know that the woman who dumped her was her real mother? It'd break her.'

'But it'd be so important for the twins to know they have relatives.'

'Then, when they're old enough, or – God forbid, if anything *did* happen to Belle – tell them then. Families aren't always a blessing.'

And indeed, look at the situation Briony had found herself in. Her father had died the year after he and Belle married, and Belle admitted to being secretly relieved. She said she had dreaded going to visit him, because he sometimes tried to slide his hand onto her bottom, so casually and carelessly he could almost be seeking a handhold to steady himself. 'Thank God Father never deteriorated in his mind that way,' she'd said as they left after seeing Briony's father for the last time. And she'd added that she realised how fortunate it had proved to be that things had worked out that way for her, with Father dying suddenly and with no prior illness.

Briony's mother was still alive, stubborn and pig-headed, and suffering from dementia. In her lucid moments, she was forever reminding her daughter that *she* owned the hotel. Briony was virtually a prisoner. Belle knew she couldn't have coped with such a scenario.

As always, that confession had been followed by guilt. Father had been exceptionally generous to her. She should be wishing she could have kept him for longer. He and Fergus would probably have got along surprisingly well, and so on, and so on.

Fergus had heard Briony tell Belle she often thought about the fact that if *her* husband hadn't died, she'd have had options. She could have walked away from it all. Too late now. She was too damn tired.

'You talk about the lack of a mother, Belle – you don't know the half of it. You might have ended up tied down like me. I'm so glad you'll never find yourself like this. You've found your second wind. You have Fergus and the children, and the world's your oyster.'

'You think we should go to Edinburgh then?' Belle had sounded scandalised.

'I'd be there like a shot, given the chance. Oh, come on, sweetie. I'd still see you! It's barely a hundred miles away. You'll come and stay with me, and one day, God willing, I'll be able to come and stay with you.'

'I suppose we're lucky,' Belle remarked to Fergus after that visit. 'Your mother wasn't gaga before she went?'

He shuddered. 'No!'

'I hope we don't go like that – the poor twins.'

'Of course we won't. They're getting nearer a cure all the time anyway. But we won't even need that. We'll be fine. Good genes. Neither of my grandparents got dementia.'

He realised as he said it, he never knew his father's parents.

And he also knew he had committed a major faux pas, because Belle's eyes struck sparks. 'Bully for you. Since I have not the faintest idea who my parents were, I may need locking up by the time I'm sixty.'

A few months back, when they'd been deep into one of their arguments about moving to Edinburgh, Belle had shushed Fergus. 'I don't want the twins to hear us yelling at each other.'

That had calmed him down instantly. He'd tried to hug her. 'Do you remember hearing your parents arguing a lot – before your mother left, I mean?'

She shrugged him off and turned back to rolling out pastry.

But he hadn't been ready to give up. 'That can be frightening for a young child, I imagine?'

She turned liquid amber eyes on him. 'I don't suppose you heard yours argue, if your father wasn't around. Well, I don't remember *anything* from before that woman went away.'

That woman. Christ, she wouldn't even use Rose's name now!

'I don't remember *her*,' she'd added, more gently. 'Although I was four, I suppose I've blotted out the memories.'

'Were you afraid of your father?'

She was taken aback. 'Afraid? No! He looked after me perfectly well. He wasn't the most affectionate of men, but he was always kind to me.'

As long as you did what you were told, thought Fergus. *Takes one to know one.*

When the twins were born, Fergus had the common sense not to suggest naming the girl Rose. But he had suggested, tentatively, that perhaps the boy should be called Arthur, after Belle's father. He'd been secretly relieved when she'd guffawed, and said that having been landed with a name like Mabel had made her especially determined not to burden any child of hers with a ridiculous name.

'In any case, he wasn't my real father,' she added. 'It's not as if I have a family tradition to keep up.'

She had been surprisingly ready to accept the idea that the twins were named after his grandmother and his father.

'They're stylish names,' she said, repeating them slowly. 'They're not weird, but they're likely to be the only ones in their school class with these names. And they both go well with Learmonth. I was at university with a girl called Victoria Plum. I don't know how parents can *do* that to a child.'

She had strongly resisted the idea that either twin should have Mountjoy as a middle name. So both were to have 'Fairbairn' in the middle.

She had then pointed out, a little spitefully, that it'd mean both were EFL. 'English as a foreign language.' So Esmée's middle name was altered to Maud, after Fergus's mother.

And he'd looked in the face of his baby daughter, who was beautiful even at two days old (as Caesarean babies often are), and announced that it was appropriate, as she was going to look like Maud Gonne. The funny thing was, now that Esmée's face was starting to lose its baby pudginess, she *did* look like a miniature version of Yeats's muse.

He and Belle had had a stonking row, in front of Briony, over whether to have the twins christened. At first, she was having none of it. 'They can make up their own minds when they're old enough. It's not as if you're religious anyway.'

'It's not about religion. It's an accepted thing to do. Were *you* not christened?' Too late, he wanted to snatch the words back.

'I have not the faintest idea. I doubt it. So what's with the "christ" bit, if it's nothing to do with religion? I'm not having my children subjected to some superstitious mumbo-jumbo for the sake of convention. We can have a naming ceremony. Nothing religious.'

'Where would you have that sort of thing?'

'Here,' said Belle. 'Here, in the sitting room. We don't need a big crowd at it. You and me and Briony, and Remi.'

Briony had caught Fergus's eye, and rolled hers. He knew that, out of loyalty to his wife, he should have ignored that look. He couldn't. He'd started to nurse an even colder hatred towards Remi, because he was certain that's where the antipathy to christenings had its origin.

But when Belle said 'my children' in that tone, Fergus knew better than to argue, and in the end it had been Briony who was the catalyst.

She had produced an exquisite white cotton lawn and lace christening gown that had been in her family for generations, and offered it as a gift to Belle, though she'd done so diffidently, adding that she'd do her best to get the loan of another for the second twin. And she had indeed commandeered a second one, equally venerable, from one of her friends.

'You must be their godmother, Briony,' Belle had said, and tears of gratitude had welled up in her friend's eyes.

So christened they were, in the town's handsome red sand-stone kirk.

Fergus saved his latest research on Rose Mountjoy in a pass-word-protected file. Briony was right. No point in trying to push it further. They needed to move to Edinburgh as soon as possi-ble, to start making new friends (and perhaps renew some old ones). The twins would be better with surrogate aunts and uncles rather than potential cousins in Italy who'd break their mother's heart.

He was particularly loving and gentle with Belle that evening.

SEVEN

The first thing that struck Tom, on entering the converted farm-house with DS Field, was how quiet it was. Eerily, neck-prick-lingly quiet. He'd noticed that in the past about houses where someone had died. A different class of quietness from what you always get at night in the countryside – and this place was in deep countryside, right enough, in the hills mid-way between Thornhill and Sanquhar, the nearest tarred road easily half a mile away. It was almost 1 am, and pitch dark; no street lights anywhere close. Tom went to the window and gazed into the darkness. No blink of a lamp from any other habitation visible. But then again, not everyone worked the stupid hours they did. He cursed Maggie McInnes under his breath. As if this couldn't have waited until the next week! He'd get neither brownie points nor overtime for working on a Friday night. Or a Saturday morning, in fact.

He cleared his throat. 'OK, Rach, what have we here?'

'Carol and Winston Bisset, both aged fifty-eight…'

'*Winston?* What sort of people call their son "Winston" in this day and age?'

'Patriots? Both aged fifty-eight, retired schoolteachers, originally from Dorset. They bought this place as a ruin about five years ago, and renovated it gradually.'

Tom snorted at that. Retired in their early fifties. If only!

Their daughter had called it in the previous day, from her place in Altrincham. She always spoke to her mother by phone, regular as clockwork, at least twice a week. They'd spoken on Christmas Eve, but there had been no reply since, either to their landline or their mobiles.

'What kind of family doesn't spend Christmas together?'

Rachel shrugged. 'Maybe they liked being on their own.'

The daughter had called the village shop, but the owners hadn't seen her parents either. She'd asked them to go up and take a look, and phone her back. They'd called to say the house was empty and there was no sign of anyone around, although they could see the car was in the garage, and the front door had been unlocked. Uniforms had been over the place with a bit more care and attention than usual in a Misper case. Not a clue. No signs of violence, or a forced entry. Valuable items in plain sight and undisturbed.

'Nicely done up,' thought Tom. Bugger, this obsession of Jackie's was turning him into some sort of nancy boy who *noticed* things like the colour of the walls. In the farmhouse kitchen, they were a warm mid-grey, with the woodwork picked out in a slightly darker shade. Big room, with one of those fancy lantern-style roof-lights above a granite-topped island unit. A handmade loaf on a breadboard, the top covered with a light bloom of blue-green mould.

Soft, opulent-looking sofas against one wall, cabinets which

were obviously bespoke along the other. A shelf with a graduated set of eight blood-red ceramic jugs. Acres of blond granite
(he'd heard that was a pig to keep clean). An oak table that had
obviously come from a high-end antique shop.

It was like a picture from one of the homes magazines that
were always lying around his own house in silent accusation.
He decided that Jackie would have to make do with paint, in
place of the flashy black and silver wallpaper she'd trailed him
into Homebase to look at. Vulgar! Discerning people clearly
didn't stick crap like that on their walls.

Making sure that Rachel wasn't watching, he took a couple
of pictures on his mobile phone. He stuck it back in his pocket
quickly as he heard her footsteps clatter across the stone-flagged
hallway.

Unlike McPhedrie's chalet, the place wasn't cold. Tom
crossed to lay his hand on the dark blue Aga, and withdrew it
again quickly.

'Oil-fired,' said Rachel, watching him quizzically. 'It'll run
until the tank goes dry.'

Tom flicked through the neat pile of documents on the
counter-top. Among them was a bill from Scottish Fuels: 23rd
December.

'One of the plods had a dekko. The tank's nearly full. You
reckon we should leave everything on?'

Tom shrugged. 'Until we find them anyway.' He
wandered through to the sitting room (two, if not three rooms
knocked into one, by the looks of it; damn it, a whole *house*
knocked into one), with its tasteful exposed stone wall and
cathedral ceiling with huge skylights; one of those fancy TVs
you hang on the wall like a painting. Sixty inches at least.
Lots of pale oak: the floor, the lamp tables, the sideboard.

Expensive-looking rugs. The sort of sofas you'd see in Barbour's sale in Dumfries reduced to two grand. Three of them.

'They must have had a designer in to do this place,' said Rachel admiringly.

As they left the room, he turned back and surreptitiously took another few pictures. Maybe he'd surprise Jackie with a few design ideas of his own.

In the three bedrooms, all the beds were carefully made up. Each room had fitted carpets, the kind you sink right into, like walking on moss. Tom opened the mirror-fronted wardrobe in what appeared to be the main bedroom. Several men's suits. Smart! These weren't from Marks and Sparks. The women's clothes looked posh too.

'What did you say these guys were?' Tom asked.

'Retired teachers.'

'You're joking! There must be more money in teaching than in being a poor bloody detective. Come on, Rach, they must have won the lottery or something. Right – I saw outbuildings. Let's see what the uniforms missed there.'

Tom slid open the unlocked door of the larger of the two outbuildings. 'Bloody hell, what have we here then?'

He swung the beam of his torch round until he spotted a light-switch on the wall. The interior was immediately illuminated by a double bank of spotlights. It was a warehouse, kitted out with well-insulated walls lined with immaculate white-enamelled metal shelving and stainless steel work-benches.

'No expense spared out here either!' The shelves were stacked neatly with brown cardboard cartons. 'Plods didn't check these?'

'I suppose they were looking for the Bissets,' said Rachel.

Tom lifted a carton down onto the nearest bench, and pulled apart the tape sealing it, tipping out the inner container.

The lid had a picture of what looked like a doll, and a quantity of Chinese writing.

Rach ripped open the box and emptied out the contents.

Both of them recoiled as a quantity of garish, flesh-coloured rubber flowed onto the gleaming steel surface.

'Fuck me! What's that?'

Rach looked askance at him. 'Blow-up doll, boss.'

'A doll?'

'For sex.'

'I know that! But it looks like...'

'A kid. Yes. It does.' She kept her voice brusque and business-like.

She shoved the obscene object aside with blue-gloved fingertips, and lifted another plain cardboard box from a different section of shelving. She hauled it open and decanted the contents onto the gleaming steel. The overhead lights were so powerful they hurt Tom's eyes. He picked up the inner box; it had a brightly-coloured illustration of the doll it contained, once inflated.

'Jesus Christ, Rach, this one looks like a *toddler*! You reckon there's filth like this in all of those?' He waved his hand to encompass the shelving, the building.

She nodded, her face grim. 'There've been quite a few of these things confiscated at airports recently. Looks like the Bissets imported a container-load. Unless they're storing it for someone. Even so!'

'God, who buys stuff like this?'

She shrugged. 'Some folk have a theory that maybe they're the lesser evil, and keep the nonces off real kids.'

A wave of nausea swept over Tom, and he headed rapidly for the outer door. He was thinking of his granddaughter.

Rachel joined him a moment later. She laid her hand lightly and fleetingly on his arm. 'You OK, boss?'

He nodded. 'Just needed a breath of air.'

'I'd be amazed if we find any prints here. The whole place has been cleaned. You can smell the bleach.'

'Like McPhedrie's house?'

'And they've had the chance to do it meticulously this time.'

Tom raised his eyebrows.

'It's so isolated. They'd have been pretty sure they'd not be observed here, whereas at Colvend...'

'Of course. Not thinking straight. Bloody hell, Rach, what sort of nasty fuckers sell blow-up dolls of *babies*?'

'Ones that don't have much right to space on this earth.'

They looked askance at each other. Tom smiled at her. '*You* OK?'

'I am. I want to catch these bastards.'

'OK, so we know why they scarpered. What we need to know is when and where. Let's take another look in the house. They must have kept records of who they were selling this crap to.'

'They obviously left in a hurry,' said Rachel. She'd opened the filing cabinet in the room the owners seemed to use as an office. She dumped a plastic concertina folder on the nearest desk. 'Stuffed with euros and US dollars,' she said, shaking it. 'Some UK currency too, by the looks of it.' She rifled through the filing cabinet once more. 'No sales records here that I can see. Must be on a computer somewhere.'

But although they searched the house and outbuildings

painstakingly, they found no computers or tablets or mobile phones.

Both Carol and Winston Bisset's passports were in the same filing cabinet as the cash.

'People like that could get hold of fake passports as soon as blink,' said Tom. 'They could be anywhere. No point in even trying to watch the airports. They could have gone on a ferry. They'd be using false IDs.'

'How would they have got to the ferry?' asked Rachel.

'Did they only have one car?'

'Apparently. The one in the garage.'

'I don't reckon they left under their own steam, do you, Rach?'

'Nope.'

Tom's shoulder blades were twitchy again. 'There's no way this is unconnected with what we found at McPhedrie's. Too many similarities. If they got away from here, they must have had a tip-off that someone was onto them. It's all been pretty high-profile, the child abuse stuff. You know what cop shops are like – most of them leak like sieves. If they didn't then someone got to them before they could scarper. Seems to me that's the more likely explanation. I think we need to go on a short road-trip, DS Field. Warrington and Altrincham aren't that far apart. Just need to get home first to pick up a few things, maybe grab an hour or two of sleep. Can you be ready to go by, say, two tomorrow?'

'Tomorrow?'

'I mean today.'

Rachel's eyes opened wide. 'Shouldn't I take one of the DCs?'

'You know they're always down my neck to cut costs. You

plus a DC on a Saturday, that's double overtime. You know I don't *get* overtime.'

Rachel pulled a face. She didn't meet his eye. 'A very short trip then. I've a hot date on Hogmanay.'

He was taken aback at first. He happened to know that she hadn't had a steady boyfriend for at least the past year. The others giggled about it in the locker-room. 'Wedded to her job,' they'd say. Or else they'd make lewd comments about how well she got on with McInnes.

He tried to sound businesslike. 'I'll have you back in plenty of time. In fact, if we head off this afternoon, we'll be back by tomorrow night.'

'You reckon the Chief'll stand us a couple of hotel rooms then?'

'This'll be a feather in her headdress, as well as ours, Rach. You got a note of the Bissets' daughter's address?'

He hated cases like this; had always dreaded having to work on one. You may know in your water – or your shoulder blades – that you're looking at a murder, but when there's no body, you're on the back foot from the start. You may have a strong suspicion that someone's come to harm, and possibly even *why* they've come to harm, but you have not one damn thing to go on, because you have no idea how or where.

In the end, they didn't get out of the office until after five that afternoon. Tom had left DC Giles to sift through the remaining papers from the Bisset's filing cabinets. The Dumfries and Galloway police budget didn't stretch to anything fancier than a three-star hotel on the northern edge of Manchester Airport. The colleagues shared an indifferent bar supper, and Tom drank more than he meant to. Then he lay awake most of the night, distracted partly by the noise of planes taking off, and partly by the fact that Rachel was in a room two doors away. She'd teased him, asking if he hadn't brought one of his jigsaws with him. He hadn't taken that well. He didn't think any of them knew that's what he liked to do to unwind. He'd snapped at her, asked her what *she* did to destress. 'Go to the gym,' she'd said, pleased with herself. And he'd gone off on one, ranting about wasting money going into a smelly, sweaty room to run on a machine when you could go out and run on the pavement, for free. She had smirked and said, 'Each to his own.' He'd wanted to slap her.

Need to apologise in the morning.

As Tom and Rachel breakfasted in the first cafe they came to, his phone chimed. He read the message, whistled under his breath, and handed it across to her. 'This could be interesting! Just as well we're seeing the daughter today.'

Paperwork from Bisset farmhouse includes insurance docu-ments, plus a will. Life cover on Carol and Winston Bisset for half a million each. The will names their daughter as sole benefi-ciary. That's the one you're due to see today, right? I'll scan the originals into Dropbox, so you can access them on your phone.

Tom licked his lips. You didn't have to be a detective to know that money was a great motivator! He read the rest of Giles's text.

Found bank statements. No money troubles that I can see, but a hell of a lot of pay-ins, big sums. Periodic large payouts too. But always a healthy balance. Only thing I did come up with: there was a report to the police in 1994 re Winston B and inap-

propriate behaviour with pupils at Willowbeck High School. It doesn't seem to have led to any action.

Despite the fancy postcode, Ilona Boston, née Bisset, lived in a duplex in a run-down building that looked more suitable for Stalinist Russia than the fashionable end of Cheshire. The Bissets' daughter had over-bleached blonde hair and eyes that were a cross between a December sky and a crime scene: an insipid blue, intensely bloodshot. Tom figured she was either a drinker, or a drug-user, or both. He sniffed the air. No sign of weed. Maybe something harder?

She was putting on a damn good pantomime of being concerned, but at the same time she didn't seem bothered that her parents had moved more than two hundred miles away to a house in the middle of a desolate moor, and hadn't even bothered to visit her for Christmas.

'We were never that close as a family,' she said, gazing over Tom's shoulder at a passing pedestrian.

'Any particular reason?' asked Rach.

The woman shrugged. Her eyes weren't on anything or anyone in the room. 'Nothing specific. You know how it is.'

Tom looked around at the shabby furniture. When he'd heard 'Altrincham', he'd thought, 'posh area; footballers' wives territory'. But as soon as they'd approached the ugly, flat-roofed 1970s block he'd realised that there were clearly two sides to such an address. It hadn't got better once they were inside. He was struck by the squalor of Ilona's house compared to her parents'. Her husband was a thug; no other description would have done him justice. The kind with tattoos on every visible surface, including his shaved head. Tom's mind drifted to what the parents must have thought when their girl married *that*. If the guy his Sharon had taken up with had been as uncouth, there's no way he'd have let her move in with him; he'd have preferred to see her a single parent than with an ape.

Maybe his feelings had shown too much on his face; within moments of their arrival, Ilona had sent the orang-utan out to the park with their three kids.

'Your parents seemed to have spent a fortune doing that place up?' he said.

'I suppose. Ma always liked things nice.'

'Did they have a cleaner, do you know?'

'A cleaner! No, we're not that sort of family.' Ilona's voice turned bitter. 'Not that they couldn't have afforded a cleaner.'

'Came into some money, did they? Lottery win or something?'

Her expression hardened to match her tone. 'Not that I know of. Dad said they'd invested wisely, and it had paid off.'

'But they were both teaching up until they retired?'

She nodded, her face impassive once more.

'Well, Dad retired a year or two before the official date. He was diagnosed with motor neurone disease two years ago.'

Tom's ears pricked up.

'I'm sorry to hear that. How far had it progressed?'

'He was in a wheelchair.'

'So could there be any question of a suicide pact?'

'They'd never do a thing like that!'

Tom caught Rachel's eye briefly.

'Are you aware of any financial provision your parents may have made for you?'

Ilona drew her bare feet up under her. Tom noticed that the soles were black with dirt.

'No idea. I hardly saw them.' She waved her arm to encompass the room. 'You can see they didn't help me out at all with the kids or anything.'

'And you're an only child?'

'Might as well be. I have a brother, but I never see him. Adrian.'

Tom wriggled his shoulders against the armchair he was perched in, then thought better of it and leaned forward a little; it didn't look too clean. 'When did you last see your brother?'

'Years ago.'

Rachel's pen was poised over her notebook. 'We'll need to visit him, in case your parents are staying with him.'

Ilona cackled. 'Some chance! Though he might welcome a visitor. I'm sure he doesn't get many. He's in Strangeways for a stretch of ten.'

'Right. How long's he been there?'

Ilona lit a cigarette, and waved it vaguely in front of her. 'A couple of years.'

'What was he convicted of?' asked Rachel. Tom was holding his breath.

'Assault with intent,' said Ilona.

'Who was the victim?'

'God knows. Some guy. Adrian didn't know him, he was in the wrong place at the wrong time.'

'Are you aware that there were formal enquiries about your father in the 1990s? Reports that he had been behaving inappropriately with pupils?'

Ilona reddened. 'Oh, that. Spiteful kids making up stories. The school didn't take any action against him. Your lot certainly didn't get involved. There was no evidence at all that Dad had done anything wrong.'

'But he moved to teach in another area?'

'You bet he did. You know as well as I do, shit sticks. He and Mum were more or less hounded out.'

'And he went on teaching until he retired?'

'They both did, yes. It didn't half take it out of Dad, all those false accusations. I always thought that was what had brought on his illness. You don't think that's connected to them going missing?'

Tom held her gaze. 'We have no idea, at this stage. We need to follow up every possible line of enquiry. I don't suppose you know the names of the children who accused him?'

'You're joking. I was a kid myself at the time, and it was all hush-hush.'

Rachel consulted her notes. 'But it happened while he was teaching at Willowbeck High School?'

'You obviously know it did. So why don't you ask them?'

'We will. You say you didn't see much of your parents. Did you have any concerns about your father's behaviour around your own children?' asked Rachel.

Ilona looked for a moment as if she was going to leap from her chair. Then she sagged back against the cushions. 'Certainly not! He was their grandad. That was rubbish, the accusations at that fucking school.'

Rachel nodded calmly. 'I have to ask you this, Ilona. We need to get a clear picture of the person we're looking for. Did your father ever behave inappropriately towards *you* when you were a child?'

The washed-out blue eyes defocussed again. 'No. Of course not.' Ilona pulled a cushion into her lap and curled herself round it. 'He wasn't like that.'

'OK. Mind if we take a look around here before we go?'

'What for?'

'It's routine in missing person cases. We won't make a mess, and we won't be long.'

'You reckon I'm hiding my dad and his wheelchair under the bed? We don't have an attic, by the way.'

'It's purely a formality.' Rachel was already halfway out of the room.

The upstairs part of the house was as dirty and untidy as the sitting room – and there was nowhere two adults could have been concealed.

'That your garden?' Tom asked when they came back downstairs.

'It's communal.'

'No sheds or anything?'

'That's right. No anything.'

'OK – thanks for your co-operation, Mrs Boston,' said Rachel. 'We'll keep you informed on the progress of our enquiries for your parents. And meantime,' – she handed Ilona a business card – 'I'd be grateful if you could let us know if you hear from them.'

'Your brother Adrian – does he use the surname Bisset?'

'I suppose. See yourselves out. Mind you shut the door.'

'She was lying,' said Rachel as soon as they were back in the car.

'No shit! About what, specifically?'

'About her father not abusing her. You can always tell. Body language. You get a feel for it. God knows why the poor woman feels she has to protect parents like that.'

'You always amaze me, DS Field. You reckon the mother knew?'

Rachel's face was stony-still. 'In my experience, the mother *always* knows, boss. Never believe otherwise. About one in a hundred has the guts to do something about it.'

'So should we be doing more about this?'

'Let's see what else we dig up, or when we find this pair.'

They made a routine call at Strangeways on their way to Warrington. Bisset Junior was as attractive as his brother-in-law, and denied all knowledge of his parents' whereabouts. Total waste of time, and like all prison visits, it took hours longer than necessary.

The prison staff confirmed that he'd had no visitors during his time there. They had no home address for him. 'No fixed abode' was all that had been noted.

'So what about this Willowbeck school?' asked Rachel as they left. 'Any point in visiting there?'

Tom consulted his phone. 'None, it would seem. Giles tried to check it out, but there's no one around who knows any details.'

'Bloody hell! No wonder there's so much of it about. Every last place is sweeping it under the carpet. Schools, the Catholic church, social work departments, the BBC.'

Tom grimaced. 'They're terrified of being sued.'

'I'd give them "sue".'

Checking out McPhedrie's address in Warrington also took more than twice as long as Tom had planned. For one thing, they discovered as the satnav took them close to the address that it wasn't in Warrington at all, but in a much smaller settlement called Lymm.

It was a large, modern house, and completely deserted. By the time Tom made contact with the relevant person in the local nick, and managed to convince them they needed to get inside, it was almost seven. Yet another frustration of not having a Chief's extra pip on his epaulettes; if he'd had epaulettes.

'Another night in a dosshouse then,' he said wearily. 'Don't worry. We'll get on our way early tomorrow.' He was beginning to relish a few days away from home, even if it *was* work rather than pleasure.

Next morning it was clear that the local CID weren't interested, and the uniforms obviously took it amiss that anyone doubted their search had been exhaustive.

'What's through there?' Tom asked, shaking a locked door off the hall.

'Cellar,' said the bored young constable.

'Can we take a look? Where did you get the keys for the inside, by the way?'

'Cleaner.' He was taking his time going through the bunch of keys, and eventually found the right one.

'Bloody hell!'

In the room at the foot of a steep concrete stairway was a fully-equipped photographic studio: lights, reflectors, cameras. There was none of the usual squalid paraphernalia Tom associated with paedophiles and child abuse. No stained mattress on the floor. No shackles attached to the walls.

In fact, the whole place was suspiciously clean. You could have eaten your dinner off the floor.

'And no one thought to report this?'

The PC shrugged. 'We were told to look for a missing person, not to report on his hobbies.'

'You speak to any of his friends, or the neighbours?'

'No one has seen him since sometime in November. But they all say that's not unusual. He spends a lot of time away.'

Tom and Rachel left their hotel at nine next morning, armed with the addresses of both of McPhedrie's ex-wives. Neither seemed interested, never mind bothered.

'I suppose they both got a good pay-off at the divorce end,' said Rach. 'Did you see the size of the diamonds in the second one's ears?'

'I have a bad feeling about this. Do you?'

'I do. I don't expect we're going to find any of the three still breathing. Now, you'll have to step on it, boss, so we can get back to the office and write our reports. Mustn't be late for my date.'

Tom felt the tips of his ears burn. 'It's not with DC Giles is it?'

Rachel guffawed. 'You must be joking! I'm a bit fussier than that. What makes you think it's with a man?'

Sodding hell! Always thought the banter about Rach and the Chief Super was no more than that.

'Jeez, Rachel, it's not McInnes is it?'

She laughed louder than ever. 'Bit old for me. I'm winding you up. It's with an old friend from Carlisle, Tom. A boy, but not a boy*friend*. There – you happy?'

EIGHT

Fergus had gone with Belle to all her antenatal appointments – and they'd been frequent. They'd checked her continually for any signs of pre-eclampsia; checked her blood pressure, checked for protein in her urine.

There had been a bit of a scene at the first visit. The doctor had told Belle he strongly recommended that she should have an amniocentesis. She had declined, with an air of finality, but the medic had persisted, trying to put the frighteners on her.

'No,' she repeated. 'I've been doing a lot of research on it, and I know there's a strong risk it can cause a miscarriage.'

The doctor had made the mistake of smirking. 'I hardly think one per cent constitutes a *strong* risk.' He'd looked at Fergus, who returned his stare coolly.

'My wife doesn't want this procedure. It's not in any way compulsory. It is her choice.'

The doctor sighed. 'Because of your age, Mrs Learmonth, there is a measurable risk of an abnormal foetus.'

'It's not a "foetus". It's my baby.'

'Surely there must be other, less invasive tests, that don't carry such a risk?' said Fergus.

'But neither do they offer the same diagnostic accuracy. It is indeed your decision, but I strongly advise you to rethink. Take some time to discuss it. I can give you literature on the increasing incidence of chromosomal abnormality in mothers over thirty-five. There is a *sharp* increase by forty-five.' He opened a leaflet and held it out for both of them to see. 'This is a graph of the incidence of trisomy 21 – that's Down syndrome – with maternal age.'

The line on the graph climbed steeply.

Belle barely glanced at it. 'We have discussed this. I don't want it done,' she said, starting to button her jacket, and picking up her bag. 'Suppose I had it done, and miscarried, and it turned out to be a perfectly normal, healthy baby? I could never forgive myself. Could you?'

The doctor hunched his shoulders. 'Well, at least make sure you turn up for your scan next week.'

'Naturally I will. I am not an *irresponsible* person, Dr Bly.'

As they were leaving, the doctor pressed the leaflet into Fergus's hand. He dropped it into the first bin they passed in the corridor, careful not to let Belle see.

Fergus had held Belle's hand tightly as the sonographer squirted cold gel on her stomach.

'You'll be booked for an amniocentesis after fifteen weeks?' asked the woman.

Fergus tensed as he saw his wife's jaw tighten; she was prepared to do battle again. 'No, I will *not*. I don't want one.'

But the sonographer was unfazed. 'Right-oh.'

He relaxed again. 'Can't you tell from a scan if the baby looks normal?'

The woman pulled a face. 'I reckon I'm quite good at spotting any problems. But obviously, it is in no way a conclusive diagnosis. And certainly not at this stage.'

The prospective parents were both quiet as the probe was slid backwards and forwards over Belle's stomach. Neither of them looked at the screen. Instead, they looked into each other's eyes.

The medic was the one to break the silence. 'Well, they both look OK to me.'

Belle sat up so suddenly that the probe slid onto the bed beside her. '*Both?*'

'You did know you're expecting twins?'

'That's not possible.'

The woman grinned. She swung the screen round so both had no option but to look. 'See – there's one head, and one bottom. There's the other head and the other backside. I assure you there are two babies. And I think you have your dates awry, Mrs Learmonth. You said you're twelve weeks? I'd say more like sixteen or seventeen. You should have had a scan before now.'

Belle had lain back again; she was ashen. 'It's impossible,' she repeated.

'No history of twins in your family?'

'I've no idea. I was adopted. I don't know my biological mother, or anything about her.'

Fergus studied his hands.

'It's not so unusual,' the woman was saying. 'The incidence of twins increases in older mothers, and dizygotic twins are extremely common with your age-group, Mrs Learmonth. In fact, around two-thirds of twins born these days are dizygotic.'

'Di...?'

'Non-identical.'

'You can tell that?' Belle asked, wonderingly.

'I'm guessing. I won't be able to tell until your next scan.'

'But you say both look OK?' asked Fergus, his voice husky.

'As far as I can see – and I'm rarely wrong. But as I said, a scan can't possibly give a definitive answer.'

Fergus and Belle grinned at each other, horrified and delighted.

Belle and Fergus had known in advance that the twins would need to be delivered by Caesarean section, because they insisted on lying the wrong way round. No matter how often the medical staff tried to turn them so that at least one was head-down, back they'd pop to lie sideways.

The obstetrician had pursed his lips. 'How far on are you now?' He consulted notes. 'Almost thirty-nine weeks. I think we'll plan to get these babies out tomorrow, Mrs Learmonth. The last thing we want is your waters breaking if they're still a transverse lie. Too big a risk of the umbilical cords getting tangled.'

Fergus assumed that meant he couldn't be at the birth, but the maternity staff had guffawed.

'It's all down to a fine art these days, your wife will only need an epidural. You can sit with her the whole time.'

He was aware that she might have preferred Remi there, but maybe he was imagining that.

'Just one person allowed with her?' he asked.

The obstetrician gave him a level look.

'How many were you thinking of?'

'I'd have liked my sister to be here too,' said Belle, glaring at Fergus, daring him to spill the beans that Remi wasn't a relative. 'But my husband has to be with me.'

'Your sister can be right outside.'

She'd turned her head away. 'This is the last thing I wanted. Why can't I have a natural birth, like other women?'

'Because these are twins, and awkward buggers by the sound of it,' said Fergus soothingly.

It was all over quickly. In an hour from the time Belle was wheeled into theatre, and Fergus planted at her shoulder, the medical staff at work beyond the green curtain rigged up over her waist, the twins were born, the twins were squawking, everything had been stitched back together, and she was on her way back to the ward.

The birth had appeared to go with text-book precision. Edmund had been born first, and was slightly the larger, at a fraction under three kilos, but both were perfectly formed, strong babies, each with a goodly thatch of black hair. They greeted the world yelling and waving their arms.

Poor old Belle, carrying that weight around for nine months!

In an instant, she'd become weepy.

In an attempt to cheer her up, Fergus had started prattling about having heard that Caesarean babies are exceptionally beautiful, because their heads haven't been squeezed. 'They tend to find everything they want drops into their laps all their lives too. Something about not having had to struggle to be born. I read that somewhere.'

Belle started to cry in earnest. 'I'm a failure. Can't even do this right.'

'Nonsense,' said one of the nurses, briskly. 'Look at the neat way he's made that incision! The scar won't be noticeable at all.

You'll still be able to wear a bikini. And count yourself lucky – your stitches are in a less sensitive place, and you won't be stretched *down there*. That matters, specially at your age.' She looked pointedly at Fergus, who blushed. 'Now, your sister can come in.'

And Remi had appeared, rosy-faced and dewy-eyed and laden with flowers, and had almost pushed him out of the way. She got to hold his children before he did.

Belle was up and about within twenty-four hours of giving birth, and home within four days. Fergus fussed around her like a mother hen.

'Should they not have kept you for a little longer, to make sure everything's all right, the stitches and so on?'

'I don't want to be in hospital. I hated it there. You don't even get wholesome food.'

'Certainly you should be at home.' Remi had materialised silently in the bedroom doorway. She seemed to be at the house all the time. In fact, she had stayed over more than once. She glared at Fergus. 'But you need maximum support. No lifting of anything heavier than a baby for the next month at least. I'm happy to stay on to help.'

And indeed, Remi had been seeing to all the cooking and laundry. She also handled the babies vey competently, and it seemed to Fergus that they responded to her better than they did to him, to begin with. One day, when they'd been home a fortnight, he watched Remi walking in the garden, an expertly-swaddled twin in the crook of each arm, in the weak spring sunshine. He almost panicked – what if she slipped? But of course, she didn't, she was as sure-footed as a leopard, and as stealthy.

So he made up his mind to be a quick and efficient learner. To be New Man. To be Super-Father.

When the twins squawked to be fed, Fergus's task was to bring them to Belle, and rock one while she fed the other. Within days, he'd become adept at changing nappies (after all, there was absolutely no reason why it should be any more disgusting than changing Gorby's litter tray), and bathing slippery infants. Remi stood over him at first, but she seemed satisfied that he was almost competent in handling his own children. 'The least a father can do,' she'd said.

'Briony has offered to help,' said Fergus. 'And she's only two steps along the road. We don't want to keep you from your horticulture.'

'Briony's busy, with Easter coming up.'

'Easter?' repeated Fergus vaguely.

'It's early this year. It's next week, in fact. Her hotel will be filling up for the season. Anyway, no need to worry,' Remi continued. 'I can easily stay for another week at least.'

For all that he hated her, Fergus was secretly relieved. She was a midwife, after all. A nurse. She'd know exactly what to do if anything *did* go wrong.

But although she was a wonderful friend to Belle, she committed the ultimate faux pas, as far as she was concerned.

'You need to get rid of that damn cat, Fergus, now you have children.'

'Get rid of Gorby? Why on earth would I do that?'

'Cats can lie on babies' faces and smother them. They get jealous.'

'That's an old wives' tale. Stuff and nonsense. And in any case, do you honestly believe I'd leave the cat with them in any situation where he could get near them? They're my children. The last thing I'd ever do is harm them. This is my way, and these are my kids, and the family cat is also part of the family, OK?'

She'd gone off stony-faced and watery-eyed, and he'd felt guilty for fully half an hour.

But everything went on as it should. Belle's stitches healed, the babies grew, the cat didn't lie on their faces and suffocate them.

So Remi went home. The twins were six weeks old by then, and Belle claimed to be feeling as good as ever. Her friend's visits continued, but at a much lower density.

Fergus would sit cradling a twin, watching in amazement as the other successfully clamped onto Belle's lovely bosom, sucking contentedly, the dog and cat curled at her feet. He'd look at the scene and his heart would almost burst with pride as he thought, 'My family! My tribe!' He was, at last, in his mid-fifties, what his grandparents had always marked him down for: paterfamilias.

He'd felt happier than ever in his life, and that glow had lasted. He was working hard, earning better money than in his heyday as a TV front man, and able to work at home, never more than a stone's throw from his wife and children.

He had a strong sense of the presence of his grandfather, in the days when he'd take him for walks on the Pentlands, always holding the shepherd's crook he carried in place of a walking stick (at primary school, Fergus's class had been asked 'Who is the Good Shepherd?' and he'd replied: Peter Fairbairn. He was scandalised that the teacher didn't know what he was talking about). Peter had taught him the name of birds and plants. He'd taught him to fish (a sport Fergus had not kept up with). He'd taught him the importance of carrying on the family line.

So the sense of duty in being a father was not an onerous one for him. It was his task to pass on to his twins that sensation of being completely safe and secure. The feeling you got inside a warm room on a stormy evening, hearing the wind and rain snatching off tree branches and battering at the windows.

It was important for children to feel this, that their care-givers were not only omnipotent but omniscient.

He was blessed indeed.

Then, within three months, Belle had turned from a peach-tree in full bloom into a cranky, tearful person who broke down many times a day, whining that she couldn't cope. The zest, the *euphoria* that had been in her while she was pregnant, had gone. She felt her life had stalled. Fergus knew that – she had told him quite frankly; he didn't know what to do about it. He felt she was possibly clinically depressed, but knew better than to suggest she see a doctor.

By the time the twins were toddling, she seemed to have pulled out of the abyss, but she hadn't gone back to being the old Belle – not in terms of either her personality or her appearance. She seemed to grow younger rather than older with every week that passed. And more independent.

NINE

Chief Super McInnes spent a merry quarter of an hour bawling Tom out as soon as he was into the office. 'Can't we just solve this? Any day now, some damn MIT from Strathclyde's going to be breathing down our necks, sneering at the country bumpkins who can't even sort a couple of straightforward Misper cases in a month.'

Tom knew why she was hacked off. They all knew. Although Dumfries and Galloway was a large area, it was sparsely populated, and they had fewer unsolved crimes than any other force in Scotland (but then, they had fewer to solve in the first instance). A safe spot to live in. A congenial place to work. That's why none of the top brass from this part of the world had got anywhere near the new plum jobs in Police Scotland. Nearly all of those had gone to Central belt guys and gals (it was the age of equal opportunity after all), or people parachuted in from the Met and West Yorkshire.

So McInnes was stuffed, basically. All rungs further up the ladder blocked.

He felt a warm glow of bitter satisfaction as he went back downstairs. OK, he had done no better. But he was far from being the only one in the division who'd not ventured off his home turf. That's what most had joined the job for in his day: no nobler vocation than protecting your ain folk.

You got the ambitious ones too, the ones who were off up the mountain the minute their probation was out. Tom might have been one of those, if things had worked out differently. He and Mabs would have been a formidable team. No way she'd have insisted on staying here, the way Jackie had (because she had to be within ten miles of her fucking mother). And nowadays, she had the nerve to accuse *him* of lack of ambition.

In his more maudlin moments, he had often wondered if that was why Mabs *did* stay in Kirkcudbright. To be near him, although she'd missed her chance of marrying him.

He knew he should apply to move on. Back into uniform if necessary, if it meant he got that extra button on his epaulettes. Though, mind you, it'd need to be the sort of role that involved a dress uniform and a leather desk chair in your office. He couldn't see himself in the paraphernalia ordinary cops had to wear these days. So ungainly, with all the stab vests and body-cams and radios and belts laden with torches and tasers and other gadgets. He'd never want to waddle around looking like the Michelin man. He greatly admired the ones who could leg it after a villain and catch him, clarted up with that lot.

When he joined the job, you didn't need to be a graduate to get on – though that era had begun. But you did have to be tall. The minimum height for men was five foot ten, and he'd made it with over two inches to spare. He hadn't approved of the height rules being scrapped in the '90s. How could some wee bachle who was barely five-two be expected to wade in and stop a fight

in a pub? When he'd started as a probationer, the men were
mostly six-footers, built like prop forwards. Cops had *presence*
in those days. You didn't tangle with one in a hurry; not if you
had any sense.

He'd lost his mojo for police work, that was the long and
short of it. Right from childhood, he used to dream of catching
dangerous criminals; wrong 'uns. Having tales of derring-do to
tell. Being a mounted policeman, even, sitting up on his fierce
high horse, back ramrod straight, like a cowboy, or a knight in a
story-book. Something to catch the attention of a girl like Mabel
Mountjoy. Girls liked a man in uniform. The reality had been
different. Seekers after truth, he'd thought they were. Bugger
that. These days, it was all about evidence. You'd know damn
well that someone was guilty, but you needed watertight proof,
with so many smart-arse lawyers around.

Not that he'd been involved in terribly many serious or
unusual crimes, even once he moved across to the CID. A
couple of fatal fail-to-stops. Arson that burned down an entire
warehouse, plus a block of flats (no fatalities in that one: a miracle). A deliberate electrocution – the old toaster-in-the-bath
scenario, except that it had been a hairdryer. He had not acted
as SIO in any of these cases.

And if his gut feeling was correct, and the Misper case was
indeed scaled up to a multiple murder enquiry, someone from
higher up the food chain would no doubt be brought in over his
head, then take all the credit.

'DCI Tom Ellis,' he muttered to himself under his breath.
'Fat chance.'

In fact, there had been remarkably few promotions to that
rank in recent years. Almost as if it was being cut out of the
system. The high fliers went from DI to Superintendent.

Usually in another force. Usually aged well under fifty. He could have gone for retirement, no questions asked. He had more than thirty years in, and in his father's day most cops would have gone at fifty anyway. But that would be admitting he'd been a failure. And what would he do with his time instead? Not too many jobs for men his age in Dumfries and Galloway. The idea of being stuck at home all day with Jackie – no, not something to be contemplated.

He paused to look out of the stair window. He'd have given a lot to be brave enough to keep going down, out to the car park, get into his motor, drive away and never come back. But of course, he didn't. He ran his fingers through his hair, using the reflection in the window as a mirror, straightened his shoulders and his tie, and went into the CID room.

He was champing at the bit to get an arrest, have someone in for questioning. He was under no illusions about being the best of interviewers, although in theory he was trained up to tier four. The trick was to get the suspect talking and keep them talking; then when they suddenly clammed up, you knew you were getting warm. He wasn't good at that; too impatient. But Rachel was tops at the interview game. She'd got one of the highest assessments in Scotland on her IMSC course, not long after she'd been bumped up to sergeant. In theory, he should have been using her as an interview supervisor now, and using DCs with the right training in the room, instead of putting Rach face to face with a suspect.

But she was so brilliant. She'd keep her cool while they lied through their teeth; she'd smile encouragingly at them. Then, after a couple of hours of that, she'd start picking their story apart and tying them in knots, and bingo; you knew she had them. She could keep calm during a 'no comment' interview in a way he'd never quite mastered. He'd sit with clenched fists, whereas she smiled ever more enigmatically, and proceeded through the list of questions.

He'd watched her do it time and again, from the observation gallery, trying to figure out what her technique was – she was far superior to any of the Tier Fives who came in to advise on the most difficult cases.

His team looked up eagerly as he entered the room. DC Giles was so eager he was practically bouncing on his chair. Tom felt his back tense up; the young puppy had already been harping on about McPhedrie and the Bissets being linked. He was a sodding menace; believed Holmes2 was a magic spell, not a computerised data-set. He was the type who'd have benefitted from a spell of the way it was in the old days, when everything was on a card index, and no one force knew what the others were doing.

'And before you start on about links between the victims again, Giles, let me remind you that what we have is three missing persons, possibly missing because of the actions of a third party, or parties. You know how many people go missing in the west of Scotland every year? Between ourselves and Strathclyde, it's near enough nineteen thousand. There is such a thing as coincidence, and it pays to bear that in mind, before you start chasing hares down blind alleys.'

From the corner of his eye, he imagined he saw Rach grin. Yes, that had been a bloody stupid comparison. Hares don't go down alleys.

He had started separate logs for McPhedrie and the Bissets. It was increasingly obvious that was a waste of time. In truth, there were seldom coincidences in police work. *If it looks like the abduction of a nonce, that's what it is; and you don't get two unconnected ones within a few days of each other in a place like Dumfriesshire.*

'I said I believed the disappearances are linked, Giles, not necessarily the victims.' *Other than that they all seem to be dirty buggers.*

Giles smirked in that way he had. The way that meant: *I'll be able to pull rank on you before you get your pension, just watch me.* 'What I was meaning is that all three are involved in child abuse.'

That had become increasingly obvious. They had discovered that McPhedrie had been working as a junior football coach for several years, in Warrington; girls' teams as well as boys'. He'd been asked to give up this work a few months earlier. It had proved impossible to get hold of the person who ran the club: he was on holiday until mid-January in Tenerife, address unknown.

They had continued to draw similar blanks with the Bissets. The education department of the local council where they had worked in the '90s was still closed. Not a chance of getting the powers-that-be to sanction yanking the council chief out of a party to chase up his head of education.

'So what I mean is, they may all be connected through being in the same ring,' said Giles.

'Right,' Tom snapped. 'In each case, we know the "who", and possibly the "why", and roughly the "when". So what we need to get our teeth into as a team – and I stress the word *team* here – is the "where" and the "how" and the sodding "*what*". Until we get to that, we're stuffed. We have no evidence at all that crimes have been committed against these people. I don't want us getting carried away with trying to find links between whatever offences *they* may have committed, until we're certain they have a bearing on the cases. It could all be coincidence. McPhedrie may have gone for a swim and drowned. The Bissets may have taken themselves off into the hills for some sort of suicide pact, if he was terminally ill, no matter what their daughter thinks.'

Rachel was looking at him quizzically. 'Not sure how far they'd have got into the hills with her on foot and him in a wheelchair, boss?'

'You know what I mean.'

'I want everyone to chase up any rumours flying around. That means you, constables. Put the word out to your buddies in uniform who're handlers. Check with all your usual snitches,' said Tom. He suspected that any minute now Giles would be correcting him, telling him that it was policy to refer to informants as *Covert Human Intelligence Sources*. He threw the *look* in his direction. 'Come on, guys, someone, somewhere must know what's happened to these three.' His tone was almost pleading.

Bugger. There'd be no peace at home to sort out his train of thought on this one. He knew from Jackie's excited twittering that there was a new Scandi-noir crime serial starting on TV that evening. He'd make a start on clearing out the garage while his wife sat glued to the set.

TEN

Belle sighed as she looked at Fergus's desk-diary, which he had carelessly left lying open. Normally, he kept it in a drawer. He was off again to another book signing later in the month. Meera would be there.

His original agent had died suddenly the previous year; heart attack at fifty-three. He'd been replaced by an Anglo-Indian high-flier: Meera Graham-Rudd . Belle hated her on sight. She looked exactly as she imagined Serena must have looked (except that Meera's eyes were the colour of obsidian, not cornflowers, and her skin was an exotic peachy-olive in place of Serena's Celtic pallor). Glossy black hair that swung down to her waist. She was thirty – exactly the same age Serena had been when Fergus last saw her.

Although she didn't like to admit it, Belle was nervous every time Fergus had to go off to London for a day or two for meetings.

He had become more attractive over the last five years. He'd lost weight, he was a lot healthier, and the success of his work (plus, she hoped, acquiring a family) had put a sparkle in his eye.

So unfair, the way men could become more attractive as they aged, like Richard Gere and George Clooney. And the way a man with gorgeous kids in tow was a sex-magnet.

She didn't understand why Fergus needed to meet this Meera dame so often face to face. She'd gone to a talk at the Wigtown Book Festival the previous September, and the author said he hardly ever saw his agent. They did everything by email. They didn't even need to use Skype.

Not for the first time, she wished that *her* work involved nothing more than sitting at a cosy desk. No sooner had they arrived home from Arran than the Dee had burst its banks and flooded the low-lying parts of Kirkcudbright. The house was safe enough, but the lower end of Belle's gallery was under three feet of water for more than twenty-four hours. Fortunately, all the paintings hung at that end were above the high-water mark.

She felt a rising sense of despair. Yet another list of things Fergus would have to pay for: the hire of an industrial dehumidifier; replastering and repainting of the walls once they dried out; new flooring.

She'd only been opening the gallery from Easter until the end of October since she had the children. She did a lot of framing, but she could do that at home, and all her materials were stored there. They had converted the garden cottage into a workshop for her – although in the end, she preferred to work on the kitchen table.

Since Damien Hirst and the other big names had started selling directly, and cutting out galleries and dealers, even emerging local artists were tending to do the same. Belle had never asked more than thirty per cent commission, but with the rise of events like the Spring Fling, and Open Studios, and non-profit collective galleries, she was selling work for few artists, after clearing out all of Roddy McCulloch's work. She didn't blame them. Although students in Scotland didn't pay fees, most graduated carrying a mound of debt. They needed the cash, as much and as quickly as possible. Belle was painfully aware she'd been privileged – she'd had an allowance from her father to pay for everything.

She had found one new artist to champion – a woman in her sixties, who lived in Portpatrick. Fergus found her paintings downright creepy – seascapes in muddy colours, and what looked like corpses scattered among the rocks. But they sold surprisingly well; they reminded Belle of Bet Low's work.

The truth was, she resented Fergus's success. She knew it was what had put new slates on the roof of Ashers, and allowed her to hang onto a gallery that barely brought in enough to pay the electricity bill. She knew she was being unreasonable, but there it was.

By any measure, her life had been a failure, a waste of time. What did she have to show for more than twenty-five years of work? A two-bit art gallery in a tiny town. One that couldn't cover its costs. She didn't feel fulfilled. Her role was always to be in her husband's shadow, to be dependent on him for paying her bills.

The only times she tried to share this with Fergus, he'd told her she was being ridiculous. He gestured towards the twins and told her that's what she had achieved: two clever children, so handsome that they looked as if they belonged in a Hornel painting (only, he knew perfectly well she loathed Hornel).

That made her more furious than ever – when did a man

ever get told that this should be his fulfilment, having sired children?

She even felt a sporadic stab of resentment when she remembered the almost triumphant way in which Fergus had seemed to believe that begetting twins was a personal achievement for *him*. She had provided two eggs, after all.

She didn't want Esmée to end up like that, depending on a man for her status and sense of self.

Belle was relieved that she wasn't expected to turn up at Fergus's book launches and signing events these days.

They had always made her feel uncomfortable, right since the first one, the launch of his non-fiction book on how to avoid getting scammed or ripped off. There had been a pragmatic reason for her discomfort that time; although neither she nor Fergus had suspected it, she was already pregnant. But honestly, having a fainting fit, and finding herself in the arms (literally) of Anita Forrest, Fergus's former boss, and someone she knew perfectly well he'd had an affair with in the past, before he knew her (though she had never asked him outright about it).

Ever since, she had – as far as possible – avoided attending such events. While the twins were too young to be depended on to stay quiet even for an hour, they were the perfect excuse.

In any case, no one was there to see *her*. She had realised one thing, ever since her days as a student, as Roddy McCulloch's consort while he held court with his adoring Glasgow School of Art fan club: reflected glory was something that made her cringe rather than bask.

She loved Fergus, but occasionally she yearned to have the bed to herself again (yet when Fergus was away, at a meeting with his agent, she couldn't sleep until he was home). She'd like to have had even a week when she didn't need to worry about anyone's requirements and concerns other than her own. And all the while, she was self-aware enough to know that her life before she met him (she had mentally divided her life into BF and AF) had not seemed free so much as barren. Latterly, at any rate, she hadn't revelled in her independence, she had hated it. She'd been assailed by fears of loneliness. That's what had *really* induced her to allow Roddy McCulloch back to live in the house after Father died, even although she had long since ceased to care for him. As long as he was there, she wasn't alone.

She had tried to apologise to Fergus for being impatient with him over his obligations to work. 'My life was so predictable until six years ago.' Let's face it: life was *dull*. 'I don't feel like the same person.'

'We're not the same people, Belle. We've both changed, now we have each other and the children. I see it as a positive change – I hope you do too?'

And she'd shuddered slightly, then nodded and said, 'Maybe that's what worries me: it feels too good to be true.'

Fergus said he worried sometimes that she felt trapped, that he knew her life had gone from being a calm loch to one with tides and whirlpools, that he was lucky enough to be able to escape into his work, while the responsibility of the kids fell on her, blah-blah.

Calm loch indeed! Stagnant pond. But in what had almost become a set routine, she smiled and said, 'Mothers always worry more, I think. It's OK. I prefer my new life.'

And the look of relief that swept across his face made her want to slap him, even as he was telling her how much he loved her.

ELEVEN

Tom Ellis's mouth was dry as he approached Ashers for the second time in six days. He could see that the kitchen and hall lights were both on. He tried to speed up his walk, to stride confidently, but damn it, he was still the overawed small boy he was years ago.

He recalled the first time he'd ever entered the house, as a tongue-tied five-year-old, dressed in an uncomfortable and over-large white shirt with a frill down the front, and a tartan bow tie, plus his school trousers. His mother had walked him to the end of the close, then propelled him towards the Big House, the brown paper bag containing his birthday present for Mabs (a jigsaw of two kittens in a basket) clutched in his sweaty hand. His mother didn't hold with nonsense like fancy wrapping paper. No one did, in those days. Waste of money. As he'd stood on the top step, he'd wanted to turn and run. But he could see, from the tail of his eye, his mother standing where he'd left her. He'd trembled as he stood on tiptoe to reach the brass door-knocker. Because he was already in love with Mabel Mountjoy, and everyone in the town was in awe of her father.

He remembered the handful of times he'd arrived for other birthdays, clutching yet other inadequate gifts. Although his mother, and the other mothers, would shake their heads over 'poor wee Mabel Mountjoy', she always had better toys and nicer clothes than any of her schoolmates.

She was sent away to her posh school at the end of primary seven. No more birthday parties for the local kids (not that he'd been invited to her parties once she'd turned nine, and the sexes tended to mix less).

He asked himself, not for the first time, if it was normal for a five-year-old child to have fallen in love. If it was normal for the same feelings to be there, scarcely submerged, almost half a century on.

And he remembered when he'd walked across those same paving stones as a young man, in his best suit, ready to take Mabel out to the cinema in Dumfries, or for a meal in the posh hotel at Creebridge. She'd been no shy virgin in those days, living in Glasgow during the week, with her teaching job. No indeed. A wild one she was. A woman of the world, much more experienced than he was, and a tease too. So the claik in the town was all about Rose Mountjoy, who had abandoned Mabs before she was even at school. 'Like mother, like daughter,' the other women said, with knowing looks.

He remembered those times all too clearly. Those, plus the fact that she'd turned him down, in the end. Turned him down without even appearing to give his proposal much serious thought. All the other girls in the area were queuing up to have him. He'd been a looker in those days, and that wasn't vanity speaking; it was the truth. But not good enough for Mabel. He had spent the months – the years – after she turned him down torturing himself over whether she had said, 'I don't want to *marry* you, Tom', or 'I don't want to marry *you*, Tom'.

He knew fine what the tittle-tattle had been in Kirkcudbright when he married Chief Inspector Maurice Black's daughter, Jackie, on the rebound, within six months. Darkest brown hair, and high cheekbones, and a thin angular body. Everyone said Jackie should have gone in for modelling. 'He'll live to regret that,' they said too. 'Netta Black's no' the easiest woman to hae as a mither-in-law.'

But he'd been determined to show Mabs Mountjoy he didn't need her. Show her what she was missing. It was one of the biggest weddings Kirkcudbright had seen in many a long year. The pics were in all the local papers, and they were a handsome couple.

And indeed, over the next twenty years or so, he'd experienced a good deal of *Schadenfreude*, as he'd seen everyone in the town sneer at Mabs. Alone in her big, fancy house, with only her ancient, grumpy father and the alcoholic poison dwarf, the so-called artist Roddy McCulloch, for company.

But the triumph of having snared someone else, a real catch, had turned to ashes in his mouth within the year anyway. He could see by then that Jackie's seeming beauty was an artificial, high-maintenance look. *Mabs doesn't look as if she even wears make-up at all, never mind getting her eyebrows dyed and her fanny waxed every week or two.*

He swallowed, and forced himself to climb the three steps to the front door, doubly nervous of seeing Mabel face to face again. Although he had been careful to stay hidden, he'd observed her a good few times, in the years since she'd married Fergus Learmonth. He had watched her from afar as she carried her advancing pregnancy, as stately as a galleon in full sail. He'd watched as she positively bloomed with motherhood. He'd watched as she and Learmonth – he couldn't yet bear to think of the man as her *husband* – had strode out from the house every evening, the twins cosy in their double buggy, and Mabel's dog, Archie, on his lead. And each time, his heart had grown a little more bitter and cramped.

'Mabs,' he murmured under his breath, savouring the word in his mouth as he used to. But she didn't call herself that those days. 'Belle' the Learmonth guy had rebranded her. Everyone in the town referred to her as Belle now – those that didn't accord her the full handle of 'Mrs Learmonth'.

He needed Fergus Learmonth's advice; there was nothing for it but to knock.

He brushed imaginary dandruff from his collar.

As he rapped the brass knocker smartly, he remembered that the last time he had stepped inside this house, he'd been carrying out orders to pin a manslaughter – if not murder – charge on Mabel. He remembered also that the last time he spoke to Fergus Learmonth was across the table in an interview room in the Dumfries nick. The last time he'd stood on Ashers' doorstep, when he called to try to apologise, Mabs had slammed the door in his face, and told him to buzz off. She had used a much stronger expression; he'd been so shocked he'd almost brought up his supper, because Mabs never swore. *Stop thinking of her as Mabs. Belle, Belle, Belle. Mrs Learmonth.*

Mabel answered the door. She looked taken aback. Her hand flew to her throat. He was struck again by how good she looked. You'd think having twins at forty-five – almost forty-six – would have aged any woman: not Mabs. She looked five years *younger*, if anything.

'You!' she said. 'What is it now? Are you spying on us again?'

Tom swallowed hard. 'Absolutely nothing to worry about. Happy New Year, by the way.'

'You've come to wish me a Happy New Year?'

Her pug ran out of the house and began snuffling round his feet. He stooped to ruffle the velvety ears, although he was not in general a dog-lover. The creature shied away from him and hid behind its mistress's shapely ankles.

Tom tried to grin, but his face seemed to stick halfway. 'Am I your first foot? I should have brought a lump of coal with me, shouldn't I?'

She ignored that. 'So why are you here? I thought the thing with Roddy was all cleared up years ago?'

'It was. It's nothing to do with him. I actually wondered if I could have a wee word with your... husband?'

'Fergus?'

'The very one.' He'd half a mind to make a joke about 'unless you've married another one since', thought better of it and smiled as ingratiatingly as he could.

'What do you want with him?'

'Just a chat.'

'He's out,' said Mabel, her voice shrewish.

'Well – could I make an arrangement to see him when it's convenient?'

A door opening down in the close made both of them pause.

'You'd better come in a minute. What do you want with Fergus?' she asked again, once the hall door was firmly closed. She didn't invite him further into the house.

'I wanted to ask for his help with something.'

Mabel snorted. 'You want his help? After what you put both

of us through a couple of years back, with your false accusations? We should have sued the police from here to kingdom come.'

'It was nearly six years ago, Mabs. I've apologised.'

'Apologised!'

At that moment, they both jumped at the sound of the door behind them opening. Fergus Learmonth strode into the hallway, the twins running ahead of him. His hair was completely silver now, but his brows were still black; it gave him the look that put Tom in mind of the guy who used to be Chancellor: Alistair Darling. Or of a badger. Tom disliked and distrusted both equally.

Fergus's face grew grim when he saw who was standing beside his wife.

'Up to your rooms, kids. Get yourselves cleaned up and ready for supper. And take those muddy boots off first, both of you.' As the children discarded wellingtons in slow motion, then vanished reluctantly upstairs, Fergus turned back to Tom, glowering. 'What the hell do you want, Ellis? You've a nerve, coming here.'

Tom coughed. Sod it! This wasn't going even half to plan. 'It was a long time ago. You got an official apology.' He tried once more to smile. 'It was you I was looking for, in fact.'

'Found another murder you want to pin on me, is that it?'

Blood suffused Tom's face and neck. 'Not at all. I was just saying to Mabs...'

'Belle. No one calls me "Mabs" these days,' said Mabel.

'Sorry. I was saying to Belle, I've come to make my peace with you.'

Fergus bellowed with laughter. 'Make your *peace* – after what you did?'

'I'm so sorry about what happened back then. I'd hoped it was water under the bridge.'

Fergus gave another mirthless laugh. 'Some bridge that'd have to be. The last time you spoke to us, you were trying to pin a murder charge on my wife, and when that didn't work, you decided I would do.'

'I apologised. You got a formal apology from the Chief Constable. Can we not move on from that? Mab... Belle, you and I go back a long way.' Ellis saw Fergus's brow crease, and decided that was the wrong tactic. 'I mean, we were at school together, for God's sake. I made an honest mistake back in 2007. *We* made an honest mistake, the police. Please.' He held out his right hand towards Fergus, who hesitated, then shook it reluctantly. 'I can see you're busy just now, with the kids and all. Can I arrange a time to come back and speak to you about something?'

'What sort of something?'

'I wanted to ask for your help with a case I'm working on.'

'Why would I help you, of all people?'

'Because I need you to. I know you're damn good at what you do.'

'I write fiction,' snapped Fergus.

'But you also help the police from time to time. I know you've helped out the guys in Lothian and Borders, and even the ones up in Strathclyde, more than once.'

'You're on the point of becoming one big happy family in Police Scotland. I thought the purpose of amalgamating the whole jingbang was to make you more efficient? I was reading in the paper that the major incident team's all set to be in place this spring. I'm sure you have some smart young graduate-entry detectives who can help you more than a mere writer can.'

'You're not "a mere writer", and well you know it. You've a knack of finding missing people that none of my colleagues have. I don't have it either.'

Giggling at the top of the stairs heralded the reappearance of the twins, faces pink and scrubbed, slippers on. They hesitated when they saw that the stranger was still there. Fergus beckoned to them. 'Come on, kids, supper time.' He turned back to Tom. 'All right, Ellis, you can come back some time when it's more convenient for us. Not at a meal-time, for instance.'

'Tomorrow suit you?'

Fergus sighed. 'All right. Come after seven.'

Tom walked back up the close with his fists balled in his pockets.

He'd done some checking-up on the case of Fergus's first wife, because he'd been determined to have something on this Learmonth guy who'd turned up out of the blue and got Mabs Mountjoy with child at the age some women were grandmothers. Too many unanswered questions in Learmonth's backstory. The ex-wife's lover – a *Russian* lover – who'd ended up as a skeleton in a shallow grave on Corstorphine Hill. The ex-wife herself dying suddenly (she was another man's wife by then). He'd made sure to ferret out all the details of that case (it had been logged, as any unexplained death would be). Dead at thirty-five, no warning, pregnant with her third child; heart defect, apparently. One of these things you knew nothing about until it struck. Dead before she hit the ground. What a way to go!

No foul play, or suggestion of it, that could be linked to Learmonth in the case of either the wife or her gigolo. Fergus hadn't been within five hundred miles of her when it happened. There were witnesses. The Russian was more of a mystery.

Fergus was set to be in a bad mood for the rest of the evening. 'Why can't the police do their own work? And why would I help him, of all people?'

'Then you shouldn't have told him to come back tomorrow,' said Belle. 'But you know you enjoy doing that sort of work from time to time.'

She was being reasonable, of course. The bread and butter of *Learmonth on the Lookout*, the TV programme he'd fronted for more years than he cared to remember, was tracking down cowboy builders and dodgy car salesmen. When he'd agreed to one more series, once he knew he was to become a father, he'd branched out a little from that, and dealt with a few cases where the missing person was a fugitive from the more serious aspects of the law.

But he'd always stopped short at the point where the police had enough information to bring it to a conclusion. Too dangerous otherwise, too distracting. Before he had a family to think of, he might have relished the adrenalin-rush that danger brought. His life was as exciting as he wanted it to be, these days.

And worst of all: Belle had confessed when they first tangled with DI Ellis almost six years before, that she'd had an affair with him when she was in her twenties. He'd even asked her to marry him. *Presumptuous, or what?*

'You realise that we need to take the brats to see the fairy lights on the boats now it's dark?' Belle said suddenly.

The twins had demanded to see the boats in the harbour

almost every night, much to Fergus's chagrin. He felt it underlined how important it was to educate them sooner rather than later; let them see *real* Christmas lights in Princes Street – and indeed in Regent Street, in due course. The dozen trawlers moored almost at the end of the High Street had their Christmas lights strung in the rigging. Fishermen were superstitious chiels; the lights wouldn't come down until Twelfth Night.

'This'll be one of the the last nights they're lit, I suppose,' agreed Fergus. 'We'll take a brisk walk round. It'll help the kids sleep.'

'It doesn't smell of the sea,' said Eddie crossly as they reached the harbour.

'It smells of fish.'

'That's not what I mean.'

'It's because it's the river,' said Belle patiently. 'The Dee. This is the estuary.'

'But the water's salt here. The teacher said.'

'That's because the tide from the sea comes up this far.'

Eddie sighed. 'So it's seawater?'

'Yeees. I suppose so.'

Esmée had decided to enter the fray. 'So why doesn't it smell of the sea?'

'Because the sides are mud banks, and there's no seaweed,' said Belle briskly. 'You, madam, are becoming a cheeky child.'

Fergus smiled to himself.

TWELVE

Tom had a lump in his throat as he took in the peaceful scene: a pool of lamplight above the table (Mabs had installed one of those fancy rise-and-fall jobs with a copper shade, instead of the functional strip light that he remembered there). And in the lamplight, a silver head and two dark ones bent over a pile of sheets of blotting paper covered in dried flowers, and a photo album – the kind with adhesive plastic sheets to cover each page. They were so focused on what they were doing that they didn't look up.

It was quite clear they'd all forgotten it was tonight he was to come and speak to Fergus.

Looking at Mabs, he felt the old thrill of desire. He should have flung caution to the winds six years ago, when the fate that befell Roddy McCulloch threw them together again. He should have swept her off her feet, and got her away from Learmonth. He should have told Jackie time was up, and applied for a job elsewhere. He'd probably have got a decent billet in the Met in those days, in his mid-forties and with more than twenty years of experience under his belt. He could have made a home for the two of them in London – or at least, the London area. A love nest. These could have been his children sitting there. His and Mabs'.

'School project,' said Mabel, defensively.

Had he ever helped his kids with their homework? He couldn't recall.

While she was shacked up with McCulloch, Tom had been able to persuade himself he pitied her. She was one of those women who needed a man, and since she'd turned *him* down, she'd had to settle for human dross. But surveying the scene before him, Tom arrived at an uncomfortable conclusion: Mabel Mountjoy had done better for herself. He'd been right when he was six. He wasn't good enough for her. He could never have given her all *this*. She'd found something he'd never had.

They were gorgeous children; the little boy's hair black as a jackdaw's back, the girl's with an auburn sheen under the lamp-light. They both gazed up at him with Mabel's amber eyes.

There had been a picture of them in the *Galloway News* the week school started. The papers were always obsessed with twins. Jackie usually sniggered and called him an old woman for studying the pics in the local rag, but she should have known, as a policeman's daughter, that you could glean fruitful intelligence about local families from the most parochial of sources. The papers and *Dumfries & Galloway Life* were a mine of information about who knew whom, and which couples had been caught holding hands, or with arms twined around each other's shoulders, or red-faced because they'd been caught in the act, as well as with the drink.

He remembered the day, more than five years ago, when

Jackie had said (nastily), 'They're saying yon Muriel Mountjoy...'

'Mabel,' he'd corrected her.

'Mabel, Muriel, Myrtle. Whatever antiquated name it is the woman has. Something that went out of date in the 1920s. Well, they're saying she refused to have an amniocentesis.'

'How could she have "refused"? No one's forced to have one.'

'It's plain daft, at her age.'

'It's the woman's choice.'

Jackie had stuck out her tongue at him, and mimicked his voice. '*The woman's choice.* Since when were you interested in women's choices?'

He hadn't known what to make of that. Naturally, Jackie – and her damn mother – were well aware that he'd had a relationship with Mabel before he married *her*. What he hadn't realised, until that moment, was how much she resented it.

'Well, it's downright selfish if you ask me. If she produces a handicapped kid, she's only herself to blame,' his wife had pronounced, slamming the frying pan viciously onto the brand new ceramic induction hob that had cost twice what a normal one would have.

He'd met Briony Hall out wheeling the twins' pram when they were a few weeks old, and peered in. 'They're both...?'

Mabel's friend had bridled and glared at him. 'They're perfect. Physically and mentally.'

Well, how the hell could she be so confident about that when they barely had their eyes open? No – that was kittens, wasn't it?

Now they were in the same school class as his grand-daughter.

And Mabs herself. There she was, in a white blouse and jeans, trim and alluring, looking much as she did in her thirties. Learmonth was looking good too, even without applying a sneaky bit of dye to his hair. Slimmer, and without that drinker's ruddiness.

The detective blinked and swallowed hard. He tried to steer his mind away from thinking about what *their* kids would have looked like: his and Mabel's.

'Your children are very well-behaved,' he said.

Mabs looked at him quizzically.

'Quiet, like,' he added. 'Maybe it's a generational thing. We brought ours up to be quiet in the house, but Sharon's kid, well!' He tailed off and reddened. 'I'm a grandfather now, did you hear? Our Sharon has a wee girl. She's in the same class as yours. The opposite of quiet.'

Mabel made a noise somewhere between approval and lack of interest. 'I didn't know she'd got married? I usually look at the pictures in the *News*.'

Tom cleared his throat. 'Well, you know how they are these days, the young ones. She and her partner don't believe in it. They say maybe they'll tie the knot by and by. It was different in our day, wasn't it?' He watched Mabel's eyes drift to unfocused. *She's thinking 'That could have been* my *grandchild,'* he told himself.

Fergus's expression had softened a little. He looked help-lessly at his children, who were staring unblinkingly at the stranger.

'Why don't you take Tom into the sitting room?' said Mabel. 'I'll help the twins clear up here. It's almost their bedtime anyway.' She trailed her fingers softly across the back of her husband's neck as she passed behind his chair. Tom slewed his eyes away. *They still have a sex life, these two. I can't remember the last time Jackie and I... not since she became menopausal and went off it. One bloody excuse after another. Sometimes, I find myself looking at Rach and wondering if she'd...? You see that all the time in these trashy TV cop dramas Jackie laps up. Banging one another like screen doors in a hurricane. It doesn't happen in real life. Not in central Dumfries and Galloway anyway. Not when your mother-in-law's that dried-up witch's dug Netta Black, with all her faculties intact, and her coven of informers as strong as ever it was, and a deep spite at you because you didn't make it to Chief Constable.*

Tom dug the nails of his middle fingers into his palms and glanced around the rest of the kitchen. New cabinets; obviously solid wood, none of your MDF, but painted in a soft colour that was neither green nor grey.

'Nice!' he said.

Mabs looked puzzled.

'The kitchen. You've had it done up?'

She smiled. She actually *smiled*. 'Fergus did a lot of the woodwork.'

'Bloody hell! Thought you were spending your days writing these best-sellers of yours?' *You'd think, with the cash he's supposed to get for his books, they could have got a man in?*

'I can't write *all* the time.'

'So I heard,' said Tom. *Caught him!* 'That's partly what I wanted to see you about.'

Fergus grimaced. 'Come on through then, out of Belle's way.'

Belle moved to the kitchen window and stood looking out over the garden. There was no moon, but in the reflected light from the street lamps, she could see the outline of the garden cottage where Roddy McCulloch had lived – and died, according to the police's forensics people, though his sister had moved his body away before anyone found it.

She was thinking about how dreary her life might have been had Roddy not died, and had she not met Fergus. Or if she'd stuck with Tom Ellis when she was in her twenties, and spent all those years as an ordinary cop's wife. She was thinking, 'God, doesn't Tom look *old!*'

Fergus pursed his lips as he led Tom through to the sitting room. The fire was laid but not lit; he stooped and put a match to it.

Tom glanced around him. The walls of the room had been painted since he was last there. The old dark-varnished wood panelling was now a warm grey shade, almost the colour of a wood pigeon's breast, and the plain-plastered fireplace wall was a dark purply-red. What he'd call plum. The oriental rugs he'd have mentally dismissed a year or two back as what you put on your floor if you couldn't afford fitted shag-pile, the stuff Jackie considered the epitome of luxury. But they blended gloriously with the wooden floor (and that had been sanded and refinished; he'd lay money on it).

The colour-scheme put him in mind of the kitchen at the Bissets' farmhouse. *Must be fashionable this year.* There were two comfortably squishy-looking sofas and two wing-chairs, all covered in a dark tartan fabric with a lot of heather-purple and dark teal in it. Heavy curtains to match. Now these didn't come from Dunelm Mill!

'My! You inherited a furniture shop?'

Fergus sounded a little defensive. 'One extra sofa, that's all. These are Belle's father's old chairs. We had them reupholstered.'

A cat jumped stiffly down from one of the sofas as Tom approached. He felt a sneeze creeping towards his nose, tried desperately to stifle it.

'Sorry. Allergy.'

Fergus Learmonth rolled his eyes. He didn't offer to remove the cat, but Gorby glared at the intruder and stalked, stiff-legged towards the door, where he set up a pathetic mew to be let out.

Mabel stuck her head round the door. 'You two want tea or anything?'

'Not for me, thanks,' said Tom.

She tossed her head, and closed the door firmly.

'So, I suppose you're meaning to send your kids to some fancy school?'

Fergus narrowed his eyes. 'The local primary's fine for the time being.'

'Well, it was good enough for their mother,' Tom said, before he could bite his tongue. 'Until she was eleven anyway.' He sank into a capacious sofa, and sighed.

'I suppose.' Fergus's smile was wan. 'That's where you two met, isn't it? I take it you're on duty, so I can't offer you a whisky?'

'This is purely a private call.'

'But you'll be driving back to Dalbeattie?'

'I'm meaning to stay over with my mother here tonight, as a matter of fact.'

Fergus grinned, finally. 'So you *would* like a whisky? Or we have – let's see: gin or vodka. Or there's beer in the fridge.'

Tom looked optimistically at the silver tray of decanters on a side table. The whole town knew that Fergus Learmonth drank an eye-wateringly exclusive whisky from Campbeltown, which he bought in by the case.

'Whisky's fine. You drink a fancy one, don't you? I remember something about that one of the times Roddy McCulloch's sister broke in here. She left a tumbler that smelt of the one he drank, and you said you wouldn't touch it if you were on a desert island and not another drop in sight? You only drank the one kind. I can't remember the name of it.'

Fergus guffawed. 'McCulloch had a taste for Glen Fruig. Belle says it would fell a pig at fifty paces. She means pig as in porcine animal, by the way. Belle's terribly keen on the forces of law and order. I drink Springbank. You want to try that?'

Tom nodded enthusiastically, and Fergus pursed his lips, then smiled wearily. 'What a memory you have. You're a bit of a connoisseur yourself then, Ellis?'

'I like a dram, from time to time.'

'Time to time is what's in it with this stuff. Costs a wee bit.' He opened the sideboard and took out a bottle, held it up for Tom to see the label, then poured two generous measures. 'Water? Soda?' His lip curled slightly.

'Water please.'

'Good man.' Fergus lifted a jug from the tray and left the room.

Tom drew his mobile phone from his pocket and grabbed a few surreptitious snaps of the room. Jackie had spurned his ideas for a colour scheme; he'd work on her. *But the decor here isn't her style. Too classy.* This could have been *his* sitting room. These could have been *his* rugs (because he remembered these at least from his tongue-tied childhood visits). *Bugger it, I must stop thinking that way about Mabs. I still love her.*

'How much?' asked Fergus, and Tom jumped visibly.

'What?'

'How much water?'

'A splash.'

Fergus nodded approvingly. 'You don't want to drown it.'

Tom sniffed his glass, savouring it. The bottle had been firmly replaced in the sideboard. He doubted he'd be getting a refill from *that* at any rate.

His host was watching him carefully. He took a sip. 'Wow!'

'Just "wow" is it?'

'Just wow. A hint of peat and no more. It's grand.' He wanted to say it made him think of warm blankets and hand-knitted jumpers. A *safe* flavour. Home. But Learmonth would think he was daft.

Fergus grinned. 'Worth what everybody says I pay for it then?'

'I'll say.' Tom gestured with his glass towards the fireplace wall. 'What colour do you call that?'

'I'd call it aubergine. Belle will know the exact name. I'll ask her when I go through again. Why – do you like it?'

'I do. Looks good with that material you got the chairs done in.'

Fergus raised his eyebrows.

'I'm going to be doing some decorating,' said Tom. 'Always on the lookout for ideas.'

'So – what exactly is it you want to see me about?'

'Everyone knows you helped the police in Edinburgh and Glasgow solve a couple of murder cases they were stuck with.'

'They turned out to be that. I was asked to help when they were missing person cases. Why – have you a murder you can't figure out?'

Tom wriggled into a more comfortable position. 'I've a handful of missing persons I can't figure out. I'm beginning to think murder's on the cards.'

Fergus sighed. 'Missing how long?'

'The first one since mid-December, the other two shortly after Christmas Day, as far as we can ascertain.'

'*Three?*'

'A single man, plus a couple.'

'Connected?'

'Could be.' Tom frowned.

'I take it you've exhausted all the usual possibilities?'

'No proof of life at all.'

'And that's police-speak for no activity on bank accounts, no mobile phone calls, no cars picked up on ANPR, and so on?'

'Not a thing.'

'You don't reckon these people have taken off voluntarily?'

'It's not sounding like that.'

'So what do you want from me?'

'Well, I know you're particularly good at tracking down people who don't want to be found.'

'Says who?'

Ellis wouldn't meet his eye. 'The guys you helped out in the other forces said where you come in useful is that your mind works differently to ordinary people's.'

Fergus grimaced at the back-handed compliment.

'By the way,' added Tom, 'one peculiar thing: in both these cases, they hadn't taken a car.'

'I take it *you* think they're connected?'

Tom shrugged. 'It'd be a hell of a coincidence if they're not.'

'So what do you reckon?'

'My first thought was kidnapping.'

'Any contact from kidnappers?'

'Not a cheep. No ransom demands, nada.'

'And no blood, I take it? No sign of violence?'

'No blood. No sign of forced entry at either property.'

'So you reckon the victims let them in?'

'Either that or they hadn't locked their doors. You know what people are like in a rural area.'

'You've no clue as to *why*?'

The detective relayed the story of the Bissets' warehouse. Fergus grunted. 'And the third person?'

Tom wrestled with his conscience. Fuck it, he needed to get this case solved. 'You'll need to keep this to yourself. We've not let bug to the press meantime, because it's part of a bigger investigation. The single guy's called McPhedrie. Ex-footballer?'

Fergus shook his head. 'Never heard of him.'

'He didn't make it to the big time. Well, he appears to be part of a child pornography ring. He had thousands of pictures and videos. Supplying as well as buying, as far as we can see. The IT geeks reckon they'll be able to get some links from the stuff on his computer to the other guys who're putting that filth out there.'

'Bloody hell, Ellis. I'd say you're looking at more than simple kidnappings then. Assassinations, more like. Can't say I feel too het-up about it either. I always feel they get what's coming to them. Scum of the earth. Worse than drug-pushers.' Fergus punched the chair-arm. 'In fact, why are you even bothering? The days when men like that would be strung up from the nearest tree; those were the good old days. Let's hope he has been done away with. One less of the bastards walking this earth.'

'I have to admit, there are some villains I don't see the point of spending good money on keeping alive. But these days, we're told we have to respect their human rights. Bloody "diversity training". We're supposed to respect all sorts. But that? No! Would you not like to see him brought to justice anyway? We might get a lot of info from him on who else is involved. Better to get two dozen off the streets than one, surely?'

'I assume you've made thorough checks on Facebook and Twitter? For contacts, I mean.'

Tom rolled his eyes. 'Got someone onto it immediately. None of the three of them seem to have gone in for that at all. We trawled all the social media for McPhedrie's ex-wives too – he'd been married a couple of times – and the couple's daughter, but absolutely nothing of interest.'

'Was this character making contact with the kids via chatrooms?'

'Not that we've been able to find out so far. But that's how they usually do it.'

'So you're asking me to investigate the victims, not the suspects?'

'Principally McPhedrie, in the first instance. But it'd be useful to get a handle on the couple too. I can give you all the details of names and places.'

'You reckon if they've been the victims of crime, it's the same person who's responsible?'

Tom picked at his nails. 'That's how it's looking.'

'But you're not asking for a hand with tracking down the suspects?'

'We have no suspects yet. I reckon it's finding out more about the victims that'll lead us to the perpetrator.'

Fergus sighed. 'OK – where do you want me to start?'

When he was on his third glass (from one of the decanters

this time), Tom finally found the courage to ask Fergus what he'd wanted to ask for the past five years.

'What actually happened to yon Russian guy?'

'You've seen the notes from your colleagues in Lothian and Borders.'

'But you didn't tell them all you knew.'

'I have not the faintest idea what happened to him. I told the police everything I knew about it at the time. He was a petty gangster who'd fastened onto Serena like a leech when she was on holiday. Told her some sob story about the mafia being after him. So she smuggled him home, and he lived off her for a few months. Hell of a drinker. A real soak. He got in with a bad crowd and disappeared. The first I heard of him being found years later was when the police contacted her aunt, and she called me, because she was in a sheer panic.'

'But you knew who it was?'

'I suspected. And I was able to tell them what he'd been wearing the last time Serena saw him.'

'Serena. Is that your wife's name? Lovely name, that. Unusual, like.'

Fergus glared at him. 'It was my ex-wife's name. And she's dead now. As I distinctly remember telling you years ago.'

Tom loosened the knot in his tie. 'So. The aunt called you – why?'

'Because she was terrified the next thing would be a bunch of reporters breathing down her neck. Exactly what you don't want if you live on an island. I was able to hush it up. The media didn't go big on reporting suicides or accidental deaths in those days.'

'And how did you come to know exactly what he'd been wearing anyway?'

'Serena told me, man! I'd gone out looking for him when he disappeared.'

'It couldn't have been that your wife – ex-wife – paid someone to get rid of him?'

'No, it couldn't. Serena's mind didn't work that way. Fuck's sake, Ellis. Do you want my help or not?'

'I do. I'm sorry. I was only curious. I'd be grateful for any help you can give me. I – we – want to get it sorted out long before the local force gets merged with the others.'

'So what do you reckon to this Police Scotland idea then?'

'It'll be a total disaster. Calls about incidents in our patch handled by some townie in Glasgow who hasn't a clue where Beeswing is. Chaos. Accidents waiting to happen. In a country like Scotland, you need the local knowledge. All that'll be lost. Wait till you see the redundancies that'll come.'

'They're saying that the police in parts of England have given up on low-level crime anyway. Burglaries, and the like – even some assaults, where they've no handle on the offender.'

Tom wriggled his back against the cushions. 'I know. It's bad. That's not what *I* joined the job for.'

'I suppose every public service has to save money.'

'It's the same with the coastguard. Local stations closed, and ignorant bozos in places like Anglesey answering all the calls. I heard about one incident where they needed a crew double-quick at an isolated beach, and the control room operator said she needed to know the postcode of the beach.'

Fergus pulled a face. 'I used to worry about Belle going swimming in the winter at places like Carrick Shore. And if there had been a problem, I wouldn't have a clue what the post-code is.' He looked anxiously towards the doorway. 'Do you want another refill?'

Tom held out his glass. He rubbed his eyes. 'I know Mabs told you I'd had a thing with her when we were young. But I've realised since – I couldn't have given her all this.' He waved an arm to encompass the gracious room. 'I know it was hers, but it never looked like this before. You have *style*, the way she does. I've never had that.' He sighed. The knowledge – and admitting it to Mabel's husband – brought a type of peace. 'You come from a good family, like her. I was reading about your father – he was famous too, wasn't he? A war photographer.'

'Much good it did him. He was killed doing his job. What did *your* father do?'

'Police constable. Here in Kirkcudbright.' He grinned wryly. 'I grew up in the police houses not two hundred yards from here.'

'So your roots are deep.'

Fergus rose and selected a volume from the bookcase, dropping it into Tom's lap. 'My father had a few books of his work published.'

He went off to refill the water-jug, while Tom leafed wonderingly through photos of the Korean War.

'Belle says it's called Passionate Plum.' Tom's jaw dropped, and Fergus guffawed. 'The paint you were asking about, man! Good luck with asking for that in Homebase. Now, about the other thing. I'll see what I can do, on one condition. This is purely a private arrangement between us, Ellis. I don't want it mentioned to another soul, because I don't have the leisure to do this more than one other time. I don't want to find I'm getting hassled from here, there and everywhere. In fact, I don't want it getting out that I'm helping the police at all. Not now I have a family to think of. Deal?'

'Deal.' Tom held out his hand, and after a brief hesitation, Fergus shook it.

The detective spent the next half-hour outlining the details of what they'd been able to discover thus far about the three missing people.

He stood up to leave, reluctantly. He'd almost been at the stage of falling asleep in Belle's warm, comfortable sitting room. He caught sight of her as he passed through the hallway. She was sitting at the kitchen table, a book spread before her. He wanted to ask what she was reading, but bit his tongue.

'Goodnight, then,' he called softly.

'Yes, goodnight.' She didn't look up.

Tom started out on the half-mile walk to his mother's house, and decided to go the long way round.

He sat on one of the benches behind the wall of the Piscy church, overlooking the harbour, hands balled in his pockets against the cold. His head was swimming, not only with the amount he'd drunk, but with having been in Mab's house all evening, having seen her sitting there, head bent over her book, and being seized with an almost irresistible desire to draw his fingers over the smooth nape of her neck.

He needed time to exorcise the demons that had gnawed at his mind for twenty-seven years.

Closing his eyes, he ran through it all again. The day in July 1985 when he'd been strolling up Dumfries High Street and noticed the most attractive girl, then realised that he *knew* her. 'Mabel Mountjoy!' he called, and she turned, looking puzzled at first, and asked hesitantly, 'Tom?' She had seemed as delighted by the encounter as he was. The WPC who was with him had tactfully moved along the street and engaged a group of youths in conversation.

After the usual pleasantries, he had asked Mabs if she'd go out with him the following evening. She'd agreed at once. On an impulse, he'd leaned forward and kissed her on the cheek, then realised that probably wasn't the done thing when he was in uniform and on duty, but the way she'd looked at him – eyes sparkling, smiling, and a little shy, he'd fallen headfirst in love with her all over again. When he'd hurried off to catch up with his colleague, he was walking three feet above the ground.

He'd sat with her on that self-same bench beside the harbour on their third date, and they'd got into a clinch so passionate that they'd had to adjourn urgently to a more private spot. And afterwards, when he'd persuaded her not to go home right away, but to sit with him again, like any other courting couple – he remembered how elated he'd felt. And also a little worried, as he carefully picked pieces of grass and twig from her hair. He'd whispered in her ear, 'Will it be all right? You know... I didn't come prepared.' She'd laughed lightly, and said yes, it would be all right, she'd come prepared, luckily; she was on the pill. Then she'd asked him suddenly, and not in a whisper, 'What were you going to do if I said you'd probably knocked me up?' He'd winced; she'd broken the romantic spell – almost. But she was smiling at him, so he'd forced a laugh too, and said they'd have been starting their family a little sooner than planned. She'd positively chortled at that. 'Just as well I took care of it then! I haven't the least intention of starting a family.'

He'd thought nothing of it at the time. It was Mabs being Mabs. Outspoken. And she'd been right – plenty of time to have kids once they'd enjoyed each other's company for a year or two more, travelled some. Probably even moved away from the area altogether, because once he'd got his foot on the first rung of the ladder, he knew it'd be easier to make the next step up if they were in a city. Glasgow, perhaps – though Mabs didn't seem to like Glasgow. Manchester. Even London; he'd heard promotion was easy in the Met if you showed you were keen.

By the time she had to be back in Glasgow during the week, for her teaching job, they were already spending time together every weekend he could get off. He'd borrow his uncle's car; you couldn't expect a girl like Mabs to ride pillion on a motorbike, and he found it uncomfortable to be a passenger in the Mini her father had bought her – no room for his legs. He found it uncomfortable to be driven by a woman, full stop. They'd go to a hotel somewhere in Cumbria or the Borders; never to Glasgow. He'd desperately wanted to meet her friends, but she was forever telling him she *had* no friends there, only her work. They'd been blissfully happy, and Tom had assumed they'd get married. It seemed inevitable. Predestined.

On that last Sunday morning, as they lay wrapped in each other's arms, warm and satiated, at an expensive four-star place in Kendal, he'd decided to ask her. No point in putting it off. He was due to take his sergeant's exams the next week, and he was sure he'd get a quick promotion, because although he wasn't a graduate, he wasn't a daft laddie either. He'd stayed on at school for sixth year, and had four Highers. He could have gone to Uni if he'd *wanted* to.

And as he was about to propose, he hesitated; he should have bought her a ring first. But he'd go up to Glasgow the first available day, and meet her after work, and they'd choose one together.

'I was thinking – I have a couple of weeks' leave in March. We could get married then, Mabs.'

She had rolled lazily onto her back and glared at the ceiling. 'What are you talking about?'

'Well, we're going to get married, aren't we? I'm going for promotion. They always prefer people who've settled down. Married men.'

Mabs had hooted with laughter. 'You want me to marry you so you'll get a better job?'

He'd become less jovial and pointed out that it wasn't *just* for that. He loved her. He'd added that if she genuinely thought it was too soon, they could live together – but she'd need to get a job in one of the schools in Dumfriesshire or Kirkcudbrightshire.

She'd laughed even harder. 'I don't want to marry you, Tom! Don't be so stupid. And I don't want to live with you either. Why can't we go on as we are?'

So that was it. He was good enough to service her a couple of weekends a month – and boy, did she enjoy it! But not good enough to marry her.

They'd driven back to Kirkcudbright in a silence broken only by arguing about whether to listen to Dire Straits or Brian Ferry, and he dropped her at the end of the High Street. She seized her bag from the back seat, and walked off. He watched until she reached the top of the close, and moved out of his sight. She didn't turn her head once.

He waited all the next week for her to phone, or even write, and apologise. Nothing. By some miracle, he'd managed to sit and pass his exams. A further week with no contact had him climbing the steps to Ashers' door on the Saturday forenoon. Her father had answered, but when Tom asked for Mabs, the old man told him, with a sneer, that she wasn't there, she was up in Glasgow with her friends, and no, he had no idea when she'd be visiting Kirkcudbright again.

So she'd broken his heart for the second time.

Within three weeks, he'd asked Jackie Black out. They were married five months later. He'd made it to sergeant by then.

He remembered the feel of Mabs' fingers soft and urgent and intimate on his body. He tried to clear his mind of the image of those same fingers stroking her husband's neck.

Then he stood up, a little unsteadily, shook his head as if to dismiss an irritating insect, wiped his eyes with the back of his hand, and walked slowly to his mother's house.

Fergus put the book of his father's photographs carefully back in the bookcase, swept by the sadness he often felt when thinking about the man he'd never known.

His mother had always seemed unduly pleased with herself for having netted a man who was already so famous, even though he was almost twenty years older than her. But his grandparents had loathed Edmund Learmonth. They were unimpressed by his vast body of published work, and incensed that he'd had the bad manners to get himself killed in Korea documenting the aftermath of a war that was already over.

He'd always wanted to photograph the footnotes to war, it seemed. The shots that had propelled him to worldwide fame in the first place, when he was barely in his thirties, chronicled Paris in the dying days of the Nazi occupation. From then on, he'd taken himself to every war zone all over the world.

'If he'd still been around, no doubt he'd have been in Libya now, or Syria,' Fergus muttered to himself. Perhaps his grandparents had been right: not a job for a married man, specially not one with a child.

'What did he want?' Belle asked when Fergus carried the glasses through to the kitchen. He kept his back to her as he rinsed them carefully under the mixer tap. Can't be too careful with crystal, and these were *good* crystal. He was also labouring under the burden of guilt he felt even now, more than fifteen years on, when he was reminded of the untimely death of his ex-wife's Russian lover, Max Grigoriev. He'd used some less than desirable contacts to frighten Max off – and that's all they were meant to do. For long enough afterwards, he'd assumed (as had Serena herself) that Max had simply grown tired of life as an illegal immigrant and skedaddled on a Russian ship that had been docked at Leith. It had come as a shock when the lad's skeleton was discovered in a shallow grave on Corstorphine Hill. But he'd felt, in some sense, responsible for his death. However much of a pest Max had been – a drunkard and a parasite, battening on Serena, he'd never have wished that on him.

'Och, some missing person thing he can't get a handle on.'

'You won't actually help him, will you?'

Fergus selected a glass cloth from a drawer. 'Maybe. It's quite interesting, in fact.'

'Is it to do with these people they're appealing for information about on TV? Some man from up the coast, and a couple from Thornhill?'

'Might be.'

'I know I shouldn't ask. Have they no idea what's happened to them?'

Fergus pursed his lips. 'I don't imagine it's anything good.'

'They've not been missing long, though.'

'Long enough, at this time of year.'

'I suppose.' Belle shuddered. 'You think they've got lost in the hills or something?'

'Or something.'

'What? Tom thinks it's more sinister than that?'

'Tom has no clue what's happened. That's why he came to see me.'

'There's so little violent crime here. I can't remember the last time there was a murder.'

Belle was forever harping on about what a dangerous place the capital was, compared to a small, peaceful town like Kirkcudbright. Total nonsense.

But Fergus had a moment of deep concern: Edinburgh *did* have more than its fair share of drugs these days. And gay bars had taken over the entire east end of the New Town so that Calton Hill was known locally as GHQ. He had nothing personally against gay men, but he knew some rum types frequented such places. He needed to think of his son's safety as much as his daughter's.

So perhaps it wouldn't be the end of the world if they stayed here in Kirkcudbright for another year or two.

He gave Belle a quick kiss on the back of the neck. 'I know – Bonnie Galloway's getting almost as bad as Edinburgh, isn't it? Now, I'd say it's your bedtime. I'll be up soon.'

Fergus went back to his study and sat at his desk, chewing the end of a Blackwing pencil.

His attitude to the case had changed as soon as Tom spilled the beans about the pictures on the footballer's laptop – though the couple's 'business' sounded equally sordid. Whatever had happened to them couldn't be bad enough. He didn't care if they were never found. Ellis had wittered on about bringing them to justice. Except, inevitably you had to contend with courts and juries that didn't do their job. His fictional DI was always moaning about that: you knocked yourself out, you built a watertight case, and some slick defence lawyer ran rings round the jurors and got the guy off. Or else they'd get a ridiculously short sentence. Fergus secretly approved of the death penalty for paedophiles; and possibly also for people who tortured animals.

The justifiable murder. Was there such a thing? How did it differ from the rule of the lynch mob? Tom Ellis had as good as admitted that there were some types of crime even the cops found hard to stomach.

And he had to agree. There had been an item in the paper the day before, some gang of yobbos who'd captured a cat, gouged its eyes out, then hanged it and set fire to it. He knew what he'd do to trash like that. People who damaged innocent animals or kids. Yes, he'd happily see hanging brought back for such crimes, no matter how much the liberal lefties wheenged.

Next week, he'd start some research on how these guys found chat rooms and used them. It'd need care, because he was well aware that no matter what the law on data protection said, there were always spooks on the lookout for any peculiar internet search histories.

He reminded himself to say something to Belle in the morning about keeping a close eye on the kids. Need to find a way to do that without alarming her.

THIRTEEN

After breakfast, Belle announced that she meant to visit Remi, since the teachers had had their in-service day, and the twins were in class once more.

'You don't mind giving them some lunch?'

Fergus agreed that he'd be delighted to do so. As soon as she'd left, he fired up his laptop. If he was going to help Ellis, he'd best get on with it. He began searching for internet chat rooms that seemed to be frequented by teenage girls. It gave him a bad feeling.

So he switched to Facebook. Fergus Learmonth the author had a presence on all the prominent social media, as well as a website. His agent saw to that, and hired some whizz-kid to keep it all up to date. Fergus himself rarely looked at those pages.

But he also had a presence on both Facebook and Twitter as Frank Stuart. He'd used that name as an alias for many years, and no one had ever rumbled him. It was the name of Serena's father, whom he had never met. Frank had died in a house-fire years before he'd met Serena, but from what she'd told him, the man was a menace anyway: alcoholic, Communist, Russia-obsessed. Clearly the key to his ex-wife's mental instability. It brought a bitter amusement that Frank Stuart lived again when Fergus had some spying to do.

He never used a photograph on his profile. He had a selection of photos of the copper-sheet dragons from the famous bridge in Lujbljana. He always used one of those, against a bland, generic backdrop. He gave no information about his education or his age.

He looked at the notebook where he'd jotted down a few details during Ellis's visit. He'd see what he could dig up on the couple from Thornhill.

There was no Facebook page for Willowbeck High School, but it took him less than five minutes to find three Facebook users who'd been pupils there at around the time the Bissets had been in post. He logged friend requests for all three, and got two acceptances almost immediately from a male and a female. He selected the woman first.

'Just wondering if anyone remembers old Winston Bisset? Heard he left England.'

A reply arrived with five minutes. 'Old Winnie the Perv? Hope he's left the planet, dirty old bastard.'

'Gee! That must have gone right over my head. Maybe he wasn't into boys?'

'Naw, it was all girls. You must have heard? Which form class were you in?'

Tricky. He'd spent time on the school's website, so had a few ideas ready. 'I was in Hollyhock House. There from '90 to '96. You?'

''91 to '94. You must have been a brainbox then. You

weren't in any of my classes. LOL. And you don't remember old Winnie? Who did you get for English then?'

'Don't remember. Have tried to wipe it from my memory. LOL.'

'Lucky you! Took your life in your hands agreeing to go to the book-room with that dirty bugger to pick up a few extra copies of *Macbeth*.'

'Shit! He tried it on with you then?'

'I'd have put his dick through a mincer. But a couple of my mates had his hands up their skirts. And worse.'

'What – he actually got his thing out?'

'They could feel it through his trousers. He'd rub himself against them until... Yuck!'

'Double shit! And he never got caught?'

'He left. His wife worked there too. The pair of them skedaddled when I was in third year. Good riddance.'

'Your pals didn't tell the police?'

'Fuck no. No one would have believed them. There was a maths teacher who was as bad.'

'Should try telling them now. Look at all the fuss on TV about Savile and the rest of them.'

'Winnie wasn't famous though. No one'd be interested.'

'Shit! Have to go. Boss is glaring at me. Nice chatting to you, Carol.'

He made a careful note to unfriend her that night. He knew from past experience that most people don't use the software that tells you who's unfriended you, and most people don't remember after a day or so anyway.

He trawled local newspaper archives for that part of Lancashire between 1991 and 1994. It was obvious none of Carol's friends had ever reported Bisset.

Nothing for it but to go back to looking at chat rooms.

On her way to visit Remi, Belle stopped for petrol. One of the mechanics from the garage beside the filling station was sitting outside, eating fish and chips from one of those hideous, sweaty polystyrene trays. The smell of vinegar on hot fat made her feel so bereft that for a moment she thought she'd faint – not from hunger, but because it had raised a memory. She was certain she had never eaten chips from a shop with Father.

What on earth was wrong with her, that she'd started having these flashbacks?

Because suddenly, she was not standing in the filling station opposite the harbour, with the fuel hose in her hand. She was in a chip shop, by the seaside. She could hear the steady pulse of the waves.

I'm walking, but only just. A toddler. People around are laughing and smiling. A man picks me up, so that I can look at the food keeping hot in the wee glass cabinet above the frying range; breaded and battered haddock; fat sausages; battered onion rings. He's squat and dark-haired, not so tall as Father, and he doesn't have so many sharp angles. His clothes smell of hot fat and vinegar. I'm frightened. I can feel the heat from the fryer rising towards me. I can hear the boiling fat gurgling and spitting. I wriggle out of his arms and run back to Rose. I hide my face under the edge of her coat. They're all laughing at me now, and I'm crying.

Belle shook herself free of the vision. That man. The same one she'd remembered on the beach in Arran. She drove his face from her mind, by a tremendous act of will.

It felt good to be driving alone. In all the time they'd been together, Fergus had ended up doing almost all the driving. Not that Belle minded terribly, but it would have been pleasing to be asked every now and again. But as soon as they approached the Volvo, he'd automatically go to the driver's side. *Ah well*. Possibly her now-ancient Land Rover Defender wasn't the ideal car for transporting kids anyway. Safe, but much less comfortable.

At least she hadn't had the usual tussle with the twins, because she hadn't even tried to bring them. She had quizzed them more than once about why they were suddenly reluctant to visit Remi's house in the village of Penreith. When they were tiny they loved going. They'd come home full of stories for Daddy about being allowed to bottle-feed the lambs.

But these days, Esmée said she didn't like Aunt Remi, because she wasn't a real aunt, and anyway her clothes always smelt like that shop in Port Alexander that Daddy said was run by hippos. Eddie usually said nothing, but a few days before, when they were having lunch, he burst out that he hated Remi because she killed the lambs to eat them.

Remi kept chickens, and raised a couple of orphan lambs each year, to eat. Fergus found that odd too, and had been unwise enough to say so, on one of the occasions she'd brought them the present of a plump organic fowl.

'You should be willing to kill anything you eat. Otherwise, eating meat is utterly dishonest. I give them the best possible life and a quick, painless death,' Remi had snapped. 'Most humans would be happy with that.'

Belle had been on the point of telling the twins where the lamb stew they were eating willingly enough came from, then thought better of it. All the same, it was unfair to deceive the child. She'd wait until Fergus was there, and confer with him on how best to deal with it.

That's as bad as telling kids, 'Wait till your father gets home'. Mabel Mountjoy, you are not a twenty-first century woman! No matter that she'd been Belle Learmonth for more than five years, she used her childhood name when she talked to herself. Because, deep inside, she was still the snooty little madam she'd been when she was the twins' age. Forever told that she was something special, but knowing in her core that she wasn't.

She knew that Fergus didn't understand her friendship with Remi. In many ways, she didn't understand it herself. She'd never had particularly close female friends. Neither at school or university, nor since. Briony had always been there for her. But Briony was more like an older relative than a friend. Not someone Belle had ever felt able to confide in.

Remi, on the other hand, was able to keep secrets. And she didn't *judge*. Not long after they'd met, Belle poured out her heart and her misery over the way Fergus had first greeted the news of her pregnancy. 'He *blamed* me,' she'd sobbed. 'He swore at me. Then he drove off. I thought he wasn't coming back, and leaving me to face it on my own.' Remi was the only other person she felt she could have shared this with. Briony wouldn't have understood.

And her friend had made all the right noises: sympathy, and contempt for Fergus. That had made Belle feel guiltier than ever, because of Fergus had come back in less than an hour, apologised, explained that it had been the shock of it talking, not his heart. He had comforted her, and stood by her, and insisted they get married at once. He'd been an exemplary provider, husband and father ever since.

She couldn't understand why her mind flipped back so

frequently to that initial reaction. It was the reality of life *since* that seemed unreal. No matter how hard she tried, she'd never been able to completely convince herself that Fergus had married her because he wanted to, not merely from a sense of duty.

But there was nothing unreal about his devotion to the children. Nor hers, though she'd lain awake many a long night questioning her own fitness as a mother. Not that she'd trade the twins for all the world, or that she'd spent a nanosecond since those first moments of panic when she saw the pregnancy test, regretting what had happened.

She loved her husband and she loved her children. In spite of that, there was always a glass wall there. She'd been pitched suddenly, on the cusp of middle age, into a life in complete contrast to the one she'd envisaged for herself after Father died. Before Fergus arrived, she'd been accustomed to being her own person, and that had been a lonely place sometimes. But she had a circle of acquaintances, most of whom were childless, like her. Some were even man-free. Without exception they were older than her, and from similar backgrounds. They were women Father had approved of. And when it came down to it, most of them had been quite happy to believe, a mere six years before, that she'd had a hand in Roddy McCulloch's death. Of the few who had not branded her as a murderer, some, like Angela Cuthbertson, were out of bounds for other reasons: Angela had turned out to be bosom buddies with Serena's aunt, of all people. One of the drawbacks of living in a country as small as Scotland. Imagine if she and Fergus had been visiting, and the aunt had sashayed in. The embarrassment!

So in her moments of contemplation, Belle never pretended to herself that it hadn't been a strain, adapting once more to having a man in the house. Adapting to sharing her bed. And kids: she had never appreciated exactly how demanding they could be, particularly when they were tiny. Such a responsibility, with no let-up. No holidays, no remission, no time off for good behaviour.

With Remi, she could be one hundred per cent herself, while envying her friend's freedom and lifestyle. That was the life she'd seen herself living: no one to answer to, no one else's interests to take account of.

For a moment, as she got close to Penreith and Remi's house, she almost turned back. But Fergus was busy; he had a deadline to meet. Once he was into editing, he disappeared into his fictional world. He'd apologise to her about it, saying it had been the same when he used to develop his own photographs; he'd lose track of time, emerging from the darkroom after what he thought was perhaps an hour to find he'd somehow mislaid half a day. If she went home early, she'd distract him.

Her friend greeted her as affectionately as she always did. Although her cottage was the diametric opposite of Ashers, Belle always felt at home there.

'Haven't seen you for ages,' Remi said, kissing her. 'You're looking tired again. Kids playing up?'

'It's not that. Ever since we came home from Arran, Fergus has been ultra-secretive. He's doing research on my mother. I know he is.'

She also knew he'd been researching false memory syndrome. When he'd left his study for a comfort break, she'd sneaked a look at his computer and seen the search history.

So when the twins had gone to bed that night, and Fergus

was deep in his work, she'd googled the subject herself, and read several articles, of varying degrees of scientific depth. But she was sure no one had *planted* any memories of Rose; they were too hazy. In any case, surely false memories require an accomplice? Someone to bounce them off? Belle had never spoken about Rose to another soul, before she met Fergus.

She was equally certain that there was nothing she'd blanked out, other than her mother's face. It wasn't as if anyone ever hurt her physically. There was nothing like that. But she had often wondered about what she thought she recalled her father saying after her mother left: '*It was Rose who wanted to have the child, then she takes off, leaving me lumbered. She and the lounge lizard aren't going to want a brat in tow.*' She wasn't even four at the time: would a child that age have understood, never mind remembered? The conversation must have dated from much later, or she had imagined it.

'Fergus dodges around the subject, instead of asking me straight out,' she added, letting Remi put her arm around her shoulders.

'It's none of his bloody business.'

'I used to think I knew a few things about Rose, but I'm not sure. Fergus keeps asking me if I don't remember her, because it's not as if I was a baby when she left – but I have these memories that are like stories I've read somewhere, years ago. Flash fiction. Or short videos, that's more accurate. In any case, I'm watching myself in them. Someone else is there, behind the camera. I can't see them. I can't see my mother's face. What do you think, Remi? You're a nurse. *Is* it therapeutic to try to remember these things?'

'Why is it so important to Fergus?'

'He's fixated on the fact the twins have no grandparents.

But it's not as if Rose was their grandmother anyway. Or "is". Fergus keeps saying that she may well be alive.'

'Don't let him bully you, sweetie. You know what they say about families anyway – you can pick your friends, but you can't pick your family. Keep remembering this: you have lots of friends, Belle. *Good* friends. Maybe he's jealous.'

'Jealous? Of what?'

'Well, from what I've seen, he doesn't have any close pals of his own. I mean, he's obviously made no effort to get to know people in Kirkcudbright, and when you're in Edinburgh you never see friends of his, do you?'

'I suppose not.' Belle felt guilty, as if she were being disloyal to him. 'But that's because he's so taken up with the three of us. I'm sure he has friends there, people he used to work with.' A vision of the elegant Anita Forrest, Fergus's former colleague (and, she was fairly certain, a former lover) rose in her mind.

Remi guffawed. 'Most likely he doesn't want you meeting them because they were friends of his and that damned ex-wife.'

'Could be, I suppose. Anyway – you don't think I should go to one of those hypnotherapists who can unlock hidden memories, or whatever?'

'Mumbo-jumbo.'

Belle sighed. With relief or guilt. She wasn't sure which. 'That's what I think too.'

'Fergus is nagging you to go to someone like that?'

'No! He thinks it's a load of codswallop. He wants me to tell him to go ahead and find Rose, if she *is* alive, or find out what happened to her.'

'It's nothing to do with him. Tell him to butt out.'

'I suppose.'

Remi put her arms round her. 'Belle, it's not your *fault* that she left.'

'I know that in my head. But I always felt it must have been because of me.'

She didn't tell Remi about what she imagined she'd over-heard her father say, in the wake of Rose leaving. She'd never told that to another human being, simply whispered it to her pug. Once or twice, she'd been on the point of telling Fergus. But she didn't want him to despise her adoptive father as well as her mother. So she'd bitten her tongue.

'I feel guilty about it all the same,' she added. 'And I worry that I haven't bonded properly with the twins. I'd never felt attached to anyone before, not genuinely. So I don't know what it should feel like.'

'Rose is the one who couldn't commit, not you!'

'But maybe it's genetic, this lack?'

Remi frowned. 'If you're adopted, how could it be genetic? Or do you mean because your birth-mother gave you up? There could have been any number of reasons for that. She may not have been *able* to keep you.'

'Fergus thinks Rose was my birth-mother. He doesn't know I know he thinks that, by the way. Don't let on. It's the real reason he's been researching her family tree.'

Remi held her by the shoulders and shook her. 'You don't believe that though?'

'I don't know. I've sometimes wondered.'

'Surely it would be on your birth certificate?'

'I only have the one adopted children get. I read up a little about it – apparently it wasn't unknown, even as late as the sixties, for a woman and her husband to both adopt the woman's illegitimate child.'

'In a small place like Kirkcudbright? Someone would have blabbed.'

'Maybe she went away to have me?'

Remi hugged her. 'Trust me, the ability to bond is not genetic! All nurture, no nature. Anyway, you spent all those years looking after your father. *That's* commitment!'

'Or a sense of duty. I sometimes wonder if that's all I feel for Fergus and the twins.'

'To your kids, yes. You don't have any duty to Fergus. If you're not happy, you should leave him. You and the kids.'

Belle's laugh sounded hollow in her ears. Or mad. 'Leave him to go where?'

'Kick him out then. It's your house.'

'I couldn't take his children away from him. He adores them. Maybe more than I do.'

'Belle, I know how much you love your children.'

'I'm ambitious for them. That's not the same.'

Remi cleared her throat. 'Are you able to talk to Fergus about this?'

Belle considered that. No point in not being honest with her friend. 'Not really. He already treats me with kid gloves because I got over-emotional after the twins were born. I don't want him thinking he has to have me sectioned. He tries to talk to me about Rose. I shut him up and change the subject.'

'Quite right.' Remi looked like the cat that found the open tin of tuna.

'Did you tell *your* husband everything? I'm sorry,' Belle added as Remi lowered her eyes and turned away. 'I know you don't like to speak about him. Though it must be a while since he died?'

'Mmmm. These books Fergus writes – they probably get published so easily because he's famous,' said Remi.

Belle bridled. 'I think his books get published because they're good.'

'But there are thousands of good authors out there who never get published unless they go it alone. Publishers and agents will only take on celebs. It's not how good you are, but who you know.'

'That's nonsense.'

'You told me before that he sees this agent of his far more often than he needs to?'

'No, not more than he *needs* to. It seems to be important.'

'Have you any reason to think he's having a fling with her?' Remi's slightly bulbous eyes gleamed.

'I suppose I'm imagining it. But look at this.'

Belle pushed a picture clipped from a magazine across the table. Fergus and an almost impossibly glamorous young dark-haired woman. They were standing close. It was impossible to tell if he perhaps had his arm around her waist.

'So this is the agent?'

'He's due to nip through to Edinburgh for some shindig she'll no doubt be at in a few days. He usually has to stay overnight.' Belle felt a little guilty about that. Fergus hadn't actually *told* her yet, and he surely didn't suspect she spied on him via his desk diary. She rummaged in her bag, and extracted another, smaller picture from the back of her wallet.

'*This* is his last wife.'

Remi studied the photo. 'They could be sisters! He gave you a picture of her?'

'Of course not! I copied one he had. He'd have a fit if he

knew I had this. He claims he's burnt all the ones he used to have.'

'Hmmmm. Pretty girl.'

'He was obsessed with her when I first knew him.'

'He doesn't still see her?'

Belle laughed; the mirthless sound clattered in her ears. 'In his dreams, I imagine. She's dead. Been dead for years. She'd got hitched to someone else by then anyway, and had kids. But I suppose for him, she's always thirty. He remembers her with no wrinkles and a perfectly flat stomach with no stretch marks or flab.'

'Well then.' Remi snatched up the photo, opened the door of the wood-stove and flung it in. 'Best place for *that*.' Belle gasped. 'I don't know why you're carrying around that cutting either. Give.' It joined the photo in the stove.

As she drove home shortly afterwards, Belle felt a slow burn of anger. Not so much over the incineration of the photos – Remi was right; she was daft to have hung onto them, torturing herself. More because of the dismissive way she'd spoken of Fergus's writing. Sheer jealousy. It was one thing for *her* to be jealous of her husband's success; totally out of order for her friend.

FOURTEEN

It seemed to Fergus that Belle was always ill-tempered when she'd been to see Remi. Maybe that wasn't the right term: discontented. And it made *him* cranky. Although he had only been in Remi's house once, years ago, he recalled that it was small and ill-decorated. Not at all like the palace he'd created for Belle. The main irritant was that she usually arrived home with a new quirk or demand on board. Typically, some hippie, socks-and-sandals, tree-hugging nonsense.

This time, it was that they should try making a borehole in the garden.

'Remi has a well, and only uses water from that for her plants. She says it's the only way you can be sure it's free of the filthy contaminants demanded by the EU.' Even Belle had to smile a little as she said that. 'I see you're smirking, but I want to try.'

'Belle, you know the river's awfully close, and it's tidal here. If you put in a borehole, you'll get brackish water.' He tried to bite his tongue, but the words spilled out. 'Or am I to pay for a desalination plant too?'

'Poor Fergus, having to *pay* for everything.'

He tried to grin. 'You know I don't mind, when it's for sensible things. You don't drink any of the water from this well of hers, do you?'

Her eyes glittered. 'There's nothing wrong with it. It's purer than the stuff that comes out of the tap, laden with chemicals.'

Their kitchen boasted the most modern carbon-filter water tap money could buy. The ceramic cartridge was an absolute bugger to change, and involved Fergus lying on the floor with his arms in the cupboard, twisted to one side of the drainpipe, banging his knuckles and swearing a lot.

'But the EU regs are there for a purpose. Her well-water probably doesn't come up to spec as safe to drink,' said Fergus. 'Or does she get it tested?'

'How do I know? You and your fixation with water. When you first came here, the stuff from the tap was impure, according to you. It had to be Evian out of a bottle, or nothing.'

Fergus laughed, in some discomfiture. Silly to fight over anything connected to Remi.

'So what have you come home with this time?' he asked, trying to keep his tone light. *Typhoid?* 'I assume her magic vegetable plots produce winter strawberries?'

'Don't be silly, Fergus.' She set down her basket. Handwoven by goblins from organic willow or some such tosh. It had cost the thick end of eighty pounds at the craft market. 'She gave me all this scrumptious kale.'

'Yum yum.'

'It's good for you! Full of iron and vitamins. I have the last of the carrots too.'

She held up a bunch of the improbably-coloured vegetables. 'So what's her secret?'

'You know perfectly well. Permaculture beds. Once you've made them properly, you never have to dig deep again. I definitely want to start a couple here. Down beside the garden cottage. And I want some of the special compost she gets.'

Fergus quizzed her, not for the first time, about what this special compost was, and where exactly it came from.

'She's cagey. She said I'd not to ask too much. All she'd say is that it's organic material. Bone meal, rotted manure, stuff like that. There's something to do with butchers, and the bits they have to get rid of. What I did get out of her is that she gets paid for taking it.'

'*Paid?*'

'It's the scraps butchers have to throw out. She says the council charges an extortionate amount to take them away – something to do with EU animal by-product rules, and all the nonsense about sell-by dates. So it's cheaper for them to subscribe to this collection service. The stuff's all taken to a central point and put through some sort of mincer, but they don't have to pay an exorbitant fee to do it.'

Fergus pulled a face. 'I bet they're putting in some fallen stock too.'

'That's illegal, isn't it?'

He nodded. 'Not half. There's a lot goes on in the countryside that's illegal. The big risk is if it gets into the human food chain. Or into pet food.' He glanced at his elderly cat and Belle's pug, snuggled together in their sheepskin-lined bed. 'I don't suppose she's getting paid a *lot* for taking it.'

Mabel grimaced. 'It seems to pay towards having a car. And her fancy holidays.'

The previous winter, Remi had gone to Sri Lanka to see the elephants.

'Bloody hell – definitely fallen stock then. I have a good idea of how much it costs farmers to have even one animal legally disposed of. More than a hundred quid. And they can be fined ten times that if they don't get rid of it quickly.' He looked dubiously at the vegetables Belle had placed on the draining board. 'Maybe we shouldn't let the twins eat any of the veg though, to be on the safe side.'

'Och, nonsense, Fergus. It's better for all of us to eat things that haven't been sprayed with poisons, like the ones from the supermarket. What harm can it do, if the stuff's buried deep underground?'

'Depends how deep,' he said, frowning.

'I found out a bit about that too. This other person who helps her –'

'Does she employ a gardener then?'

'Someone helps her dig the trenches for the permaculture beds. He has one of these miniature diggers, so when a new bed's to be made, she takes out a trench about six feet deep.' She shuddered suddenly. 'That's the same as a grave, isn't it? And the scraps from the butchers' go in first, with layers of compost and leaf mould and seaweed, even before the topsoil goes on. Miles away from the roots of the vegetables. There can't be any harm in it, surely?'

'I suppose not,' said Fergus grudgingly.

He noticed that his wife was suddenly looking uncharacteristically dubious. She was gazing at the carrots.

'What?'

'You don't genuinely think anything harmful could get into the veg?'

Fergus was never one to pass up an advantage. 'No idea. But I think maybe it's best not to take the risk. Not while the twins are so young.'

'Shit!' said Belle suddenly.

Fergus was taken aback. It was rare for her to use even slightly colourful language. 'What?'

'It's parents' evening. We'll need to have supper early. Damn! I forgot to arrange anyone to come and sit with them while we go to that. Go and get changed.'

'We won't be long. Either Briony'll be able to come up here for an hour, or we can drop them down there. You know they'll be no trouble.'

Fergus was pensive as he went upstairs to find a suitable outfit for being interviewed by the twins' teacher.

They'd first met Remi at Kirkcudbright Food Festival, when Belle was pregnant. She'd headed for a colourful vegetable stall, set a little apart from the rest, like a guided missile.

The dark-haired woman in dungarees who was presiding over it smiled broadly at her. 'All organic, guaranteed,' she said. 'Terribly important when you're expecting, and you can't trust the stuff in the supermarkets.' She split a carrot in two, and pared one half with a few deft strokes. 'Taste.'

Even Fergus had to admit it tasted better than anything from Tesco.

The woman was well into her spiel by then, 'Now: folic acid. What are you doing to make sure you're getting enough?'

'I have tablets to take,' Belle's voice sounded a little faint.

The woman frowned and shook her head. 'Tablets! Here – dark green veg are best.' She tucked two bundles of spinach into

Belle's bag. 'Make these into soup, and there's enough there for a couple of smoothies too. You do make smoothies?'

'Er...'

'Haven't you got a blender?'

Belle nodded.

'Well then, use that. You don't need one of these fancy machines they peddle on TV. You should be having plenty of pulses too: chickpeas, lentils. You don't eat red meat more than once a week, do you?'

'Yes,' faltered Belle. She arched her back; Fergus knew she was trying to unkink the dull ache that settled there most days, and winced in sympathy.

The woman tutted. 'You shouldn't. You don't know what muck's in it these days, even the stuff that's labelled organic. What's your address? I'll bring you a couple of my chickens – you can be sure they're absolutely free of toxins. You're looking a little peaky, by the way, if you don't mind my saying. Here–' she gestured to the substantial canvas chair behind her stall. 'Sit down for a moment.'

Belle admitted she felt tired all the time. 'In fact,' she said, 'some days I keep thinking, *I can't do this.*'

Fergus was looking at her sideways, wondering why she was pouring out her heart to a stranger.

'When's it due?'

'It's twins.'

'Ah! That's why you're so big. But that's marvellous. Not your first though?'

'"Fraid so. I'm a *very* elderly primip.'

'You'll be having the babies at home?'

Belle had been almost apologetic. 'They say it must be in hospital, because of my age.'

The woman rolled her eyes. 'With a good midwife, you're safer at home. Far less chance of infection. I know which way I'd prefer to come into the world – a calm, safe, gently-lit place that smelt of my parents, or a noisy hospital with bright lights and the stench of disinfectant and stress. No wonder there are so many disaffected young people these days.'

'Maybe if it had just been one baby, or if I'd been a few years younger,' said Belle guiltily.

Fergus tutted. 'We've been told it should be a hospital birth, so we're going to take the experts' advice.'

'Lean forward for a moment with your elbows on your knees.' The woman massaged Belle's back.

'Ooh, that's lovely. It's exactly where it hurts.'

'Of course it is. You're not wearing a belly-band?'

Belle stared at her in amazement.

'Your midwife didn't tell you to get one? You poor woman! I wonder if I have one lying about at home? Tell you what – the quickest way is to buy online.'

She produced an iPhone, typed in an address, then held the screen out for Belle to see. 'Order one up as soon as you get home, express delivery. You'll find it makes a tremendous difference.'

The woman grasped Belle's wrist, as if it was the most natural thing in the world, and slid her index finger over the pulse point. 'Your pulse is a little fast. You need to rest more, and get yourself onto a healthier diet.'

Fergus was aware he had the *look* on. Belle glared at him, but he was staring at the stallholder. 'And what do you know about it? My wife's been going to all the doctor's appointments that she's supposed to.'

The woman turned a smile of surprising sweetness on him.

'Doctors, what do they know? I'm a midwife. I'm Remi McGregor, by the way.'

She held out her hand, and Fergus had no option but to shake it.

'So you've used these belly-band things when you were pregnant?' said Belle.

Remi roared with laughter. 'I've never had any of my own! Too busy delivering other people's.'

'You work in Dumfries?' asked Fergus.

'Good God, no. I left all that behind several years ago.'

'You don't look nearly old enough to be retired,' said Belle.

Remi pulled a face. 'I'm not. But I'd had enough of the NHS, thank you very much.'

'So what do you do now?'

Remi gestured to her stall. 'This. I managed to get a cottage with a lot of land, and I grow all my own veg in permaculture beds.'

'Permaculture?'

'The best way to grow food. You dig once, and then you only have to feed the topsoil. Almost effortless. And exceptionally productive.'

'Do you come to the farmers' market here every month then?'

'No. Far too busy. But you'll need fresh veg supplies from me a lot more often than once a month at the moment anyway, since you're eating for three.'

In the end, they'd gone home laden with vegetables from her stall, plus a dozen free-range eggs. Fergus's eyes had popped a little at what they were charged, but the produce *did* look superior.

Remi had insisted on typing Belle's name and address into

her contacts file, and promised to bring two chickens and more greens before the middle of the week.

By the time that happened, Belle had bought a belly-band, and was walking and sitting and sleeping a lot better. She'd perked up in spirits too, and her hair was glossy instead of dull.

A month or so later, Belle was wearing a floaty chiffon top Fergus hadn't seen before. It was in shades of russet and scarlet, and it suited her colouring extremely well.

'I don't recognise that one – new?'

'Remi gave it to me.' Her tone was defensive. 'Why?'

By then, she was seeing the woman at least once a week.

'It's not your usual style. It suits you.'

But the damage was done.

'Remi gave it to me because it's too big for her. You're saying I look fat in it?'

'You're not fat, Belle. You're pregnant. You look beautiful. It brings out the colour of your hair.'

She made a small, almost-mollified sound. Then she smiled brightly once more. 'Remi's changed my life.'

Fergus's heart sank. Had *he* not changed her life, even a little? 'Remi! She looks more like a man than a woman.'

'Och, nonsense. Just because she can't be bothered with make-up.'

'Apart from that silly thing in her eyebrow. What the hell's that about?'

Remi had a gold stud in the end of her left eyebrow. When he was speaking to her, Fergus couldn't take his eyes off it. Ridiculous, in a middle-aged woman.

'It's fashionable.'

'Don't you dare even think about getting something like that done.' He realised as he spoke that it was the wrong approach.

She bridled up. 'And don't you dare tell me what I can and can't do.'

'But Belle!' His tone was almost wheedling by then. 'You wouldn't suit a stud in your face. It's not your style.'

'I have no intention of getting one. But you don't get to dictate what I do.'

'It looks so daft at her age.'

'You haven't the faintest idea what age she is.'

'Amaze me then.'

'Guess.'

'A hundred and two.'

'Don't be silly, Fergus. She's exactly the same age as me. Well, a couple of years older.'

'I'm duly amazed. So why's she *really* not still working?'

'She is.'

'As a midwife, I mean.'

'She told you. She got fed up with the NHS. Not enough staff or resources, everyone rushed off their feet and stressed out with paperwork, and everything driven by targets. She says it's too regimented, that birth's a natural thing, a celebration, not the excuse for injections and machines.'

Fergus harrumphed. A midwife was a neat, clean woman dressed in starched clothing and wearing sensible shoes, not a latter-day hippie festooned in clashing bright colours, and lace-up canvas boots. Remi's upper arms were firm, like a body-builders. A navvy rather than a midwife, in his opinion. She had a tattoo of a pentagram on her left arm. She looked foreign: Middle Eastern, or Indian.

When he visualised her, he didn't think 'midwife' but 'witch'. He shuddered at the sudden recollection of Serena saying that's what the kids in Glasgow called her when she was a child: *Witch*. He'd often used that nickname for her himself, when they were together.

'Midwives were the wise women, way back,' said Belle happily. 'They knew all about herbs and healing. That's the side that interests Remi now.'

'Well, you, thank God, will be in the care of competent medics not an amateur herbalist, my darling.'

But he had to bite his tongue again, because he could see for himself how much better Belle was since she'd been eating Remi's produce.

'Where did she dig up that handle anyway? It's a man's name isn't it?'

Belle was vague. 'I think it's short for something. She's half-European.'

Half European, half woman.

'What?'

He hadn't realised he'd spoken aloud. 'So, is she a lezzer?'

Belle's eyes flashed, and for a moment he thought she was going to slap him. 'Shouldn't think so. What business is it of yours anyway?'

He shrugged. 'She certainly has no time for men.'

Belle's smile was cold steel. 'I think you'll find that doesn't automatically mean she's gay, Fergus.'

Remi seemed to him like a real ball-crusher; in fact, perhaps she originally went into midwifery because she wanted to work in the one place where a woman's always ready to *blame* her husband.

'So where in Europe is she half from?' he asked. Important to keep the peace.

She pursed her lips at him. 'Why?'

'Just wondered. I mean, she doesn't look as if she's from around here.'

'She's from one of the places that used to be part of Yugoslavia.'

'And the McGregor bit?'

'She was married to a Scot.'

Fergus raised his eyebrows. 'She doesn't wear a wedding ring.'

'He's been gone for a few years. She's lived in Britain since she was in her teens. Did all her training here.'

'When you say "gone", do you mean from her, or this mortal coil?'

Belle looked slightly uneasy. 'He went missing. Well, presumed dead. He went off, she doesn't know where, and she never heard from him again. Vanished into thin air.'

Fergus raised his eyebrows. 'Was this after she moved here?'

'That he disappeared? I'm not sure. I've never liked to ask her too much about it. It clearly upsets her, even after all this time. She's accepted that he's dead, but she's never known exactly *how*. Or where.'

'What does she live on? She's far too young to have a pension. And she's never making a living from selling vegetables in the odd farmers' market. Not even with what she charges you, if those are her usual prices.'

Belle shrugged. 'She had to wait seven years, or some such rubbish, to get her husband declared dead, so that she could claim his estate. He'd left it to her, I mean, in his will. I think maybe there was family money too. Both her parents are dead. They were doctors – I suspect she has a bit of a complex about only being a nurse. Not that being a midwife is any less worthy than being a doctor. She's an expert on why natural birth's important for bonding. In fact, she believes a lot of the break-down of the family's down to the drug companies and technologists getting too involved in the procedure.'

Fergus snorted.

'Anyway,' added Belle, 'I assume she got a good inheritance from her parents. I never like to ask. It's none of our business.'

He made a mental note to research this woman's history as soon as possible, but to say nothing to Belle until the birth was safely over. It wouldn't do to upset her.

And although Fergus loathed Remi, he'd been glad enough of her presence three weeks later.

His mind often drifted back to the ghastly experience of the day in mid-December 2007, when a heavily-pregnant Belle had said she couldn't feel the babies moving. She had the card with the community midwife's contact details. Fergus dialled the number.

'Can you drive her into the hospital in Dumfries? Just to be on the safe side.'

And he had, of course, breaking the speed limit along most of the A75. During the journey, she'd texted Remi's number from her mobile.

'They won't let her in because she's not a relative,' said Fergus.

'They will. She's going to say she's my sister.'

'She can't say that!'

Belle glared at him from tear-heavy eyes. 'She could be. How do you know she's not? That's the thing about being adopted. Maybe that's why we get on so well.'

He'd held Belle's hand tightly as the sonographer ran the probe of the monitor over her stomach.

Then the door had opened, and a nurse stuck her head round. 'Your sister's here, Mrs Learmonth.'

He remembered how his wife's breathing had steadied when she saw Remi. The sonographer glared at the newcomer.

'They can only find one heartbeat,' said Belle in a strangled voice.

Remi and the medic locked eyes.

'What if one has died?' cried Belle. 'How can they get it out without harming the other?'

She'd already been bombarding Fergus and the sonographer with the same question, and neither had replied, because all three of them knew the answer, and knew that the others knew: it was a hopeless situation. If one twin had died, at this stage of the pregnancy the other was almost inevitably doomed.

And Fergus hadn't known how to reassure her. They'd both gone, in the space of barely three months, from being people who congratulated themselves on not feeling the need to breed, of not falling into that gender trap, into parents who couldn't countenance the thought that anything might befall either of their unborn twins.

Remi exuded an air of calm. 'Let me have a listen.' Gently, she pushed the monitor probe aside and wiped Belle's stomach with the sheet. From her bag she produced what looked like an ear trumpet, and applied it to the bump, her face a picture of concentration.

After seconds rather than minutes, her face broke into a grin. 'Here.' She held the implement in place, motioning Fergus to put his ear to it. 'You listen.'

He could hear two distinct pulsing beats.

Remi beamed at him. 'Well?'

'I think I can hear two?'

'Surely you can.'

'So why did the monitor not pick them both up?'

She smiled at the sonographer, who was glaring at her from beyond the bed.

'Technology's all very well, but nothing beats experience. Both heartbeats sound absolutely fine to me.'

The babies chose that moment to start dancing a jig. Belle was sent home, assured that nothing was amiss.

From that moment onwards, Belle had hung on every word Remi said, long after the birth, right up to the present day.

FIFTEEN

Fergus smiled to himself as he and Belle marched smartly along the road towards the school. They were both a lot fitter than they'd been when they met, although they'd sometimes giggled to themselves when they picked the twins up from nursery; they were of an age with some of the grandparents. In fact, a lot of the grandfathers were younger than him, because Kirkcudbright was like all small towns: not a small share of early breeders.

He reflected once again on how his life had changed: a stable marriage; a wife who was truly his soulmate; children; a new career; fame. He felt like the *real* Fergus. Since he was in his late teens, he'd been the false Fergus; brash; arrogant; selfish; contemptuous of women.

He had always assumed that the twins would have all their schooling in the capital. Not that the local primary wasn't an excellent establishment, but he'd felt there had been an element of *blame* in the feedback when the staff discovered the twins could already read and write competently. He and Belle had been able to read and write before they started formal education, and both agreed that it hadn't blighted their lives either socially or educationally, so although they hadn't deliberately set out to make their children literate, they had done nothing to discourage the twins' thirst for learning. They had merely fed natural inquisitiveness. They'd giggle together over the portrayal of young Bertie in Sandy McCall Smith's *Scotland Street* series, which the twins loved (such a relief to find adults' books that it was safe to read to young children).

Neither child had expressed any interest to learn either Italian or the saxophone – although Esmée had nagged her way to permission to start ballet lessons, which meant a weekly trek to Dumfries.

When Fergus was young, he had assumed that every house was like his grandparents' – piled high with books. The classics: Scott, Stevenson, Trollope, Eliot, Austen, Dickens... all the way up to DH Lawrence. In his mother's house, fiction started a little later, and was mostly unsuitable for children. PG Wodehouse. Orwell. Henry Miller.

After the twins were born, Belle had said, 'There are no children's books in the house. I'm sure all mine got thrown out.' And Fergus had laughed, and held up his finger and said, 'Wait till you see what I've got in the attic,' and carried down triumphantly two full boxes of Ladybird books, all the ones he'd almost jettisoned when he was selling his flat in Learmonth Terrace.

The twins knew all of them by heart by the time they were three. Belle was convinced that was how they'd learned to read so easily and quickly.

Fergus vowed to tread carefully, whatever the feedback they were about to get on the kids' first term at school; he knew Belle worried that they needed her less than when they were tiny.

When they were going through the terrible twos and thrawn threes, she had always dealt with it. They were decidedly *her* children, once she'd got over her groundless qualms about having no role model as a mother.

Now that they were cadet adults, he knew he played a bigger role in their lives, and Belle must resent it a little. They positively looked forward to school, which was a relief. And because it was a small school, with small classes, there was none of the nonsense he'd read about in other schools, separating twins in case they became too dependent on each other.

Naturally, they were close. That was how it should be with twins. He was also, in his heart of hearts, relieved that they had each other to play with.

'I suppose you realise that you have two very gifted children?'

Fergus and Belle mumbled that yes, they'd thought that. The teacher rambled on about reading ages of eight, and the fact that Edmund also seemed to have a grasp of number skills far beyond his years.

'*Number skills?*' Belle's tone was puzzled.

Fergus smiled. 'Arithmetic. So is he getting stretched enough?' He could feel Belle looking askance at him. He clasped her right hand firmly in his left.

'I've been getting the primary two teacher to give me work for him.'

'But won't he get bored once he gets through that?'

'They are obedient children, Mr Learmonth. Not the sort to make a fuss. They get on with work, and if they finish before the others, they read quietly, or write in their jotters. In fact, Esmée tells me she is writing a book. Her gifts seem to be more on the creative side – although she will also do extremely well academically, I have no doubt.'

The teacher produced folders, with the twins' familiar, neat handwriting (so similar that it was difficult to tell which was which).

'They are exemplary pupils. A delight.'

'And they're fitting in well socially, as far as you can see?' Belle sounded more diffident than Fergus was accustomed to. 'You know, with twins, they can become a little self-contained?'

'They're popular. Both fit in well – though I'd say Esmée is the more confident of the two.'

Fergus grinned. 'Esmée is a bossy-boots. We'll work on quashing that a little, for her own good.'

On their way out, they passed the next couple waiting to be called in.

'Oh, hello, Anne,' Belle greeted the woman a little hesitantly. Fergus saw his wife's eyes flit briefly to rest on the man, then away again even more quickly. 'Feels like being interviewed by the police, doesn't it? The thought police.' She laughed hollowly. 'Bye then.'

'Who was that?' asked Fergus once they were out of earshot.

'Anne Bullivant. Can't remember her husband's name. Do you not remember their daughter came to the twins' birthday party?'

Fergus shrugged. One four-year-old looked much like another to him.

'You must have heard the gossip about them in the town?'

He shrugged again.

Belle tutted. 'I don't suppose you talk to anyone in the town.

Anyone would think you haven't lived here for almost six years. I remember telling you about it anyway. In one ear and out the other. She's the one who had an affair with a fishing boat skipper, then decided to confess all to her husband.'

'I'd hardly remember you telling me about that, Belle! None of our business.'

'I can't stop wondering why she'd tell him. Who would it help?'

'If you had an affair, you wouldn't tell me?'

'Who am I likely to have an affair with, at my age?' She cleared her throat. 'How about you? You're clearly besotted with the Meera creature.'

'Bollocks. But I'd say that your handsome detective pal would be more than up for a fling with you.'

'Tom Ellis?' Her voice rose to a higher pitch than normal. 'He's not handsome.'

'I'd say he's the type women go for. He obviously still carries a torch for you anyway.'

'You speak such rubbish.'

'So anyway, our young Eddie's going to be maths whizz-kid, according to Miss what's-it?'

'How can she possibly know that?'

Belle was quiet for the rest of the way home, although they walked hand in hand. She'd formed a mental picture of a heavy rubber torch, the kind the police carry. Or maybe they didn't, nowadays? Tom might cosh her across the head with it and carry her off slung over his shoulder, like a caveman. What utter nonsense Fergus came out with sometimes.

She often got irritated by the way he talked up the twins'

smartness too. 'I suppose you'll be arranging for them to sit the Cambridge entrance exam by the time they're ten,' she'd say bitterly. And he'd look at her in surprise and say, 'You and I are both smart. We have smart kids – that's something to be proud of, surely?'

Then it would descend into a quarrel.

'You seem to want to push them, and everyone says that's bad.'

'Everyone being Remi? What the fuck does she know.'

'That's right, teach them to swear.'

'Bet they hear worse at school.'

'That's no excuse.'

'I know. I'll watch my tongue. I'm not forcing them to learn, Belle.'

She could admit to herself, now, when it mattered: she was envious of her children. What kind of mother did that make her? She envied the fact that they had two parents; two *real* parents. That they were confident and sassy without being obnoxious. That they were indeed smart; smarter than she'd ever been. That they'd get an education at least as privileged as hers had been, but that they'd *make* something of it, not stagnate.

She easily became irritated with Fergus because he'd been sent to an expensive single-sex school. But then, so had she. St Leonards hadn't become co-ed until the year she was leaving. When she thought back to her time there, she realised that although she couldn't say she was *happy*, she had relished the fact that it was girls-only. Peaceful, like a nunnery. Perhaps they should find one of the few remaining girls' schools for Esmée? But she knew that was a ridiculous thought. It would be cruel to separate the twins, even once they reached their teens. She realised, with increasing feelings of guilt, that she was jealous about that too: she'd yearned to have a sibling, never mind a twin.

These days, she worried more than ever about how her children perceived her. Someone who played at being a bohemian, instead of admitting she was as middle-class and money-oriented as most of the successful artists she'd mixed with in the early days?

She had even developed angst about when it would be appropriate to introduce the twins to trivia like the niceties of drinking coffee, so that the first time they went to Italy as a family there was no risk of their making fools of themselves the way she had on her first trip there, ordering a cappuccino after lunch.

Since Fergus never drank coffee, he saw this as an exceptionally esoteric problem. The twins drank tea, as he did; not yet lapsang souchong without milk. Even in tea-drinking, there are age-appropriate conventions, though both parents had looked on in awe and trepidation as their offspring tucked into strong cheeses, such as Stilton and Aged Gouda, with evident enjoyment, from around the age of three.

So Belle was in awe of her children, as well as loving them as completely as she knew how.

'I'm sorry we don't always see eye to eye on their education.' She tried to keep her tone level, but could hear her voice shaking. 'I know you want to send them to somewhere like Fettes, but I don't feel they need to go to a school like that.'

Fergus chortled and squeezed her hand. 'Have you seen what the fees are these days? I doubt they'll be going there anyway. Why are you against it, in particular?'

'You were there, so you shouldn't even have to ask. There are all those rumours starting to come out about child abuse.'

'Nonsense. There are always those stories. I bet there were stories about St Leonards in your day too. Bet there was a bunch of raging lesbians teaching there.'

They had almost reached the house, and could hear the twins having high jinks in Briony's care.

They looked at each other. They'd made it a rule to be as careful as possible not to let the twins hear them rowing, particularly about *them*.

Fergus often thought about his own father (not that he could remember him; he had no memories at all of Edmund Learmonth), and the way his mother's parents (and his mother, when she thought he wasn't listening) talked of him as if he'd been a failure as a husband and a father. Taking himself off into danger at the time when his wife needed him most, with her child newly born, then getting himself killed, all for the sake of having his name against another handful of gory photos of a post-war zone.

But he was sure his father didn't *want* to be killed. It wasn't even as if it had happened in the front line in the Korean War. That conflict was over when he was caught by a random sniper's bullet.

His grandmother would refer to her son-in-law, with a curl of the lip as 'that irresponsible so-and-so'. It was only later in life, when Fergus understood what a snob she had been that he realised the real problem: his father had attended a state school, and didn't finish his degree before he went off to become a photo-journalist, hitch-hiking his way round the world with a camera-bag and little else in the way of luggage.

And he'd have seen things that traumatised him, for many, many years. Death and destruction. People at their lowest ebb, wrecked lives and dead children. In all likelihood, he'd been suffering from PTSD, years before it was recognised or given a name.

And had Edmund senior not been killed, Fergus may not have been a lonely only child. But that was what he'd grown up with – a father whose name couldn't be mentioned. An embarrassment, like a suicide. His mother hadn't even kept any of the books of Edmund's photos that had been published, though he'd found two of them in the library at Fettes College, and had managed to collect his own pristine copies of every one in existence, by the time he was twenty-five. *Two years in Burma*, discovered in a musty second-hand bookshop in Liverpool, even had Edmund's signature in it, plus a hand-written dedication. 'To Dorothy, with love.'

That, presumably, was another story. Although he'd done some research into the names of people his father might have worked with, he had never found a Dorothy.

Those books gave Fergus his definition of himself. To hell with the Fairbairns and their snobbery – much though he'd loved them. Edmund was his father. *His genes are my genes. One day, I'll write a biography.*

Soon after completing his collection of Edmund Learmonth's books of photographs and travel writing, Fergus had bought his first serious camera, a battered but fully functioning Hasselblad 500 EL. He still owned it, and the photos it produced were infinitely superior to anything you could get from digital equipment. But it was years since he'd developed his own film and prints. These days, he simply didn't have time.

He had often wondered, over the years, what his grandmother had made of his career. Journalism! Not a career for a *gentleman*. She'd have preferred to see him a lawyer, or a Cambridge don (or possibly not; Esmée Fairbairn was, improbably, a devout Scottish Nationalist – Edinburgh or St Andrews would have been her idea of the apogee).

As an antidote to his own upbringing, Fergus had vowed to be a thoroughly modern father.

To that end, he had made a conscious effort to be more modern in his dress. Before he met Belle and became a parent, he dressed like someone a generation older than he was. It was a mix of snobbery and self-defence; a barrier; a challenge.

But gone were the tweed suits (not literally: they hung accusingly in the spare room wardrobe), in favour of jeans and chinos and casual shirts. The shirts were invariably well-pressed (he had always ironed his own shirts; his grandmother had taught him to do so, probably around the age of ten). Since he'd lost weight, he suited his new style.

Arthur Mountjoy had been fifty when he adopted Belle, and his tactic had been to turn her into a middle-aged woman while she was a child. Fergus knew that his kids had made him *young*.

Life could be perfect, if Belle would only see sense about moving, and Remi would disappear into one of her own permaculture trenches. Bitter carrots *that* would grow!

SIXTEEN

Fergus had not been averse to agreeing to visit the chalet at Colvend with Tom Ellis. He'd rolled his eyes, and pretended it was an imposition when the detective asked, but in truth he was keen to see it. Always useful to get new ideas for crime scenes. Once he was gloved up, he tried to think himself into the persona of DI Joyce Maxwell, the main character in his detective novels. It wasn't so easy to do with someone else there.

The place was disappointing. Clean as a whistle.

'Your lot have been over this?'

Ellis grimaced. 'Not before someone else had. Someone who knew exactly what they were doing too. Look...' He crouched and pointed to the faint scuff on the tiles. 'Our only clue. Looks as if someone was dragged across here, wearing outdoor shoes.'

'That's all you've got to go on?'

'That and the fact he was dressed up to the nines. His best clothes, favourite cufflinks, the lot. His cleaner was able to tell us everything that was missing,' he added, in response to

Fergus's quizzical look. 'There's a fitted box with slots for them, and they're the only ones not there. She said he'd never have left them at his other house.'

'So he dressed himself.'

Tom was immediately interested. 'Why do you say that?'

'No one else would have bothered with the cufflinks, specially not his best ones. Was he heavily into self-promotion?'

Tom shrugged. 'No idea. We've got remarkably little on his personal life. Typical Z-list celebrity. Hundreds of acquaintances, no friends, it seems.'

'I'm trying to visualise a scenario where he'd voluntarily get dressed to kill, then end up getting dragged out of his own house, presumably unconscious.' Tom had told him about the chloroform.

'Or dead? Maybe he was dressed to *be* killed.'

'You reckon?'

'Can't think of any other explanation for the fact there's been no proof of life since.'

'And no evidence of forced entry?'

'As far as we could see, he'd let them in. Unless he never locked his door.'

'You're sure it was a "them"?'

Tom pointed to the photo of McPhedrie. 'He's a hefty individual. I doubt if one person could have lifted him.'

'But they didn't – he was dragged.'

'Must have been lifted into a vehicle. We looked carefully for any signs that the gravel outside had been disturbed.'

'And nothing else was missing?'

'His mobile phone, and a pricey watch.'

'And you have an idea of *when* this happened?'

'As far as we can make out, the early hours of the sixteenth of December.'

Fergus walked around the main room, stroking his beard. 'I'd say you're looking for at least two men and a woman, then.'

'Ah! Why a woman?'

'Best clothes and so on. A good-looking woman, smartly-dressed. Possibly quite slender and petite.'

'I wonder...?'

'What?'

'I was wondering if they were posing as police. Plain-clothes ones. He must have expected them to catch up with him at some point. The basement of his other house was kitted out as a photography studio. Presumably he was supplying pics as well as ogling them. From what I can glean, he was a cocky bastard. No way he'd agree to go in for questioning dressed in trackie bottoms and a sweatshirt.'

'But if they'd pulled that trick, surely they could have persuaded him to walk out to the car?'

'I suppose.' Tom ran his fingers through his hair and sighed. 'I'm clutching at straws here.'

'I'll have another try at finding out more about McPhedrie's background. Need to be away in Edinburgh for a day or two, but I'll get to it the moment I can.'

The time he was spending with Tom Ellis counted as 'work' in Fergus's mind, since it added local colour, although he was sure Ellis didn't deal with much real crime. Not the sort of crime books were made of, anyway. But hours spent with the police were rarely wasted, in fact. They helped him keep the ambience of the books fresh and realistic. They lent authenticity. He had never strayed from facts in writing police procedure, even for dramatic effect. For the same reason, he couldn't bear to watch crime fiction on TV.

Some days, he thought back to things he'd tried to write while he was a student, and wondered if, in the end, he had wasted more time than he had left. That was before the days when everyone had a word processor. He hadn't even had an electric typewriter. He remembered, with nostalgia, the physical release of ripping a sheet of paper out of a manual machine, crumpling it and hurling it towards a waste bin, missing and producing, by the end of the afternoon, a snowball-field of rejected pages in a corner of the room. Hitting the delete key never brought such closure, such satisfaction. In his view, literature had been in decline since the arrival of the word processor. It had made it all too easy. Nothing was ever lost. The delete key was too damn convenient, so no one used it enough. It didn't have the same value as a safety-valve for frustration, on the days when the muse wouldn't play catch.

He had told Belle over and over that he couldn't work in Kirkcudbright. It was too bland. It had no dark underbelly. The only thing that smelled bad was the fish factory.

In the small hours, he'd panic that maybe even Edinburgh wouldn't do it for him now. He was too late starting. Whatever 'it' was, it had dried up.

From the day Belle agreed to marry him, his first crime novel had practically written itself – although he had scrapped his first ideas for a main character; too stereotypical. At that point, Joyce Maxwell had arrived, almost fully-fledged. Some days, he'd produced five thousand words – good, useable words – at a sitting without feeling that the well had run dry. He'd felt confident enough to let Belle read what he'd written day by day and she – a true connoisseur of crime fiction, better-read than he was in the genre, and highly selective – had told him it was *good*. He'd demurred that she *would* say that, but she'd replied that she was savvy enough to know that false praise is as little use to a writer as it is to an artist. 'Believe me, if I didn't think it was as good as anything else I've ever read, I'd say so.'

And his productivity had remained high. That made him superstitious. When the TV series based on his first book, *The Debatable Lands*, was being filmed, he had resisted the invitations to go and watch.

In the book he was trying to finish, his main character, DI Joyce Maxwell, faced a dilemma: she didn't want a husband, but she did want to have a child before she was forty. She was considering obtaining sperm from Denmark, because she found the typical Dane aesthetically pleasing: tall, blond, athletic. 'So why doesn't she get herself a Danish man?' Fergus asked himself. He wasn't satisfied that he'd found the answer to that one. He contemplated the Danish and Swedish noir that had been on TV recently. Hardly a single male actor who measured up to that physical description. He chuckled to himself. 'That's why then. It's because there are as many bald, overweight wimps there as anywhere else.' But he knew in his heart that wasn't the reason.

Quite against her creator's wishes, and in spite of his prejudices, DI Maxwell had made it plain that she preferred women.

She was based in a fictional town in the Scottish Borders, that wild, unkempt area that hadn't made up its mind if it was in England or Scotland. He'd been taken aback when *The Bridge* hit TV screens in 2012, just as his agent had managed to secure a deal for a televised version of *The Debatable Lands*. The themes were similar: two rival police forces vying to get the kudos of solving crime in no man's land. But Mathew Emery, the agent who preceded Meera, had assured him that no one else would see a clash – and he always knew what he was talking about.

DI Joyce Maxwell was no Saga Norén. Neither was she remotely like Tom Ellis – but Fergus found Ellis almost a figure of fun.

Joyce had a side-kick, another woman, who ran a pub, and although she'd bounce ideas off her, never in a lifetime would she have involved her – or any other civilian – in solving a case. Fergus read a lot of crime fiction, to keep abreast of his game. He despised the storylines where a journalist, or the local postman, or whatever, got deeply involved in helping the police. When did Inspectors Rebus and Morse ever have a civilian tagging along in their investigations?

Although he had chosen a small town similar in size to Kirkcudbright as a setting for the books (he'd called it Longridgetown), he knew in his heart that he'd have preferred to be writing about Edinburgh. Its dark places were so qualitatively different from the dark places of a small town. More satisfying. More complex. Small towns offered too much closure, too little mystery. However, although he was forever being pestered for what his publisher referred to as 'Edinburgh porn' (the expression had caused Fergus to choke on his own breath the first time, until he realised the man meant Sandy McCall Smith's *Scotland Street* books), and he knew he could do it from memory (when he dreamed, it was almost always of Edinburgh), he felt the capital had become a little over-played.

He had never been one to make a detailed outline before he started to write, although he had read over and over that crime writers *must* plan fully before putting finger to key. He always had an overview of where each plot was going – but that was sufficient. He'd have found it stifling to have a skeleton of each chapter, pin-boards covered in index cards, sheets of wallpaper tacked up lengthways and back to front, with timelines drawn on them in different colours.

Often, when he was contemplating a real-life dilemma, he'd ask himself: what would DI Maxwell do? Much of the time, she felt more real to him than those around him – even his own family. Because he knew her with a depth he'd never know Belle – *could* never know Belle. He'd beat himself up a little about that in the early days, but he recognised all it meant was that he was truly a writer.

He believed Belle understood his work, and how he *had* to work: both the artist and the sculptor. First he had to fill the canvas. An expansive process; the one he'd been immersed in since the end of July, completing a coherent first draft. Then he needed to chip away at the extraneous material, reveal the form. That was the submersive part of the process, when any interruption was disastrous. It was akin to the days when he did a lot more in the way of photography, and did his own developing and printing. That was the stage when he lost track of time. He could go into the bathroom he'd converted into a darkroom, with blackout blinds, at eight in the evening, and emerge to find it was dawn.

For the current book, which was due with his editor by the end of March, Fergus had been researching murder cases where no body was ever found – Arlene Fraser being the most famous. *The Reivers* featured a case where the bodies of the first two victims were never found. 'People are sick of blood and gore,' he'd told Belle. 'There was an article in the *Guardian* about it. Cosy murder mysteries, that's what the market wants nowadays. But not *too* cosy, and not set in country houses.'

Belle had thrown him a level look. 'Waterstones is packed end to end with blood-and-gore ones.'

'Yes, because that's what was being written a year or two back. I want to be part of a rising trend, not an outdated one. I want to concentrate on the mystery, the detection. TV's nauseated people with an overload of police procedurals and bodies turning up in pieces, or burned, or whatever.'

He knew that Belle was worried about how he'd react to seeing *The Debatable Lands* on the small screen.

Everyone who knew him, and knew his contempt for televised crime fiction, had been amazed when he'd agreed to allow it to be made into a six-part series – although he'd retained a high degree of involvement, even after handing over the co-authored script. Only his oldest friend, Anita Forrest from Albion TV, believed him when he said it was purely for the money.

He sometimes met up with Anita when he was in town. It was only five years since they'd worked together, after all; he had signed up for a further series of *Learmonth on the Lookout* before the twins were born, because he realised it would be some time before his books would bring in the sort of money a family required.

Anita had smirked, digging him in the ribs with her elbow as they sat in the Café Royal the previous August. 'I suppose you'll soon need to be thinking about two sets of school fees. Astronomical, these days, I'd guess. Though most places give you a discount for siblings, don't they? Shall you send them to Fettes?'

'Belle doesn't like the sound of it.'

Anita pulled a face. 'Didn't have her down as a Commie.'

He'd felt disloyal, even as he giggled. 'She's not. But her new best friend is probably a card-carrying member of Militant, so no doubt that comes into the equation. I want the twins to have the best start we can give them. What are you grinning at?'

'You. Who could ever have guessed that Fergus Learmonth would take to fatherhood like a squirrel to nuts. It's restored faith in human nature among your former colleagues, I can tell you. But back to this TV script – surely you're not short of money? I was reading in the *Scotsman* that your last book sold over a million copies in its first year?'

'It's done OK. In fact, I've been lucky with all three. But you do realise I only get a pittance for every one sold?'

'Even a pittance times a million mounts up.'

He felt guilty about that, for a brief time, most days. Writing didn't feel enough like work. He could hear his grandmother's voice in his head, telling him about schoolfellows who were now Writers to the Signet, more than one who was a judge, another half dozen who were successful surgeons.

When he was fourteen, and set on becoming a photographer like his father, she'd told him, 'But you must have a *job*, Fergus. A real job.'

He had yet to finish writing his monograph on the Scottish architect James Gillespie Graham (based on the thesis which had earned him a PhD from the University of Edinburgh more years ago than he cared to remember). Possibly a retirement project, if he could ever afford to retire.

Sometimes, he longed to have the freedom to abandon DI Maxwell for a few years, and write in another genre altogether. Historical fiction, perhaps? Success was a trap as well as a reward, in writing as in any other calling.

SEVENTEEN

When Fergus's agent had told him the previous summer that she'd fixed him up with a talk at Wigtown Book Festival, he had been tempted to say no.

He loathed such events – although he knew at the same time that they were an unavoidable evil in the life of a successful writer. Reading from his work, answering questions that could border on the inane, signing the few dozen copies he could expect to sell, maintaining a smile so fixed it became a rictus.

In the end, inevitably, he had agreed.

Belle and the twins had travelled through to Wigtown with him, but he had forbidden them to attend his talk. Instead, they had walked down to the bird observatory, where the only birds that deigned to show themselves were half a dozen seagulls and a crow.

'At least the book signing groupies were denied their ration of drooling over the twins,' she'd said shrewishly when they met up with Fergus afterwards. 'Isn't it amazing – a middle-aged woman on her own with kids will send every man in the vicinity off on urgent business he's newly recollected, but put those kids with a middle-aged *man* on his own: iron filings to a magnet. Harpies!'

So until the last moment, he'd put off confessing that Meera had set up a high-profile event at Waterstones in Edinburgh. Belle wasn't best pleased.

'You could have told me before this!'

'You should all come with me. We can make a long weekend of it at the flat.'

'You said it's on Thursday evening?'

He nodded.

'Well then, that'd mean taking the twins out of school for two whole days.'

'That's hardly going to blight their futures. The school won't mind. Give the teacher a break.'

'You're the one who's always going on about how important education is.'

He sighed. 'You wouldn't need to come to the bookshop, Belle. I know you hate these events. You and the twins could go out somewhere – to the cinema or whatever. Cheat the harpies out of their treat again.'

He hoped she'd smile, but she didn't.

'I suppose Meera will be there to hold your hand?'

'Meera will be there, yes.' He struggled to keep a calm tone. 'She'll be there because she's my agent, and she wants to make the most of all the PR opportunities.'

'Why – so you can sell another dozen books, on top of the millions you already sell?'

She immediately crossed the room and put her arms round him. 'Sorry, Fergus. I'm being a bitch. I know it's important to build your career. I'm jealous.'

He held her at arm's length and laughed. 'Jealous of what – the fact I make money? It's for *us*, sweetheart. I wouldn't bother doing it otherwise.' He studied her face. 'Jealous of *Meera*? Jesus, Belle, you have absolutely no grounds for that. She's not my type at all. She's a good businesswoman, that's all. Besides, why would I want to look at another woman? I only want to look at you. That's why I wanted you to come with me.'

'What time does the Waterstones thing finish?'

'By nine.'

'I suppose you'll have to take what's-her-name out for a meal afterwards.'

'I won't have to do anything. If you honestly don't want to come, I'll drive through to town on Thursday morning, and back home after the stupid book signing.'

'Then you won't be able to have a drink.'

'So I won't have a drink.'

'Tell you what – we'll definitely come with you next time. You need to give me a bit more notice.' She hesitated for a moment. 'Fergus – do you think it's because you're well-known that your books are such a success?'

He grinned. 'Undoubtedly that helps. It's lucky, because age wasn't on my side. Damn few publishers are keen to take on a first-time novelist much over fifty.' He drew her onto his lap. The Aeron chair creaked ominously. 'Look, I know I've been damn lucky. I was reading somewhere that it took Ian Rankin something like eleven years before he started making serious money off Rebus. So I managed to hit the ground running, for whatever reason. At least it means you and the twins will be financially secure.' He kissed her lingeringly. 'I'll hold you to the promise to come with me next time. And I won't be away for more than a few hours on Thursday.'

Fergus knew that Belle often got up in the night, walked into the garden and stood there in the dark that wasn't completely dark: the silver hour, just before dawn.

He watched her a little nervously from behind the bedroom curtain, to make sure she was safe. She'd put on her warm dressing gown and sheepskin boots.

He knew he mustn't let her know he'd noticed. He mustn't ask if she was feeling all right, because she would fly off the handle. Or laugh; that was almost worse. He knew he mustn't intrude on her privacy.

She was standing on the path in front of the garden cottage. He was fairly sure she wasn't merely laying ghosts. After the Roddy incident, she was keen to have the damn building knocked down. He'd been the one to create problems with that – even getting to the stage of saying that if she did so, people would believe she was guilty after all. They could gut the inside, he said, take it back to the walls and refinish it, because it would add value to the property.

Nowadays, he'd happily have taken a sledgehammer to the place himself, but the twins had colonised it as their play-space, and he was often grateful for the peace and quiet when he was on a roll with writing, comfortable in the elegant room that had been Belle's father's study.

When she came back to bed, he'd cuddle her warm, as he always did, and draw her frozen feet against his legs.

It was cold, but not unbearably so, sheltered by her garden's ancient eleven-foot walls. And not too dark, because it was never completely dark in the town. Belle smiled, remembering the night she had fled from the house, barefoot and wearing nothing but her nightie, terrified by the knowledge that an intruder had been in her home, to where Fergus was sleeping in the garden cottage. The night it all started, in fact, because that was when she had invited Fergus to stay in the main house with her, and it hadn't been terribly long afterwards that she allowed him to invite himself into her room. And then: twins! She laughed softly to herself.

At the end of the plot, sheltered by the garden walls and the cottage, she had decided to create two permaculture beds, exactly like Remi's. She intended to do all the deep digging herself.

Fergus was good at helping in the garden, and was often to be found spade in hand, sleeves rolled up, sweat streaming into his eyes, doing the first serious gardening he'd undertaken since his mother died.

But this was *her* thing. She knew the trenches needed to be deep. It would be back-breaking work, but she was fitter than she had ever been. And once it was done, she'd never have to deep-dig again, simply hoe the weeds out. Remi said it was so worth it. You filled the trench with good stuff and it'd go on producing, if you paid attention to growing the appropriate vegetables in the correct sequence.

In truth, one of the reasons she liked to potter in the garden under the reflection of the street lights was to give Fergus a break from her presence. She knew she wasn't the easiest person to live with, and often worried that he'd leave her. But she couldn't change. It was as if there was a glass wall between her and the person she yearned to be. Like those swimming pool cafes that were all the rage for a while, where you could sit drinking your coffee and watch the swimmers on the other side of the glass, although no sound got through.

The house and garden were all Father had left her – apart from her gallery. She felt she didn't have the *right* to sell it. In any case, Ashers symbolised home for her – that's why she couldn't bear the thought of losing it completely.

She knew in her heart that she'd probably have lost it anyway, if Fergus hadn't come along, because she'd not been able to afford to maintain it. And it would be wildly impractical as a holiday home – it needed to be kept heated and aired, and the garden would quickly become a jungle if untended. She knew they couldn't *afford* to keep it as a holiday home.

That's what her head knew. Her heart knew differently. *If I didn't have Ashers, where could I hide?*

And she had an epiphany. All her memories of Rose were linked to this garden; every last one. On an impulse, she hauled open the shed door, trying to minimise its squeak, and checked that the miniature watering can, sole surviving remnant of what had been a child's gardening set, was in its usual place on the shelf. She ran her fingers over its rust-pitted enamelled surface, feeling for the loose spout lying on the shelf beside it; that dated from the day Esmée had thrown it on the paving stones in one of her tantrums. One of the few times Belle had lost her temper with her daughter. She had even slapped her – though not as hard as she'd wanted to.

The incident had made her decide against moving her doll's house from the attic into Esmée's room until the girl was older. The furniture in it was quite valuable; she had collected most of it as an adult.

She fell to wondering for the thousandth time what had

become of the tiny trowel and fork that had originally been the watering can's companions.

Rose must have bought the set for her. Father had taken no interest whatsoever in the garden; it was simply a necessary social evil for a solicitor of standing. Something you got a man in to do. Perhaps Rose spent so much time out of doors because she simply couldn't bear to be in the house with Father?

An element of her childhood made sense for the first time: before Rose left, there had been no housekeeper, and no man coming in to tend the garden. She had often wondered what on earth had possessed Father, marrying someone so clearly not suitable for him, a much younger woman of no education.

When she and Fergus went out walking, they were usually hand-in-hand, a twin on each free hand. But Belle couldn't recall ever seeing Rose and Father touch each other, far less hold hands. In fact, she was certain they had slept in separate rooms. She shuddered, and started to walk slowly back towards the house.

She had been reading, recently, a book about London's Foundling Hospital. In reality, she'd been fortunate. Had she been born a century earlier, she might simply have been abandoned on the steps of such an institution. Two out of three of the children thus jettisoned had died long before they were old enough to be apprenticed into some menial trade. Hers had truly been a Tom Jones story; a fairy tale.

Belle took hold of a bare rose-stem and drew her fingertips over the thorns. Physical pain was so much easier to deal with.

Father had never put any pressure on her to study law. He had seemed to take little interest in *what* she studied, in fact. Would she have been a good solicitor? She laughed bitterly at the thought. At least with a profession like that she'd have had a more conventionally successful life. And not have met Fergus or had the twins.

Belle loathed having her photo taken; that was possibly one reason why there were so few pictures of her even as a child. But Fergus had persuaded her that it was only fair to the twins to leave them a record of their entire childhood, and she was an irreplaceable part of that.

He adored her graduation photo – when he first saw it he'd said, 'Wow, if I'd met you then, no other man would ever have snatched you away.'

And she'd tossed her head and said, 'No man did. It's you that had tied the knot three times before, Fergus Learmonth. A loose knot, by the sound of it.'

Bloody Serena had obviously been the diametric opposite. Nothing she'd liked better than posing for him, specially in the early days, by the looks of it. Although Fergus swore he had now destroyed all the portrait shots of Serena that he'd taken, he'd brought a handful with him from Edinburgh when he first moved in. He didn't suspect she'd found his stash. Must have been a wrench to burn the lot; some were works of art. He'd won prizes for them.

She sucked the blood off her fingers.

It was *Ashers'* garden that was important. Not just *a* garden.

And this, after all, was the twins' inheritance too. At least they'd have a photographic record of *their* early lives. Although Belle had virtually no photos from her childhood, Ashers' dining room bookcase held more than a dozen albums, charting the twins' progress from birth onwards. They'd have memories. They'd have *roots*. Unless Fergus went off with another woman. The Meera creature...

She shook her head to banish the idea. Fergus would *never*

do that, no matter what suspicions Remi tried to plant in her head. The only woman who could possibly have stolen Fergus from her was dead, long ago.

She drew the thick woollen dressing gown more tightly around her, and headed back to the house, to her bed. To Fergus.

EIGHTEEN

Fergus left Kirkcudbright at first light, eager to steep himself in Edinburgh for as long as possible before his meeting.

During his working career, he had spent time in many of the world's great cities: Toronto, Paris, Barcelona, London, New York. But he remained convinced that no other city – with the possible exception of Granada – could command such love as the city of Edinburgh. It had held him in thrall since his earliest memories of walking in Princes Street Gardens with his grandmother, below the louring mass of the Castle Rock, and weeping against her skirt because he was afraid the rock was about to crumble and crush them. His people had been Edinburgh people since time immemorial. It was in his DNA. Even the twins loved it, instinctively. Life at the centre, not the periphery. Life, like good writing, should begin *in medias res*.

He loved the unpredictability of urban meandering; the thrill of the unexpected. And, to be fair, you could find that in Kirkcudbright too; the sudden glimpse of a brightly-planted window box; a pleasing fanlight; a polished brass door-knocker.

But in Kirkcudbright, it was all contained within one or two streets of pastel-painted quaintness. In Edinburgh, you could walk for miles along pavements ringing with frost – from the Dean Village through the New Town, and out along the elegant terraces lining the London Road, until you were almost satiated with the rich detail of the place. And in an era when all cities had begun to look more or less alike, morphing into one another, Edinburgh was blessed with a sufficiency of *otherness*.

He knew he was being unreasonable in comparing a town of under three and a half thousand souls with Scotland's capital city.

It was the perspective of buildings he missed most. Kirkcudbright had more architectural pretensions than a lot of small Scottish towns. But it lacked the grandeur of a Princes Street, or a Lawnmarket, where you could look up from within a canyon of ancient stones and see (with amazement) an exquisite sliver of sky (perhaps adorned with a tiny silver plane). And yet, in ten minutes' walking you'd find yourself in what seemed like open countryside. You could turn, and there was the ridiculous top of Our Dynamic Earth, and the new Parliament, cheek by jowl with the old Palace. And a few steps across Holyrood Road, the stamping-ground of some of the city's most notorious drug dealers.

Good restaurants, congenial society, the kitschness of the Christmas market in Princes Street Gardens, and the one o'clock gun; the Traverse Theatre and the Usher Hall. The fragrance of history that wafted in your face as you walked down the Royal Mile and looked up, to be confronted by the timeless, improbable blue of a strip of North Sea framed by buildings, and crowned by the Bass Rock. And presiding over everything, the all-pervasive, yeasty aroma from the Caledonian Brewery, held down by a temperature inversion.

Quite simply, he could not imagine another town where he'd be happy to live out the remainder of his days, and raise his children – unless it were Granada, and Belle was probably correct about that; impractical, until the twins are grown and independent. He sighed. That might mean never, for him. He'd be near enough eighty by the time they were through with all of their higher education.

He closed his eyes, thinking of the few genuinely hot days you got in a Scottish summer, when there was the same soft velvety dusk you found in Granada, that same subtle amethyst haze lying over the horizon, where the paving stones and the earth and the stonework never cooled completely, but happed you in warmth until midnight.

All the same, if he could find an Edinburgh home that didn't totally clean them out, maybe they could find a tiny house in the Albaicín with a tiny garden. A patio with a fountain. A balcony; a view across to the Alhambra, floating in the misty dusk like a mirage.

The whole thing was a mirage. They'd taken the twins there the previous year, and it was every bit as crowded as when he and Belle had stayed at the Parador on their honeymoon. You could barely move for the pressure of people. Even in the Alhambra gardens, they were moved on the whole time. Like viewing the Crown Jewels. No time to stop and appreciate the scent of the roses. No opportunity to photograph the iconic fountain on the Patio de los Leones without people getting in the way.

The problem with older marriages is that there's so much history apart; it gets in the way of the history you build together.

Fergus sat at one of the table windows in Frederick's Coffee House, his laptop open in front of him, studying the local Solicitors' Property Centre webpages.

If he could have somehow transported Ashers to the capital, there could not have been a greater paradise on earth. He knew that if there was one thing that would be a necessity, it'd be to find a place with an equally fine garden, not merely a courtyard with pots. Which, up in town, equalled pots of money.

And it had to be close to the centre. He had no wish to live in what he considered the suburbs: the Grange, or even Trinity. As for further out! He was a city boy, through and through. He loved *real* cities, with cathedrals and steeples and history and cobbled streets. He loved the way the street lights formed pools of chiaroscuro. He loved the way *l'heure bleue* expanded for what felt like forever; the way a city never slept. Life-affirming! But he also recognised that his wife found it enervating and almost frightening.

He knew where she was coming from with that fear. He'd lived in London for a few years, when his TV career took off after he'd split up with Serena, and he had loathed it; the sense of unconnectedness, rootlessness; the press of people everywhere, the lack of cohesion. A city of ten million individuals and no community, it had seemed to him.

Edinburgh was the perfect size – though he wasn't particularly keen on the more perjink parts of the New Town either. They lacked character these days. The Old Town he ruled out, with the exception of Ramsay Garden – and it would have to be a truly exceptional apartment; one of the ones with stupendous views over Princes Street. He couldn't recall when last what he'd call a truly desirable flat there had come onto the market. No real shops near it, or even a decent pub. The epicentre of a tourist hell for most of the year.

For the part of town they would settle in, he had in mind a relatively self-contained zone, on the well-mannered border between the Western New Town and Stockbridge and Dean; an area that had *edge*. That, surely, would win Belle over. La Vie Boheme – except that all the street lamps worked, and there were no overgrown trees hanging above the pavement to create sinister pools of shadow. That part of town was truly a city of light. And the play of cool northern sunlight on Edinburgh's grey stone. His heart leapt.

He had found an advert for an entire house in Saxe Coburg Place. The agent's blurb said it 'required modernisation', which probably meant rewiring, replumbing, replastering, replacing windows. Maybe replacing the damn roof. They could almost stretch to buying it, even if houses in that area were going for at least twenty-five per cent above the asking price. And if Belle would agree to sell Ashers, they could afford a renovation programme that would make it a palace. Maybe he could talk her round? Once she saw that Ashers wasn't the only house in the country with those elegant high ceilings and fine plaster-work on the cornices. The Saxe Coburg house had a garden too, not so terribly much smaller than Ashers'.

He looked longingly at the estate agent's photos. All right, it was overlooked; what town centre garden wasn't? But he could imagine what an Eden Belle would make of it, with her green fingers. And there was the entitlement to a key to the locked communal gardens opposite. The twins could run about there, and be even safer than they were in Kirkcudbright, where there was plenty of open countryside, but no park.

He closed his eyes for a moment, and pictured the view from his office window, looking down Ashers' long garden. Yes indeed, it would be a Herculean task to duplicate all the things in it that Belle held dear. The stag's horn sumach they planted the year they married, close against a mature mound of Japanese maple, its leaves the colour of a fine claret (and even now, in January, there was a rumpled carpet of burgundy and gold on the ground around it). A bed of sempervivum (how he loved that word!) that also had burgundy leaves and surprisingly delicate pink flowers. The viburnum still in bloom against the south-facing wall.

Roses. There must be roses – Belle's favourite flower. And they'd have to find a buyer for her house who'd cherish everything about it, including her garden. The thought that the garden she'd tended, the one they'd tended together since they met, the one where the twins had lain out on the grass on a blanket every fine day of their first summer (they could walk competently by the next one) would live on after the family had left. That would be equally important to her.

The main thing was: living in town would give Belle the chance to feel she was in the thick of things again. She'd taken a long time away from work to look after the twins, and the art world had changed out of all recognition during that time. Now her gallery was barely ticking over, he wanted her to have the chance of a larger, more highly-textured world. Anita Forrest had told him that his former colleague Nick Cochran's wife, Claire, was thinking of opening a shop which'd sell shabby-chic furniture and paintings and soft furnishings: the sort of thing that'd suit Belle's excellent taste and eye for art.

Bugger! The basement flat of the Saxe Coburg house was being listed as a separate sale! Even that might be doable, if the entire nest egg was invested in it. And of course, they could dispose of the Bruntsfield crash-pad.

He'd need to convince Belle quickly. Houses in that part of town didn't hang around.

It was close to the Stockbridge Colonies, where he had lived with Serena during their ultra-brief marriage. His heart skipped a beat, then he told himself severely he was not the same person who'd lived there with Serena. That person was as dead as she was. And Belle need never know about the house in the Colonies.

He finished his coffee quickly, and dialled the agent's number. Then he texted Meera: something's come up. See you at half six at the venue.

The Saxe Coburg house had a good vibe, from the pavement. He waited impatiently for the agent, taking in the neatly-kept locked communal gardens. That, in itself, led to a sense of belonging.

A white Toyota Yaris drew up, and a girl in a skirt so short that he got a glimpse of knicker got out. He averted his eyes.

'Mr Learmonth? Sorry,' she gushed with false sincerity, thrusting a glossy brochure into his hand. 'Hope I haven't kept you waiting long?'

What a disappointment, once she'd unlocked the door. The house was a veritable wreck inside, and more than that, it didn't have a pleasant ambience. In fact, it gave Fergus the creeps – and not many things were capable of rattling him. Even the ground floor rooms were dark, despite the tall windows.

'Did the last owner die here in the house, do you happen to know?' he asked the agent.

Her eyes slewed away. 'Die? My goodness, no. Why would you think that?'

He shrugged and turned back to the stairway. No point in bringing Belle to see this one; she'd reject it out of hand. But there was plenty of time. He needed to be sure she was fully ready to move.

He apologised to the agent, and left abruptly, ripping the schedule of particulars in half and slipping it into the nearest bin. There would be other houses. Edinburgh prices were climbing alarmingly, but he was more confident these days that his earnings could keep pace, particularly if *Bordering on Murder* got picked up for TV. He'd already decided to accept the three-book deal that would mean changing publishers, moving up a rung. Trying his hand at a different genre could wait, as could his monograph on Gillespie Graham, and the biography of Edmund Learmonth, senior, he planned to write.

And without a doubt he could manage to work in Kirkcudbright for the time being. He didn't actively dislike the town for its small size. After all, his favourite classic Scottish novel was *The House with the Green Shutters*. He chuckled to himself.

It might mean more frequent trips to Edinburgh, and to Newcastleton, the Longridgetown of his novels (the police station there had been closed the previous year, but that suited well; better to have a fictional nick in a fictional town). They'd need to take Briony up on her offers to look after the twins from time to time, now that they were older. Then Belle could come with him; it'd be like their all-too-brief courtship.

A chance to stroll past his old flat in Learmonth Terrace would leave plenty of time to get to the book signing.

The place looked inviting in the sunshine. Although he had enjoyed living there, he felt no nostalgia for it. Serena had stayed with him there for a few weeks after the Russian had vanished, but it had been strictly as a guest; a stranger. He glanced at the communal garden where he'd made a bonfire of the photos of his wedding to her. He should have burned the lot, even the studio portraits he'd won prizes for. Yes, he could have put them in the bank, in the deposit box where he kept some important but private documents, such as his first three marriage certificates and divorce certificates (he'd brought home his mother's and grandmother's jewellery, all the family heirlooms, for Belle to wear). But he was likely to die first, being a man and eight years older. He'd never have wanted his wife to see those photos; in some, Serena had been wearing scanty clothing, if any. The last thing he wanted to do was hurt Belle in any way. Enough people had done that in the past.

He walked briskly along Queensferry Road to the west end of Princes Street, relishing that particular brand of cold that gets into your bones in winter, the chill that lingers on the north face of a building in February. He barely glanced at St John's Church in passing. He had little time for churches, but he had always envisaged Esmée as a bride in St John's; he'd be so proud, leading her down the aisle on his arm, his radiant daughter in a simple white satin dress. If he was around. He shivered. *Pull yourself together, man. You take care of your health these days. Of course you'll be around in another twenty years or so, and able to put one foot in front of another steadily enough for that.* Eddie waiting at the front of the church, as best man. No, that was silly. It was the groom's best friend who did that. And there was no way that Fergus could picture the groom, for what man would be good enough for his daughter?

He'd been wise enough never to share that vision with Belle, particularly since his choice of St John's as the venue was based on the fact he'd married the first Mrs Learmonth there; she was a member of the Episcopal church. *Piscy, Piscy, Amen, Down on your knees and up again!*

He racked his brain. Who was *his* best man that time? Ruaraidh Cruikshank, the one he'd played rugger with at university. He hadn't seen him in more than thirty years. Didn't even know if he still lived in Edinburgh.

He sleepwalked his way through the reading and book-signing, and was on his way back to Galloway before nine-thirty.

Belle was waiting up for him, anxious about the state of the wintry roads. She knew he'd have taken the shortcut off the A75; the one she had forbidden him to use.

These days, she never mentioned the real reason for not wanting to take the shorter route: the crash at Tongland Bridge that had written off her father's car and taken away his confidence forever. But she regularly relived the sickening sensation of the microseconds that seemed like hours, as the lorry crunched into the front wing of the ancient Bentley, and kept coming, until it was brought to a halt by the old car's sturdy chassis. Then the silence, and the sound of something dripping, and the immediacy of the panic: she had to get out, she had to get her father out. The workers from the hydro-electric station beside the bridge had arrived by then; all was well. Gentle hands helped both of them out from the twisted metal. Neither she nor Father had been seriously injured (although the driver's side of the car had taken the brunt of the impact), and the fireball she'd been bracing herself for didn't come.

The injuries had all been psychological. Her father had never got behind a steering wheel again (though the fault had been entirely the lorry driver's), and she herself had never driven along that road since.

She wiped away a tear of relief as she heard Fergus's key in the front door.

'How was it?'

'Tedious as these things always are.'

'Sell many books?'

'A couple of dozen – but Meera's always telling me that's not what it's for. It's all about raising my profile.' He laughed and drew Belle into his arms. 'I had time to walk around the best area for house-hunting. Next time, the three of you come with me, and we'll *all* explore it.'

But Belle wrinkled her nose. 'Och, Edinburgh. It's full of snooty folk.'

'So's Kirkcudbright.'

She had no answer to that. She'd seen the changes in the place since she was a girl. It was a pleasant town to retire to, as Lord Cockburn had said in 1844. '*Small, clean, silent and respectable.*'

But Edinburgh. That was a different proposition. A two-faced town. All fur coat and no knickers. It pretended to be a city of posh fanlights and Morningside accents, and two branches of Waitrose. But it had changed; changed hugely even since the days when she and Roddy used to go through on the train to view an exhibition at the Gallery of Modern Art.

Jenners wasn't Jenners any more, merely any old chain store. Princes Street had a beggar every ten metres. And those dark chasms of Old Town streets you'd see in photos from the 1940s! Those hadn't changed, even with the Clean Air Act. As black and full of menace as ever.

She led the way into the kitchen, crossing to switch on the

kettle. 'I like to be able to go for a walk in the evenings. In safety. Not always wondering if someone's going to snatch my bag.'

'I can't think of many places where it's safer to walk than Stockbridge and the New Town, in the evenings or any other time. Just as safe as here – and at least there are places to walk *to*.'

'I know you're always on telling me we could go to the theatre, and to concerts. But how can we do that? It's fine here, because Briony will always babysit, or Anna can come in.' Anna was the eighteen-year-old daughter of one of the local doctors. She was charming, reliable and trustworthy, and the twins adored her. Even Archie and Gorby adored her: she was the main reason they'd been able to take holidays or weekend in the Bruntsfield flat over the years without worrying about the cat. Belle was triumphant now, sensing victory. 'What do you mean to do in Edinburgh – hire in some stranger? No thank *you*.'

'There will be Annas in Edinburgh. I still know people there. Lots of them have teenage daughters. We'd never have to leave the kids with a stranger. We didn't know Anna until she started babysitting for us.'

'We knew her family though.'

'Nick and Claire Cochran – you remember we ran into them in the Botanics one day? I used to work with him at Albion. Their daughter's sixteen now. She'd be perfect. Utterly dependable family. In any case – how often do we go out *here*? There's nowhere to go.'

'That's because you're too much of a snob to go to anything here. There's the choral society. There are plays. What's so wonderful in Edinburgh?'

Fergus snorted. The one and only time he'd agreed to attend a concert by the local choral society, he'd slipped out halfway through, leaving Belle to sit stolidly lthrough the rest of the programme. He could be the most *irritating* man. Even when he'd lived alone in towns like Edinburgh and London, she knew he hadn't belonged to clubs and societies. He'd never been a *joiner*.

'There are theatres, cinemas. Murrayfield – but I know that cuts no ice with you. But the exhibitions, the Festival. And a fast rail link to London.'

Where his agent and his publishers were based.

'The twins are almost five,' he added. 'It's not like leaving babies.'

'There's no way we'd be able to afford a detached house there,' said Belle, with an air of finality. 'We'd be tacked onto other people's houses. Then if anything happens, you've only yourself to blame. Fires and things.' She shuddered. 'And we have no friends there. Well – I haven't anyway.'

'We'll make friends together.'

They had tried meeting up with some of Fergus's old colleagues on the odd Bruntsfield weekend, trailing the twins along with them. That had not been an unqualified success, because no one else their age had small children. In fact, some were grandparents.

'The people we know here are from our sort of background. That's important.' She was suddenly pensive. 'I mean, *we're* from the same sort of backgrounds, aren't we?'

'That's why we hit it off so well from the start. Too well in fact. The main reason we had to have a shot-gun wedding, at our age!'

She smiled, at last. 'I suppose so. So why not Glasgow? There are excellent schools there, and the *Herald* says house prices aren't so ridiculous.'

Fergus didn't know how to counter this. He was aghast. She knew he loathed Glasgow almost as much as he loved Edinburgh.

And it had to be faced: she used to believe that when Fergus got that faraway look in his eyes – the look that bleared the blue – he was thinking of Serena. But she'd come to realise that the parts of Fergus that were blank on her mental map of him should all be marked 'Edinburgh'.

'I've always found cities are lonely places,' she said carefully.

'Not Edinburgh – it's too small. More like a series of villages.'

She fixed him with a gimlet stare. 'But you keep saying that's why you're fed up with being here. And this isn't even a village – it's a *town*.'

He didn't reply, so she was on a roll. 'I suppose your idea of a "village" needs to have a branch of Waitrose, and a Valvona & Crolla, and a cheesemonger, and several bookshops?'

He wasn't taking that lying down! 'One bookshop would be welcome, yes.'

The only one in Kirkcudbright had closed the previous year. She started to busy herself with warming the teapot, but Fergus walked over to where she stood and slid his arms round her waist.

'Leave that, and come to bed. As long as I'm with you and the children, I don't need Valvona & Crolla.'

She moved towards the stairway with him eagerly enough, but before they started to climb, she pulled him round to face her. 'I've been thinking – I know you feel you can't work properly here, and it's important for you to be able to get on with it. You could always spend the week in Edinburgh, in the flat. Then we wouldn't disturb you, and you'd get more done.'

His spine had turned to ice. 'What — go without you and the twins?'

'I know you've been finding it hard to work recently. I realise we're a distraction.'

'*You* want that?'

'Of course I don't. But I don't want to feel I'm holding you back. We're neither of us going to fade away if we're apart for a few days most weeks. You lived on your own without me and the twins for a long time, Fergus.'

But that hadn't been the same Fergus.

Even on the days when he missed his home city most, he knew he could never leave Belle or the children. Not even to stay in the crash-pad during the week, as he knew other authors did, to get peace to work. She couldn't manage without him, and he couldn't manage without her.

'Did your friend Remi suggest this?'

She laughed, instead of becoming angry. 'I don't need anyone else to tell me that we're getting in the way of your work, and the flat's there anyway. It might as well earn its keep. It's a sensible solution. You spent most of your life able to please yourself, and here you are having to work around things like children's bath times, and homework. I know it's boring for you.'

'I'm not bored with the kids! I'm bored with Kirkcudbright, if you must know. I want us to be able to do even more together, as a family.'

She slid her arm round his waist as they climbed the stairs side by side. 'I want that too.'

NINETEEN

At noon, Tom Ellis carved out sufficient time away from his desk to stride quickly up to the High Street, to Waterstones. He purchased a copy of *The Debatable Lands*, and spent the first hour back in the office reading it, a sheaf of papers at hand to cover the book quickly if anyone disturbed him.

He had convinced himself it was work anyway. If he was to get help from Learmonth, he had to understand him better – and what better way to understand a writer than to read his work?

Crime fiction was always tripe. But Jackie had read the second Learmonth book, *Bordering on Murder*, so he'd heard extracts, because she was the type of reader who couldn't resist relaying a story as she waded through it. The main character, Joyce Maxwell, was a female DI who was bisexual, and kept slipping away to London for dirty weekends with different men or women, or both at the same time. Well, how unrealistic was that? He'd never heard of a single colleague who swung both ways, the women even less likely than the men, though it was a known fact that McInnes batted for the other team.

He'd sneaked into Waterstones a couple of times over the past few years, ever since Learmonth's first novel was an overnight sensation, just to look at them.

He was finding it difficult to admit, even to himself, that he was enjoying Learmonth's style. He'd wanted to hate it, and find inaccuracies and improbabilities to sneer at. But three chapters in and he was hooked. He could see why Jackie was a fan. For a moment, he thought he might even give the book to her to read once he had finished it. In the end, he decided he'd keep it in the office, in his desk drawer. He might pass it on to Rach instead.

Apart from her sexual peccadilloes, Learmonth's detective was disturbingly true to life. She didn't wander unaccompanied into sinister, deserted warehouses or disused railway tunnels at night, in pursuit of dangerous, armed criminals. She didn't have an affair with any other cops (though Jackie was right about the dirty weekends in London). Her civilian sidekick was exactly that – a supportive companion, not someone who helped her solve cases. Tom was uncertain whether or not they were supposed to be in a lesbian relationship; Learmonth was clever in the way he handled that. Subtle. Maybe the fact that the side-kick was a female bar-owner was meant as a clue? But surely in a relationship like that the detective would be the 'man', the butch one? Learmonth's detective, DI Joyce Maxwell, was almost ladylike. She swore very little – a lot less than Tom himself did. Although the writer had been clever enough never to give a precise description of what DI Maxwell looked like, she didn't sound like one of those muscle-bound, mannish women who always wore trousers, even off-duty. He found himself visualising her as looking like Belle.

He couldn't even fault Learmonth on his grasp of police procedure. Rach watched things like *Scott & Bailey*, and *Inspector Morse*. Even reruns of *Taggart*. Tom would hear her discussing them with Giles. They found the improbable scenarios amusing. Tom found them infuriating.

He'd read in the *Galloway News* that *The Debatable Lands* was being serialised on TV. Maybe he'd watch that, with Jackie. Maybe he'd mention, casually, that he knew the author. But Jackie would roll her eyes and say, 'Everyone knows *him*. He's married to that one you used to go with. Marjory, or whatever her name is.'

As soon as he was home that evening, he'd go online and order himself a treat. The latest 1500-piece Jan van Haasteren jigsaw, perhaps. Or one of the larger Ravensburger ones. After all, those counted as work too. He had a technique: he looked at the picture on the lid just once, in a desultory way, before putting it away. Then he concentrated on studying the shapes of the pieces, and the logic of colour and form. You often had to try several solutions before you found the right one. But there always *was* a single right one. Exactly the same as his day job.

He allowed himself two minutes of wondering if Mabs Mountjoy would have married him if he had been a writer, rather than just a cop. Perhaps he'd write a book now: *The Zen of Jigsaw Puzzling*. Chortling to himself, he slammed his desk drawer shut and strode through to the crew room.

His team was still drawing blanks. He'd had two DCs going through every bit of potentially relevant ANPR footage for the weeks before they reckoned the victims had disappeared, finding the last times their own cars had been picked up. Thankless task, because apart from finding McPhedrie travelling north at the beginning of November, there was nothing.

There was, predictably, no local CCTV. He'd even had uniforms going door to door to see if anyone en route to either house had a dashcam that might have been left on in a parked car. He'd seen footage from a few of those, and it was often of exceptionally high quality. But they came up empty-handed.

There were no records of any of the three leaving the country – he had even made the airports and ferry companies search for all data on passengers who needed wheelchairs, since presumably Winston Bisset couldn't manage without one.

Nil.

No activity on any of the bank accounts. No new phone records.

He had eventually managed to track down council officials who knew about the allegations against Bisset, but they'd been of little help. New head, and both the school and the education authority maintained there was no paper trail. Some dame in the council office said she vaguely remembered something about it, but since there was absolutely no proof of wrong-doing, it hadn't been followed up or documented.

'So why was he asked to leave?' he asked.

'He wasn't. Our records show that Mr and Mrs Bisset both resigned their posts at Willowbeck High School in 1997, because he had accepted a post elsewhere.'

By now, Tom was convinced that they weren't looking at kidnappings or last-minute getaways by sex offenders who thought they'd been rumbled. There was no chance of finding any one of the three alive. He was sure the brass must have figured this out too, but so far he'd been left in charge.

In charge of a case that was going nowhere.

'Boss!'

He headed across the room. The rest of the team were gathered round DC Susie Dolland's computer screen.

'What?' asked Tom. The others moved aside to let him see Susie's screen.

'There's something interesting on Twitter,' Rachel said.

@Housekeep.net #uselesscops. Dumfries police failed to round up the nonces in their area. So we have.

Tom felt the colour rise in his face. 'What's that all about?'

'Our Misper case, presumably,' said DC Dolland.

Tom liked Susie Dolland. He liked her trim, petite figure, and the blonde hair that framed her face like a shiny golden bell. But he was at the end of his patience. 'So what the hell is "Housekeep.net"?'

'The Twitter user name for "Housekeeping.net",' said Susie, unhelpfully.

'And?'

'There's more.'

@Housekeep.net #uselesscops The authorities are doing nothing about cleaning up. We have the answer. One shot and the grot's gone.

'Fuck! How did you latch onto these?'

'We do a regular trawl to see anything that mentions Dumfries and Galloway police. And the useless cops hashtag caught my eye.'

'Well done, DC Dolland. Now – can we find where these are coming from?'

Stuart Pirie, the IT nerd, had joined the group. He rolled his eyes. 'Not a chance, I'd say. I'll see what I can do, but I'm not optimistic.'

'Do you reckon they're telling us these people have been shot?' said DC Giles.

'What?' Tom asked irritably.

'"One shot". Do you think that means they've been shot? McPhedrie and the Bissets, I mean.'

Two or three people around the table looked at Giles admiringly. Dolland and DS Field didn't.

'It's the Scuzbuster slogan,' said Susie. 'You see the ads for it on TV all the time. It's that woman with the irritating voice. "One shot and the grot's gone". She always says that. Or shouts it.'

'We don't *know* that anything at all has happened to our Mispers,' growled Tom. 'They're as likely to be sunning themselves on the Costa del Crime and sniggering at us.'

'So what are this lot trying to tell us?'

'Have you seen them mention any of the missing persons we are supposed to be searching for?'

Giles coloured up. 'No, but...'

'Jumping to conclusions is no fucking good in police work. If you think you're Inspector Morse, doing it all by "intuition" and fannying about listening to opera, you're in the wrong job, DC Giles. Here in Dumfries and Galloway, we look at the facts, and only the facts. Thus far, we have found precisely nothing to indicate that any of the three missing persons is dead.'

'There's been no proof of life for weeks now,' added Giles.

Even Rachel was looking at Tom dubiously.

'So? If they all scarpered to the Continent, do you think they won't have other bank accounts and cards? And anyone I know who's gone for more than a couple of weeks in Majorca has bought a pay-as-you-go phone over there, because it's cheaper.'

'So what are these Housekeeping guys on about?'

'Who the hell knows? Right. I'm going to see if I can get a

bit more of a handle on this,' said Tom, retrieving his jacket from his office. Rachel stood up expectantly. 'It's OK, DS Field. I'll see to this one myself.' He tapped the side of his nose.

He left the building in a cold fury. Not that Giles's fan club had *tried* to make a fool of him. He'd managed that all by himself.

The afternoon was unusually warm for January, and the sun skinkling off the water in the estuary had almost given Tom Ellis a headache. He'd walked around Kirkcudbright some, before deciding he had to visit Fergus Learmonth again.

He was about to raise the knocker on the front door when he heard voices from the garden. So he walked round to the side gate, and found it unlocked. He was careful to close it after him, remembering the fuss Mabs – Belle – had made at the time of the McCulloch shindig in case they let her precious dog, or Learmonth's cat, get out.

Mabs seemed startled when she saw him standing there.

'Not at the gallery?' he said, but his throat was so dry the words hardly came out.

'What?'

She sounded in a bad mood, suddenly. The children had stopped playing, and were ogling him.

'I thought you might be at your gallery,' he repeated.

She shrugged. 'No point in opening before Easter. No customers.'

And with what Learmonth was reputed to be earning, no pressure to find any. She could play at being a businesswoman. He dug his nails into his palms. *Stop it, Tom. It's hardly her fault. She wants to be at home with her kids anyway.*

The little boy had a football, which he was rolling under his foot, a little disconsolately.

'You're looking for Fergus, I assume?' said Mabs.

'If he's not busy.'

'He is. He's working hard on getting something ready for his editor. Is it urgent?'

Tom cleared his throat again. 'You could say that.'

'I'll see if he can take a break. Do you want to come in, or will you wait here?'

'I'll wait out here, if you'll trust me with your kids.'

She pulled a face and went indoors.

The wee boy was looking at him optimistically. 'Do you play football?'

'I do.'

'Will you play with me? Daddy never does.'

Fergus emerged a few minutes later to a charming scene of bucolic joy. Tom Ellis and Eddie were having the time of their lives, kicking a ball. He swallowed the mouthful of bile that came from seeing his son having such fun with another man. And one who appeared to be super-fit, the way he was careering up and down the garden.

Jealousy was replaced by guilt. He never kicked a football around with his son; he'd always despised the game, and hoped Eddie would end up with a college blue for playing rugger.

The boy was squealing with delight, and Belle, who had gone back outdoors, was laughing. 'You mind my greenhouse, or you'll be for it.'

Ellis had his jacket off. *There it is, folded carefully over Belle's arm.* The cop's face was flushed with the exercise and the cold air. He'd loosened his tie and unbuttoned his shirt at the collar. *He has that type of blond hair that never shows grey; straight to Scandinavian silver. With those navy blue eyes, he must have been a looker when he was young. Still is. The type of man women turn their heads to watch in the street or a restaurant. He's eight years younger than me, and he's known Belle since she was the age the twins are now.* Bastard! Making spaniel's eyes at his wife all the time, and playing with his son in a way he'd never got the hang of.

Fergus couldn't keep the curtness out of his voice. 'You wanted to see me, Ellis?'

Tom dribbled the ball back to the child. 'You can play with your sister instead.'

'Girls don't play football,' said Esmée.

'Havers. Better at it than most men, the good ones. My granddaughter's the same age as you, and she's a promising player. In fact, maybe she could play with Eddie, give him some tips?'

Fergus winced as he looked at his wife's flushed, joyful face. Would she, could she, have been happy with a pedestrian chap like Tom Ellis? She'd probably have had grandchildren herself by now.

Tom glanced at Belle, abashed, retrieved his jacket and walked up the garden to where Fergus stood at the top of the back steps.

'What is it?' Fergus repeated.

'You've got a computer in your office, haven't you?'

'Naturally.'

'I wanted to show you something.'

The two men sat side by side, studying the screen.

'You reckon this is genuine?'

The detective nodded. 'That's the general consensus.'

'So how did you find them? I assume you can't possibly monitor everything on Twitter?'

'Partly by chance. My guys routinely do a bit of a hunt on anything that mentions Dumfries and Galloway.'

'Hell's teeth! "Housekeep.net". What's all that about?'

'Housekeeping, apparently. Now read the older ones.'

@Housekeep.net #uselesscops #savilereport We have to take action because the police are fannying around doing nothing.

Tom laughed bitterly. 'Bet the guys who worked on the Yorkshire Ripper case are bloody glad Twitter hadn't been invented back then.'

@Housekeep.net #uselesscops Warrington cops investigating these paedos since 2009. Enough is enough. We cleaned it up.

'Warrington?' asked Fergus.

'Triple murder down there before Christmas. It's looking as if the victims were all paedophiles. Keep reading.'

@Housekeep.net #uselesscops #paedos We'll do your work for you from now on. We'll find them, wherever they are, and cleanse the country a little at a time.

@Housekeep.net #uselesscops #paedos We'll deal with them efficiently. Normal people shouldn't have to pay to keep human trash in prison.

@Housekeep.net #uselesscops #keystonecops You think we use Twitter or FB to make our plans? Dream on. We're always a step ahead.

@Housekeep.net #uselesscops #nonces We have branches throughout Britain. No cleaning task is too big or too small. We're watching you.

'Your IT guys must be able to track down where these are coming from?' said Fergus.

'Not as easy as that. God be with the days when all we had to do was match up print to typewriters. But you can tweet from anywhere. A phone, an iPad. Needle in a haystack. Needle in the combined haystacks of the entire UK, more like, the entire *world*, for all we know. And the price you can pick up sim cards and phones for these days, it'd not be expensive to use them then dump them.'

Tom spent a wild moment visualising his staff trawling through every electrical equipment recycling centre in the county. But you'd never use a recycling facility for that, would you? Nearest bin.

'What the hell is "Housekeep.net" anyway?'

Tom looked embarrassed. 'We can't get a handle on who they are. That's the worst of the dark net.'

'So are they some sort of secret society?'

'God knows. Vigilantes. We know about most groups, but these seem to be something different. That's the downside of starting to lose community policing. We believe there's a link with the murders in Cheshire. What we haven't a clue about is whether the same people are responsible for disappearing our local victims – if indeed they *have* met the same fate. Totally different MO, if that's the case. The only similarity is that the ones in Cheshire were lured to a meeting point. We're working on the assumption *that* case is down to vigilantes. They're doing that a lot more these days. Posing as kids in chat rooms, setting up meetings, ambushing them.'

'No more than they deserve.'

'But it's entrapment, Fergus. It means that even if we can start to put a case together, the nonce is likely to walk because the bloody vigilantes have filmed the meeting and put it on YouTube.'

'Doesn't exactly look as if the local ones were lured out in that way. You reckon that Housekeep's men or women? Certainly sounds as if it could be more than one person.'

'We're working on the assumption it's more than one.'

'I suppose you pointed out yourself, it'd be difficult to manhandle a guy the size of McPhedrie out of the house and into a vehicle single-handed. So no idea on how the House-keeping guys are recruiting members, if they're all over the country, as they claim?'

Tom shrugged. 'Not a clue. They obviously don't advertise their existence – at least, only to taunt us. You'd need to be invited to join, I imagine.' Would he join if he was asked? He would not. And yet... he couldn't bring himself to condemn anyone outright for taking child abusers off the streets.

'You still SIO on this, Ellis, even if it turns out they've been done away with?'

'Seems so.' Tom gave a half-hearted laugh. 'I suppose everyone's taken their eye off the ball in the scutterin' about to get organised for the handover to Police Scotland.'

'But you can handle it?'

'I've had the training. Went through the SIO Development Programme several years back. I'm well able to handle a Category C case. But if this gets bumped up to a Category B, no doubt some fucking graduate entrant will be brought in over my head. Sorry. Excuse my French.'

Fergus chewed the end of a pencil. 'Secret societies! The Masons still a big influence with your lot?'

'No! Never were many in this area. Though you hear stories.'

'Could never be doing with all that stuff. Grown men playing wee boys' games, dressing up and swearing stupid oaths.'

Tom grunted in reply. Jackie's father had been a Mason.

Belle went back indoors after she heard Tom leave by the front door. Her husband wasn't in his study. She stood quietly for a moment, taking in the sheer *Fergusness* of the room: the orderly bookshelves; the notebook on his desk, filled with his neat, elegant writing; the fountain pen carefully capped, lying beside it. She ran her fingers tenderly over the back of his desk chair.

She felt guilty about Tom Ellis. But she could never have made him happy. She'd have been too discontented. In those days, he didn't care about art and he didn't seem to read much. She couldn't have taken his work sufficiently *seriously*, or respected him enough. And he had deserved better than that – although it didn't sound as if he'd found it. Poor Tom!

Hearing sounds from the kitchen, she switched off the desk lamp and went in search of Fergus.

He was standing at the worktop, and the air in the room was fragrant with spice. Belle slid her arms round his waist and rested her head against his shoulder blade.

'What you up to?'

'I fancied something Thai. I'll make it mild, so the kids can have the same as us.'

'You're a marvel. What did Tom want?'

'You.'

'Don't be daft.'

'You seemed to be having great fun.' Fergus couldn't keep the bitterness out of his voice. 'Reliving old times?'

Belle sighed and moved away from him. 'I wish I'd never told you about the relationship I had with Tom. *He'd* certainly never have let on. It was so long ago. And it was nothing.'

'It wasn't nothing to him. He's soft on you.'

'*Soft* on me? What sort of antiquated expression is that, Fergus Learmonth?'

He laid down the knife he was chopping onion with, wiped his hands on a cloth and turned to face her. 'You must be aware of it. The way he looks at you like a leopard seal sizing up a penguin. I used the wrong word. He's got a *hard* spot for you.'

'Don't be crude. And you're talking nonsense. He was just happy to play with Eddie.'

'Yes, I noticed that too.'

'Well, you should play football with the poor kid.'

'I've never played football, ever.'

'If you're nursing some ambition that he'll play rugby, like you, forget it.'

'Well, all right. So I'll kick a ball around with him now and again.'

Belle was looking thoughtful. 'Maybe he should be allowed to play with Tom's granddaughter.'

Fergus snorted with laughter. 'This is the same Tom who wanted to lock you up for manslaughter a few years back? The same Tom who wanted both of us locked up, and waded in with the false accusations?'

'You seem pally enough with him these days.'

He was immediately sombre again. 'He's on the trail of some particularly nasty types. It goes to show what life's like these days, even in the wilds of Galloway. I certainly don't want the kids playing anywhere outside this garden, unless one or other of us is with them the whole time.'

'Who's over-protective now?'

'It's common sense.'

'What did Tom tell you – are there child abusers here?'

'Probably. It's everywhere nowadays, if you believe all you read. But no, he's investigating something even more sinister.'

When Fergus was a journalist, he was aware of stories about paedophiles and child abuse, but he used to think they were given too much priority. It couldn't possibly be as common or as serious as they made out. Then there had been the rumours about it at his old school, but he'd never had any of the masters, or the older boys, interfere with him in any way. He'd dismissed it, in his own mind, as attention-seeking.

But nowadays, he was as violent as any other parent at the very thought.

Belle was silent again. He tried to dismiss from his mind the idea that she was brooding over the encounter with Tom Ellis.

Tom's step was light as he walked back to his car. When he'd taken off his jacket, and Belle had held out her hand to take it, such a natural gesture, their fingers had touched, and their glances had slid together and locked. She'd looked away first.

'I wanted to say, Tom. I'm sorry about – you know. The way I treated you back then.'

And he'd replied, his voice sticking in his throat, 'Me too. It's a long time ago. You have a couple of smashing kids. You're happy, Belle?' It was the first time it had felt natural to call her that.

'Yes.' Her tone had been decisive. 'You?'

'Och, you know how it is. I could be happier. I'm *stuck*, Belle.' And he'd held her gaze again for a long moment, until the little boy had come to tug at his arm, wanting to play.

But she *remembered*. That had been the hardest thing to take, to think she had completely forgotten what had been between them, all those years ago. She *remembered*.

It should have brought him closure, whatever that was. He'd been to umpteen training courses about it over his career. How important it was for relatives of victims. The acceptance that the dead person wasn't coming back. The knowledge that the killer had got his just deserts.

He didn't feel calmer. He felt lonelier than he could ever remember feeling. He contemplated, not for the first time in recent years, whether it might feel less bleak to live alone, so that he didn't have to hide his emotions all the time.

The worst of it was: he *liked* Fergus Learmonth, in spite of everything. In different circumstances, they could have been friends.

Because marriage had changed Fergus Learmonth too, easily as much as it had Mabs. Belle. Gone was the truculent, confrontational, self-righteous man he'd tangled with nearly six years before: well, almost gone. Fergus had mellowed. Probably the success in his new career had helped. Folk said he raked in near enough half a million per book, but then they'd say anything. You could tell from the state of the house that writing paid well anyway. We'd all be mellow if we made that sort of loot.

Had *he* mellowed? *What's the opposite of 'mellow' anyway?* He'd stagnated. That was the word for it. Rotting on the vine.

TWENTY

Belle was all for opening the letter, but Fergus said that Edmund should open it himself, since it was addressed to him.

It sat on the kitchen table, burning a hole in Belle's imagination until Fergus brought the children back from school.

Esmée was clearly put out, as her brother ripped open the envelope, his father hovering at his shoulder.

'I think it says I've won a competition,' Eddie said timidly.

'What competition?' asked Belle.

'The school said we could send a photo to the Natural Scotland magazine competition. It was ages ago, when they took us to the park in Castle Douglas. We got to use one of the school cameras, and the teacher picked the best ones to send.'

'But that's wonderful, Eddie. What was in your photo?'

'Two swans.' The child was blushing with pride.

'And the school sent it in for you?' Belle was dewy-eyed with pride. 'Will we not get to see it?'

Fergus began to read the letter. 'There's a presentation ceremony. We'll see it then.'

Esmée was performing pirouettes across the room. 'I don't suppose you'll get a *real* prize.'

Eddie bit his lip, but his father slid his arm round his shoulders. 'You've won *first* prize. I'm so proud of you. And yes, madam, he does get a real prize. He's won a camera all of his own. And he gets a trip to Glasgow to collect it.'

'Can I go too?'

'We can all go, I think. Edmund Learmonth, you are a wee marvel. You're keeping up a family tradition. I won a couple of prizes for photos too.'

'I believe you were more than five.' Belle's voice was a cross between mischievous and waspish. 'I don't think these were pics of a swan either? A bird with no feathers.'

Fergus reddened. He was sure he'd hidden those pictures of Serena carefully when he'd brought them back from Edinburgh in his original flitting. 'What do you mean, Belle?'

She smiled grimly.

'I burned the lot after this pair were born. You know I did.'

'Yes, I know.' She laid her hand on his shoulder.

'I want a camera too,' said Esmée, reaching up to tug at her mother's arm.

'I want doesn't get,' said Belle.

'That's not fair!'

'We don't like whiny children in this house. It's perfectly fair.'

'If he gets one, I should get one the same.'

'Eddie did something special to earn his prize.' Belle's voice was sharp. 'When you do something special, you get prizes too. Look at the swimming certificates I framed for you to put on your wall.'

'But they're not *prizes*.'

'It's a tough life, Esmée.'

Fergus smiled to himself. He knew Belle didn't mean to spoil the girl, but he was relieved to hear the rebuke in her voice. He'd tried to tell her more than once – clumsily – that her daughter wouldn't love her any less if she didn't give in to her all the time.

And he was delighted to know that his son was also gifted 'on the creative side'. So much for teachers! He whistled softly to himself as he went back to his desk.

Fergus heard a crash outside, followed by a loud whoop. What had those damn kids done now?

He sighed, saved the chapter he was working on, and marched towards the back door, ready to administer punishment.

Belle was sitting on one of the low walls beside the steps, holding her side. He started to quicken his pace – she had hurt herself. But when she turned towards him, he could see she was helpless with laughter. Both twins were lying on the grass, giggling.

'Get up, kids,' he said brusquely. 'You'll catch chills, lying on the wet ground.'

Belle had managed to catch her breath. 'They're OK. We're all hot from running about.'

'What was that noise? It sounded like broken glass.'

'Mummy kicked the ball against the greenhouse, and it broke.'

Fergus looked at her sharply. 'You wrecked your own greenhouse?'

'Don't know my own strength. It's only one pane. It's not the end of the world.'

'She scored a goal,' said Eddie proudly.

Well, damn it! All it needed was for the Ellis creature to turn up and show off in front of her, and tell her 'girls play football too', and look at her from under his calf's eyelashes, and there was Belle, kicking a ball and making a fool of herself, and breaking things.

Esmée arrived beside him and tugged at his arm, drawing it round her shoulders.

'Don't be angry, Daddy. We were having fun.'

'I thought "girls don't play football"?'

'DI Ellis said they do. Mummy's quite good at it,' said Eddie.

Fergus felt a surge of love for his son, sticking up for his mother. But the anger was still strong. 'Obviously, if she breaks windows.'

'One pane, Fergus! I can replace it easily enough,' said Belle, disentangling Esmée from him, and drawing his arm through hers. She steered him back up the steps. 'Keep away from that bit of the garden until I get the glass picked up, kids. I'll just be a minute.'

'Tom was right,' she said, once they were indoors. 'We don't play enough games with them. They're so young!'

'Ellis said that? Bloody cheek. What business is it of his?'

'He didn't say it in so many words. But you saw how made up Eddie was to have someone play with him.'

'*Made up?*'

'Happy. Och, come on, Fergus. Don't get into a mood.'

He looked down into her smiling eyes. He knew he should be delighted that she seemed genuinely cheerful.

'You might have got hurt.'

'Nonsense. Esmée was enjoying herself too. Probably we should take the ball somewhere else next time.'

'You could get your pal *Tom* to come along.'

'Don't be childish, Fergus. Maybe we should encourage both of them to play football at school. Some team game anyway. Esmée's too competitive, in the wrong way. Though maybe that was my problem when I was younger – I wasn't competitive *enough*. I want to prevent her – prevent both of them – from making the mistakes I made. By the way,' she added casually. 'I've been pondering what you said, about Remi's name being unusual. I think possibly she changed her name. In fact, she was so evasive when I asked her about being married, I'm wondering if she was.'

He looked askance at her. *At last, she's starting to see the other side of her pal.* 'I'm going to pay her a visit tomorrow – you coming too?'

'Why on earth do you want to visit her *now*? You've never shown any interest in going before.'

'Just curious to try to learn about what she's actually up to with this permaculture fad.'

Belle looked thoughtful. 'Maybe a good idea to go on your own then. See if you can get more out of her about what she's putting in the ground, since you're so suspicious.'

TWENTY-ONE

'So how many of these beds do you have now?' asked Fergus.

'This'll be the tenth.' Remi's expression was guarded.

'I'm interested in this permaculture business. Belle's keen to start experimenting with it in our garden, so I need to know what's needed.'

She led him outside. Although her cottage was untidy, outdoors everything was as immaculate as an operating theatre. The whole length of the plot was divided into rectangular beds, each neatly edged with wood. Three of them had tunnel cloches rigged on top, and there were also two large polytunnels. Beside each of those was a large solar panel, set on a frame above a black plastic tank.

Remi laid her hand on one of the tanks. 'You'd be amazed how much power there is from the sun, even in winter. These heat water for the pipes that run through the tunnels. I need to protect the crops. This far inland, we get frost long before you do at the coast, so I need to help keep the ground warm. But the tunnels are wonderful. You can work in them all winter, fine and warm. My solar heating means I can keep them frost-free, and it doesn't cost me anything. So I don't have paraffin fumes, or the dampness you get off a paraffin stove – cause botrytis, those do. Rots the plants.'

'Seems like an excellent system,' said Fergus.

Beside the tunnel nearest the house, there were two beds that looked new plus a trench several feet deep, and apparently freshly-dug.

'And these permaculture beds, you don't have to dig them again once they're made, Belle was saying?'

'You need deep trenches to start with.'

'Sounds like a lot of work.'

'It is the first year, yes. But after that you only have to keep the weeds under control and give it a wee feed. No artificial chemicals required. No need to dig deep again.'

'What – never?'

'See that bed nearest the fence?' She pointed to the bottom of the garden. 'That's been going ten years now, and the veg off it get better and better.'

'So how deep do you need this trench?'

She gestured to the fresh one. 'Depends what you mean to grow. I go at least five feet, because we have an excellent depth of soil here, in the valley.'

'Why do you need it so deep?'

'Because I put so much organic material in it before I start, and you don't want the roots of the plants to touch that.'

'I don't think we'd manage to go that far down at Ashers. We'd probably hit the water table.'

'You only have to excavate that much if you're adding something like my special compost. Two to three feet's fine otherwise.'

'You never dig that out by hand?'

'You're joking! There's a man in the village with one of those mini-JCBs. He does it for me, and gets paid in veg and organic meat.'

'Barter economy, eh? There's a lot to be said for that.' Fergus tried hard to keep his tone jocular. 'So once you have the trench, what next?'

'Then plenty of good material in, a wee bit of topsoil, and off you go. After that, you never need to do more than hoe the top ever so gently to control weeds, and maybe give it an extra feed from time to time. But the stuff that goes into the trench first is what provides all the goodness.'

'So what *does* go in?'

'Everything under the sun. Leaf mould from the bins in my garden, and from the neighbours who don't use theirs. Kelp from whatever beach I can get it from. Well-rotted manure from the livery stable up at Drumshawes farm. Oh, and the special fertiliser Petronella Wyse from the village brings me. And a load of good topsoil on the top.'

'Petronella! Does everyone in Penreith have a fancy name then?'

'She's English. She helps me a bit with the work here. It's too much for one person once we get to spring and summer. A tremendously strong girl – you'd never think to look at her. She's only a slip of a thing, all mascara and lipstick. She freelances as a model.'

Fergus whistled through his teeth. 'More to this place than meets the eye. And this special fertiliser? What's in that then?'

Remi tapped the side of her nose. 'Och, it's scraps from restaurants, and from the butchers' shops round about.'

'Scraps?'

'Bits of meat that have gone past their sell-by date. Bones. Meat that's been left over. That sort of thing.' She twinkled at him defiantly. 'What's that look for? You pay a fortune in these greedy garden centres for a wee sack of bone meal. An absolute fortune. A tenner for a thing about the size of a bag of sugar.'

'And you get this special fertiliser cheap?'

'I get it for nothing,' she said proudly. 'In fact, I get paid a small amount for taking it. I'm doing all these local butchers and restaurants a favour. You know what the council charges to take it away? "Hazardous waste" they class it as. Did you ever hear the like? Total nonsense. Some fat man sitting at a desk in Brussels decided that. So they charge whatever comes up their backs to take it away. Thousands. Put the local shops out of business, it would. Hazardous waste, my foot. You can't beat a good layer of fertiliser to bring on vegetables in our climate.' She suddenly gave all of her attention to a loose thread on her sleeve. 'I'm not a rich woman, Fergus,' she added. 'I won't get any pension for a good few years yet. I just have the interest on a few investments.'

Fergus glanced involuntarily towards the almost-new Vauxhall Corsa parked at the side of her house.

'You need a car here. The bus service into Dumfries is a disgrace.'

This was the same woman who became almost violent if anyone suggested that she grew her vegetables for money, or because she couldn't afford to buy them.

'I'm not greedy, you know,' she added, her voice shrill. 'I give away far more than I sell. I even deliver a lot to the food bank in Dumfries. That's the problem with young children these days, no fresh veg, only the stuff from the supermarket, sprayed with who knows what poisons. And the mothers haven't a clue. So I supply plenty of fresh veg, and I've had wee booklets printed, with advice on how to cook the various items. These parents have no idea how to prepare good, wholesome food from scratch. I often spend an hour or two in there, when I've made a delivery, teaching these young mothers how to cook properly.'

Remi unfastened the doorway of the closest polytunnel. Inside, he could see vivid green growth.

'Green kale,' said Remi. 'And on the other side there's purple sprouting broccoli. Then there's Black Tuscan kale and calabrese. I'll give you some of everything that's ready.'

'Must keep you busy,' Fergus said, watching her take a lethal-looking knife from her pocket and start to harvest leaves.

'There's always plenty to do! Need to get on with sowing more winter lettuce and radicchio. And in no time at all, it'll be time to start the early peas and cabbage, then the runner and French beans.'

The vivid greens almost hurt his eyes. Unbidden, it popped into his mind that he'd read somewhere that the place where the victims of the plague in Mary King's Close were buried, under what's now Edinburgh's treasured space called The Meadows, is a particularly green and verdant spot.

'Does this fertiliser not smell bad?'

'You don't notice. It's not an enormous volume. They mince the meat and bones up first, you know. Once the seaweed and the manure's on top, you'd never smell a thing. It's quite *fresh*. A lot of the meat would probably be fine enough to eat, but they're not allowed to sell it. It's because of these stupid EU rules.'

'And you've got that in all these trenches?'

'Every one,' said Remi proudly.

'Must be a damn big butcher's then.'

'Och, it's from more than one. They go round and collect it from several – probably all over the county. But it's great stuff. I never have to add a thing other than a wee top-dressing of Growmore once in a while. The ground bones are the secret. They release the goodness slowly, so it feeds the soil for year after year.'

'And you've started new trenches already this year?'

'Just the three.'

'How do you square that with everything having to be organic or biodynamic, or whatever?' Fergus asked, so suddenly that she jumped. 'Putting meat in the trenches – you can't be *certain* where it's from.'

Remi regained her composure instantly. 'Mother Earth isn't squeamish. But she is an ace cleanser. Nothing but pure, clean nutrients reach the roots of the vegetables. She sends all the bad stuff downwards where it can't harm us.'

'Downwards?'

'Towards the core, where it's purified by fire. It's a perfect system.'

Fergus had decided that she was possibly clinically insane, but probably not dangerous. The back of his neck prickled at the thought of a dangerous person being Belle's friend.

'I'm getting a delivery for the new bed next Tuesday,' said Remi. 'But I won't plant anything in it, or these two others, until next year – or maybe a green manure crop in the summer. You need to let them settle a bit for things like potatoes and carrots – it's too hot for these otherwise; burns the roots. It gives the worms and bugs a chance to start their good work of carrying the nutrients into the soil.'

'So – the million-dollar question: how can I get some of this special fertiliser for Belle's garden?'

A faint red flush crept over Remi's throat. 'Not sure. My supplier doesn't sell to others. In any case, I'm not sure it'd do in a town garden, Fergus. It really is only suitable for out here in the sticks. Besides, you already said, you can't go down nearly deep enough.'

'I bet the environmental protection guys would have a field day if they knew, wouldn't they? I'm sure there must be a damn sight more than a few butchers' scraps involved.'

Her cheeks burned. 'I've no idea what you mean.'

'Illegal disposal of fallen stock, Remi. God alone knows what you've got in there. Diseased meat. Animals that had TB. Maybe worse.'

'Oh, nonsense. Petronella assured me it's perfectly pure.'

Fergus glared at her. 'You know what, Remi? I'd say you have enough permaculture beds now.'

He was in a fug of fury as he left the house. There was so much more to this story than some left-over bone and offal. God knows whether things like BSE could cross the barrier into veg, but who in their right mind would take the risk? And then, there were her damned 'organic' lambs and chickens. What was she feeding them?

Remi and her fixations about only drinking organic, biodynamic wine. And yet she'd risk *that*.

He pulled into the first lay-by with bins, and dumped the carefully-wrapped package of leaves. He had no qualms about Belle finding out. He intended to tell her in no uncertain terms that he was sure his suspicions about fallen stock, diseased meat, were correct. Perhaps that was where the absent husband had ended up. Maybe that was what first gave Remi the idea. Bloody hell. Maybe they'd all been eating carrots raised on Mr McGregor. Terribly Beatrix Potter. No more vegetables from *that* source were being fed to his children!

His mobile phone pinged. He glanced at the screen. Barely one bar of signal. He saw that he had several missed calls from home, and swore under his breath. It was unlike Belle to call him on the mobile, because she knew as well as anyone that the whole of Galloway was a black hole as far as the phone companies were concerned.

He checked his text messages. 'Please come home the minute you can.' It was timed more than an hour before. He revved the engine, turned the car awkwardly in the narrow road, and drove as fast as he dared towards Moniaive, where he knew he'd get a signal.

Both Belle's mobile and the landline went straight to answering machine.

He started the car again and raced back towards Kirkcudbright.

As he opened the front door, he was confronted by both twins, hand in hand, their pink, swollen faces streaked with tears. He felt his heart skip several beats, then begin to race. *Oh, God – Belle!*

'Belle!' he called, and she appeared in the kitchen doorway, then ran to him and buried her face against his shoulder. He felt the tears soak through his shirt.

'I'm so sorry,' she snivelled. 'So terribly sorry.'

'What on earth's wrong, darling?'

'It's Gorby.'

'He's dead,' wailed Esmée, rushing to her mother's side, and clinging to her legs. Edmund joined her and set up a fresh howl. Then the pug joined in.

'For God's sake,' said Fergus sternly. 'Hush, all of you, and tell me what's happened.'

'He was in the garden beside me, right as rain at lunchtime,' mumbled Belle, 'then he seemed to have some sort of fit, and fell over. I grabbed the kids and we ran with him to the vet – didn't even wait to get the car out – but they could do nothing for him. They said it was probably his heart, and that he wouldn't have suffered. In fact, they said he wouldn't have known anything about it. I'm so sorry, Fergus,' she repeated. 'I did all I could. And it's not as if he was alone. He was right beside Archie and me, and the children.'

Fergus's panic and sadness vanished under a tidal wave of relief. 'It's all right,' he said, embracing his entire family. 'He was nineteen, for God's sake. I thought something had happened to one of *you*. You're OK, the twins are OK. That's all that matters.'

That night, he bought fish and chips for supper, though no one had much appetite. He packed the twins off to bed early, then sat on the sofa with Belle on his lap. She was still weepy.

'I know you feel bad that you had to take them with you to the vet, but it's probably good for them to experience death for the first time that way, you know,' he said, stroking her hair. 'In a safe environment. They'll be more able to accept it as a natural thing. You should get an early night too,' he added as she yawned.

After she had gone upstairs, he allowed himself to shed pent-up tears. But there was also the feeling of a great weight lifted. The last living thing that carried memories of Serena was gone – not that she had genuinely cared about the cat. She'd only insisted on keeping him when they split up to spite Fergus.

He hadn't dreamt about her for more than a year. He could not summon the courage to dig a grave in the dark.

Next morning, the family, including Archie, attended the bleak little funeral ceremony.

The twins, who had been allowed to stay off school, stood silently holding hands, their eyes tear-swollen and red. Fergus felt an inappropriate glow of satisfaction: his children loved their mother's little dog, but at heart they were cat people, like him.

He had managed to dig deeply enough through the chilly earth to make a sufficiently roomy hole. Even in old age, Gorby had been a huge cat. Big-boned.

As he began to fill in the grave, Belle laid her hand on his arm. 'Hang on a moment.' She strode to the greenhouse, and returned carrying a long brown paper sack, which she tore open to reveal a sturdy-looking bare-root rose. 'It's "Peace",' she said, handing the plant carefully to Fergus. 'I know you like that one. I phoned the plant people, and they dropped it off yesterday afternoon.'

That night, Fergus woke with a start from fitful dozing. 'That's it!' he said aloud.

'What?' asked a drowsy Belle.

'Something I thought of. I'm going to work for a little while. You go back to sleep.'

Fergus had tried to following the Remi McGregor trail before, with little luck – but he wasn't so naive as to believe that everyone leaves footprints on the internet, even in this day and age. Belle said she reckoned the woman had changed her name. Needle in a haystack.

On an impulse, he searched for 'midwife sacked'. On the third page of Google results, he found her. She might have changed her name, but not her appearance. There was a newspaper photo; although grainy, it was unmistakably his wife's friend.

Her real name was Paula Garrett, and she had been a senior midwife at a hospital in Birmingham.

The case dated from 2005. Five babies and a mother had died in the hospital she worked in – they were recorded as unnecessary/unexpected deaths. It was found that she had been so set on women having natural births that she didn't summon doctors until it was too late. A panel of the Nursing & Midwifery Council found her guilty of gross misconduct, told her she had brought the profession into disrepute, and struck her off the nursing register, although they accepted that she now had 'genuine and deep remorse' over the deaths.

The formal inquiry that followed found that a 'lethal mix' of failures at the hospital had led to the unnecessary deaths. 'All showed evidence of the same problems of poor clinical competence, insufficient recognition of risk, inappropriate pursuit of normal childbirth and failures of team-working,' the chairman had concluded.

The *Express* had interviewed one of the bereaved mothers:

While most babies in the UK are born safe and healthy, such stories reflect a major problem today: substandard maternity care causing avoidable damage, even death, notably when a 'low risk' pregnancy suddenly becomes an emergency.

In these circumstances, women can be caught in the crossfire of a 'turf war' between midwives and obstetricians over which is best – natural childbirth or medicalised labour.

At its extreme, midwives have refused to refer women to clinical specialists. The report said these failures included 'a growing move among midwives to pursue normal childbirth at any cost'.

At the heart of these tragedies were 'extremely poor working relationships between midwives and obstetricians'.

The report spoke of a 'them and us' culture, with repeated instances of failure to communicate important clinical information about patients'.

Susan, one of the mothers whose baby died while she was in Garrett's care told the Express: *'Paula Garrett was on a mission to deliver my baby naturally at any cost; at one point she told another midwife I'd requested not to have an epidural anaesthetic, which was untrue. I was in agony for hours on end. At another point, a young doctor who was coming on duty offered to help but he was shooed away by Paula Garrett, who said he wasn't needed.'*

Fergus broke into a cold sweat: suppose Remi had persuaded Belle to hang on, and not have a C-section? Thank God his wife had been in the hands of professionals. He sat for a long time, deep in thought: should he tell her what he'd discovered about her friend?

To take his mind off that, he started to search for Ruaraidh Cruikshank, who had been his best man first time around the marriage carousel. He trawled LinkedIn, Companies House, and then Facebook, to make sure he had the right man. Ruaraidh was indeed alive, with an address in Musselburgh (but that'd be a business address). He was a director of twelve companies. Fergus smiled to himself. His grandmother would have approved of such a trajectory much more strongly than of the one he himself had taken.

Maybe next time he was in town, he should look him up. Or maybe not. He'd lay money on it that his former friend had transmogrified into one of those tweedy, ruddy-nosed types Belle loathed. He'd have a flashy car (Volvos were never flashy: they were *safe*), and a holiday home in Madeira, and be on his third, ultra-high-maintenance wife. He'd belong to the most exclusive golf clubs (but rarely play golf). He'd have turned into the type of man at whom Sandy McCall Smith poked gentle fun in his novels.

He switched off the iMac and went back to bed.

TWENTY-TWO

Fergus was conscious of the fact that it was difficult to hide a large silver car in a small village, but he decided to trust to luck. At half past one, a dark red transit van with 'B Forsyth, Handyman' on the side, and a ladder on the roof, passed him, slowed, and pulled into Remi's driveway. The type of vehicle that doesn't register with anyone as unusual, because it looks legitimate.

He watched as Remi and the driver and another man wheelbarrowed two loads round into the garden. It took barely ten minutes to unload it.

While he watched, he turned the details of Ellis's cases over in his mind. They'd all been straightforward missing person cases – in every one, a person who had good reason not to be found. He'd wondered, at first, if that's what they were dealing with, and Ellis was wide of the mark.

What didn't compute was how completely they'd managed to vanish. Ellis had confirmed none of the three had accessed any bank account the police were aware of, since they were last seen. All three had left their passports behind, and their cars. No one had noticed a strange car in the area.

When the tradesman's van pulled back onto the road, he followed at a safe distance. Not far past Moniaive, it turned off onto a narrow, unmarked side road. He pulled in, not wanting to find himself heading into a dead-end where he'd be trapped. There were two of them, after all, and if they were up to the nefarious business he suspected, then he didn't fancy facing them single-handed. He noted down the GPS coordinates.

The next afternoon, he was back in Penreith. He cruised slowly along the village street, scanning house-fronts and shop-fronts for CCTV cameras. The Spar shop had a camera discreetly placed above its front door. He'd find out what he could about that, then mention it to Ellis, once he'd had a dekko at whatever was up that track.

After all, if he hadn't found the private camera on the back road out of Kirkcudbright six years before, the police might have managed to nail his wife on a charge of manslaughter. They'd never have unravelled the strange story of Roddy McCulloch's sister, Alison, moving his body from the garden cottage at Ashers, and dumping it in woodland. He frowned. Why the hell was he helping the inept cop who had tried to pin Roddy's death on Belle? In the end, Alison hadn't even been charged, because moving a body turned out not to be a criminal offence, and according to what he'd been able to glean afterwards, the powers-that-be hadn't felt it was in the public interest to charge her with failing to report a death, given her poor mental health. At least she'd left the area altogether soon afterwards. One less weirdo.

Fergus waited patiently in the queue in Spar, then asked casually about the CCTV camera. He made up complicated story about his wife's car having been stolen, and someone saying they'd seen it in the village. He wondered if it'd be at all possible to view the video? The woman behind the counter laughed.

'There's no card in it. The bobbies were doing one of their crime prevention drives a couple of years ago, and they advised us to put one of those up. You can get them for a couple of quid online. It's a dummy. So what kind of car is it?'

'What?'

'Your wife's car.'

'A dark green Audi quattro.'

She shrugged. 'Not seen anything like that.'

Unwise to raise suspicion by asking her anything more. So he strode casually up the street until he met an elderly man hobbling towards him.

'You look as if you know this area well?'

'I'd hope so. I lived here all my life, man and boy.'

'There's a track off the main road a mile and a half in that direction. Two stone gateposts, but no gate on it. I was wondering what's up there?'

'Why do ye want tae ken that?'

'I heard there's some interesting Andy Goldsworthy sculptures near here, and they're up a wee side road.'

'Och them! Sculptures! A rickle o' stanes. That road's signposted. About four miles up yonder.' He gestured with his walking stick.

'So what's on that other road I noticed?'

'Naething ava'.'

'Really? It looks as if it's been a tarred road.'

'Aye, maybe once upon a time it was. Ye're meaning the road up tae the auld slaughterhoose. Shut doon since the '60s. A' these EU rules, tellin' us whaur we could and couldna kill oor beasts.' He spat on the ground. 'Naebody gaes up there noo.'

No use reminding people like him that Britain didn't even join the EU until 1973, and the animal welfare and food hygiene regulations didn't come in until later again.

Fergus thanked him and almost sprinted back to the car. *A fucking abattoir!* He was right with his suspicions about what that bitch was putting in her damn permaculture beds. He'd lay money on it. And God alone knew where else it went. He'd already been an investigative journalist when the BSE scare hit the headlines in the late '80s. And look how easily that had got into the food chain!

The building reeked of death. Fergus drew a deep breath. *What else can you expect of an abattoir, even one that has been abandoned for more than thirty years?* Impossible to imagine that any of the animals slaughtered here met a peaceful end, or a mercifully quick one. No soothing music for them; no serpentine ramp to hide the horror that lay ahead until the last moment. The brutishness of the place seeped from the very walls.

He swung the torch beam across the sand-strewn floor, noting the area of deep staining that formed a rough rectangle in the centre. The light bounced off the polished stainless steel contraption positioned at its inner edge. He knew at once what it was. You couldn't call it a mincer: a bone-grinder. The sort you'd find on a less-than-salubrious pig farm. Newish, by the looks of it. And recently cleaned. He sniffed. No smell of bleach. Possibly clued-up enough to have used hydrogen peroxide. But there was no sign of a generator, so how the hell...?

He flicked the nearest grubby metal light-switch, and the three fluorescent tubes overhead began to judder into life. He threw the switch again, quickly. The power was connected, after all this time? Weirder and weirder.

He returned his attention to the stain. He didn't doubt for a moment that it was blood. Relatively fresh. So all his suspicions had been correct. 'A bit of butchers' waste,' that witch Remi, had purred a few days ago, as she told him about her 'special compost'. 'Same as the blood and bone meal you buy in the garden centre, but a bit fresher. And a damn sight cheaper. In fact...' She had tailed off. 'At least I know what I'm getting.'

Butchers' waste be damned. Far too much blood for that. Diseased animals, without a shadow of doubt. Such things went on; he knew that. Cash-strapped farmers will always bend the rules.

Thinking of where the detritus had *gone* made his stomach heave. For a moment, he thought he'd vomit. But Fergus had a strong stomach. He'd faced worse than this, in his days as a journalist. DI Joyce Maxwell faced worse on a weekly basis.

Remi *must* have known, or at least suspected.

He shook himself, took a step backwards and angled the powerful light toward the rough stonework of the outer walls. Something glinted against the sand. He strode across, bent and picked it up, examined it in the torchlight, then dropped it again quickly, swearing under his breath. *AMcP*. The last thing he'd expected, although – he could admit it to himself now – the thing he'd feared.

He gripped the torch under his arm and stretched a tentative vinyl-gloved hand to pick up the object once more, reaching his free hand into his pocket for a plastic bag. Not a good idea. He placed the cufflink, shaped like a football, back on the ground exactly where he'd first spotted it.

The hair on the back of his neck prickled; he felt he was being watched.

This is where it happened. He knew as clearly as if he'd seen the executions take place.

He left the building swiftly, fumbling to snap the hefty padlock closed. Another blast of wind reverberated against the rusty metal wall-panels, making him jump. *Pull yourself together, man! It takes more than this to spook Fergus Learmonth.* He'd never been afraid of standing up to thugs and blackguards more or less single-handedly, in his former persona (though there had usually been a cameraman and a sound engineer twenty paces behind him, and he'd been ten years younger then).

The dying rays of weak sunlight vanished abruptly behind a cloud. He almost sprinted towards the car, cursing himself for having parked it at the outer edge of the vacant ground, though glad he'd had the foresight to park on gravel, not on the churned mud closer to the building, where it would have left tracks, and to turn it, ready for the return journey.

As he reached the Volvo, he was almost calm again. At the last moment, he peeled off the blue vinyl gloves and overshoes, dropping them into the supermarket bag he'd left open on the passenger seat. He patted his pocket to check that he'd remembered to put back the set of skeleton keys he'd blagged from a contact in Lothian and Borders Fire Service when he was with Albion TV. Forcing himself to breathe steadily, he replaced the heavy, rubber-cased torch under the driver's seat, and secured its Velcro strap. He remembered to record the precise location on the GPS device that was a permanent fixture on the dashboard.

He pulled out onto the dirt track, relieved to hear the automatic door locks snap. Usually, the sound irritated him, and caused him to mutter darkly about health and safety gone berserk. But the main reason for sticking with Volvo (he could, if the notion had appealed, have afforded a much flashier marque) was its reputation for safety. That was what counted most, now that he had a family.

On the way up, a red kite had been hovering a mere ten feet above the tarmac, its russet-barred wings illuminated by the late sun, and he'd thought how much the twins would have loved to see it. They'd have demanded that he stop, and had the doors open, silent as mice, their field glasses trained on the bird, to see if it was ringed.

Until he was well into his fifties, the word had meant little to him. 'Family' denoted the past. Now it was the most important thing in Fergus's world. It was both the present and the future. He was fired up with fresh determination to extricate his wife and children from Remi's malevolent influence.

Why the hell would they have built an abattoir here? I suppose it was easy for the farmers from all around to bring their beasts. But how would you ever have got trucks up this road? Even a trailer would be difficult. Maybe they drove the animals on foot, the way they did in the old days.

As he'd driven towards the abandoned building half an hour earlier, tinkering with the visor, trying unsuccessfully to keep the low winter sun out of his eyes, the track had seemed endless, particularly after the grass-split tarmac had petered out and the space had become too narrow to turn the car. With the evening mirk closing in, the slope on the right-hand side seemed even more precipitous now, the post-and-wire fence collapsed along most of its length even more frail. The nearside bank was a jungle of scrubby bushes and brambles. *Hell's teeth!* It would be irritating to scratch the car's immaculate silver bodywork, but even worse: Belle would laugh at him if that happened. He drove as fast as he dared, seatbelt unfastened, leaning forward, straining to spot the worst potholes before he was upon them, foot hovering over the brake.

The landscape seemed unfamiliar, not only because darkness was falling, but because everything was changed now. What his wife's bosom friend was mixed up in had segued from sordid into seriously criminal. Perhaps she was even a member of this 'Housekeeping' group? And although he didn't entirely disagree with her reasoning on that, he'd do everything in his power to prevent Belle being drawn into something so dangerous by association, however peripheral.

Despite wearing a cashmere sweater and a thick coat, Fergus was shivering. On the open moorland, the wind cut like a knife. He fired up the car's heater and glanced at the hillside opposite. Not a single house-light to be seen. Not one sign of civilisation, apart from the standing stones outlined against the bitter lemon afterglow (so cold, compared to the amber of high summer). What a bloody awful place this would be to breakdown.

A lone sunbeam burst from below the cloud, making the scene even more desolate; a quilt of mist had settled on the floor of the valley below. An anaemic gibbous moon already hung in the sky.

Fergus was not easily spooked, but he was spooked now. This entire countryside gave him the willies, especially at the time of year when the sun – such of it as you'd see – was white rather than golden, and sent no heat that far north. 'Scotland's Riviera', the tourist brochures said, backing up the claim with photos of the palm trees in the Logan Botanic Garden. *Fuck that!*

Then, quite suddenly, the deeply-rutted mud surface gave way to gravel, then to the grass-crowned tarred road. Less than half a mile to the B735.

He sighed with relief as he turned onto a road with a solid surface and a number, and a signpost announcing that Moniaive was a mere five miles away. And what next? He cursed himself inwardly for getting involved in this to begin with, succumbing yet again to the blandishments of an out-of-his-depth cop. Yes, helping out with the odd bit of work on missing persons cases, as he'd done since his TV days, played to his strengths. It also helped give an immediacy to his writing.

But he wanted nothing to do with what had happened here. It wasn't as if the victims hadn't deserved it, after all. He'd walk away, ignore it. Yet what *would* DI Maxwell have done? She'd never condone the idea of summary justice.

Fergus reached a decision: he'd phone the police as soon as he reached someplace with a mobile signal.

In his mind's eye, he could see the small gold bauble he had picked up and laid down again: half of a cufflink, in the shape of a football, with the initials AMcP engraved in the centre. It must have rolled to the side of the floor where they didn't spot it – though that was strange, since they'd taken so much trouble to clean everything up. Perhaps it was all a deliberate part of their plan to torment the police, along the same lines as the tweets from Housekeep.net.

In Moniaive, he pulled up and glanced at his phone. Three bars of signal. He only got better at home because he'd ranted at the mobile company so long that they gave him a free booster box; he got five bars in the house, little more than one if he walked to the bottom of the garden.

He found Tom Ellis's private number in his contacts list. His finger hovered over the call button.

No. He'd go to see him instead.

Then he pictured Belle and the twins in the tawny light of the kitchen at home. She'd be bustling back and forth to the stove, getting dinner ready, and the twins would have heads bent over their homework. They were the most precious things in his world, and there was nothing he wouldn't do to protect them.

One thing Fergus was sure of: his skill in assessing who was capable of the ultimate violence. It's what had kept him safe when he worked at tracking down crooks and scammers. What had kept him *alive*, damn it!

But the people who had done this: they weren't admirable people. They probably weren't people who gave a damn about family. Not if something threatened their own safety.

And they could be anyone, from anywhere. He'd crossed the paths of enough thugs and villains to know that the stereotype of the shaven-headed, bull-necked, tattooed lout could be 180 degrees out of kilter. They probably looked and acted absolutely normal. They could be local. They could be any man he passed in the street in Dumfries, or even Kirkcudbright. Killers. They could be watching him right now, through binoculars. Ruthless. The most dangerous type, vigilantes, because they had what they perceived as a high moral code, but that wouldn't extend to clemency for anyone who got in their way. They could even hurt Belle or the twins.

And the people who'd been despatched at the abattoir –

what did it matter, in the end? Human trash. They'd got nothing more than natural justice. Like as not they'd have been done away with in prison anyway. You heard about that a lot these days, paedophiles, child porn merchants, found dead in their cells, and few questions asked. And he was as certain as he could be that Remi, much as he loathed her, had no inkling of what she had *actually* been burying in her permaculture trenches.

It doesn't do to dig too deep.

And, in any case, why should he do the police's job for them?

'It's none of my business,' he muttered to himself. 'And Ellis is hardly my friend anyway, the way he looks at my Belle like a collie eyeing up a lamb chop.'

He owed Tom Ellis nothing, nothing at all.

He felt a brief sting of professional shame: there had never been a missing person case yet where he drew a complete blank. It went against the grain to pretend he had failed this time.

And yet, and yet... *you can't have everyone and his Rottweiler running around taking the law into his own hands.*

Wearing a fresh pair of vinyl gloves, and with his scarf pulled over his nose and mouth, he tore a fresh sheet from near the back of his notebook, holding it up to the car's reading light to ensure there was no trace of impression from his earlier writing. He printed the GPS coordinates on it in black biro, then, as an afterthought, added the number-plate of the van he'd followed. If the trail led back to Remi, so be it. After contemplating what he'd written for a moment, he crumpled the sheet of paper into his pocket and selected a fresh one, subjecting it to the same scrutiny before printing only the identifying coordinates on it. Let the police do some detecting, for a change. He selected one of the plain white envelopes he always kept in the glovebox, addressed it to DI Tom Ellis, peeled the paper strip and sealed it. He applied a self-adhesive stamp from the book in his wallet.

Instead of going home by the most direct route, he veered through the suburbs of Dumfries until he found a postbox.

Once he was back on the outskirts of Kirkcudbright, he dialled Ellis's private mobile number.

'Sorry, Ellis,' he said, 'I've drawn a total blank. There's not a lot more I can do to help. But I'd say you're right to be treating this as a murder enquiry. I suggest that whoever's covering for the perpetrator will get cold feet, because of the publicity.'

By the time he was home, he had reached another decision. No more nonsense from Belle about Edinburgh being dangerous. They were moving, whether she liked it or not. He'd be more assertive. He was the man of the family after all. It was his duty to protect them.

TWENTY-THREE

In the days since Gorby died, Fergus had watched Belle's pug sniffing disconsolately at the hearthrug where the cat used to lie. The twins were still pink-eyed.

It would be no disrespect to his pet to get another cat. In fact, it was the greatest compliment he could pay Gorby.

He went into the study and fired up his computer. When he'd originally got Gorby, he'd been told he was a Norwegian Forest Cat cross. He'd always believed that the cat's intelligence and companionable nature were due to that breeding – not to mention his size.

A quick search on the internet, a phone conversation, and a few hours later he'd returned from a mysterious errand to a cat-breeder in Gretna.

'One each?' asked Belle, amused.

The twins had spent the past hour crawling around the floor playing with the kittens, one pure black, the other white.

'Did you not get one for yourself?' she added.

'They were the last two left from a litter,' said Fergus, a little shamefaced. 'I could hardly take one and leave the other. The breeder said they need to be kept contained, or they'll wander off to hunt. I suppose they might get stolen too, if they got out. I think I'll need to make the garden even more secure, because these wee buggers will soon be climbing in a way Gorby never did.'

Esmée looked up from petting the black kitten, which she had decided was hers. 'Daddy said a bad word.'

Belle laughed. 'Daddy used to say a lot more bad words, before you two came along. He's a well-behaved Daddy these days. You do realise, Mr Learmonth, this probably puts the kybosh on Bruntsfield visits for a while?'

Fergus looked at her questioningly.

'We can't leave the kittens to just *anyone*'s tender mercies. We'll need to organise the sitter well in advance, and make sure she knows how to look after them. She'll need to come here and meet them.'

Belle seldom interrupted Fergus when he was working. But that afternoon, she couldn't help herself. Too long to wait till he finished for the day.

As soon as the twins had gone back to school after lunch, she followed him through.

'Fergus?'

'Yes, sweetheart?'

'I know you've been doing some research on Rose.'

He reddened slightly, but didn't deny it.

'How long were they married before I was adopted?'

'A little over three years.'

'OK. Thanks.'

'Why?'

'Just curious.'

'Do you want to know more about her?'

'Not now. Thanks.'

'Not now or not ever?'

'Not ever, Fergus.'

She started to walk towards the door, but turned back and dropped a kiss on top of his head. He caught her hand and drew her onto his lap. 'You all right?'

She leant against him, and relaxed. 'I'm fine. I love you, you know that, don't you? Even if I sometimes bowf at you.'

She heard the chuckle rumble in his chest. He swung the desk chair round, so that they were both looking down Ashers' long garden.

'I know it,' he said. 'And do you know how much I love *you*?'

They sat like that for a long time, content, until the sunlight started to dim. Belle's memory was full of that stranger's face again; the man on the beach at Whitefarland Bay. The man in the chip shop. And she'd realised, at last, why it seemed familiar. It was echoed in her children's faces and colouring. She buried her face against Fergus's shoulder.

'You don't honestly want me to go up to town during the week?' he said.

'I thought it would be better for you. I know you miss Edinburgh.'

'But I'd miss you more. I know you love this place – it's where your roots are. It's not the end of the world if we stay longer.'

'I know. And I know your work's important to you too. You need to be where you are *happy*.'

'I *am* happy. You know I'd never leave you, Belle. I'm in it for the long haul. I don't want to be away from you for even a day.'

'I don't want that either.'

He nuzzled her ear. 'No more daft suggestions about living apart then. We're OK, aren't we, sweetheart?'

'We are. But sorry – I'm keeping you from your work.'

'It doesn't matter, Belle. This is more important. Shall we go upstairs for a while?'

She giggled. She felt young again. 'We can't! It's almost time to collect the twins.'

'Just as well I had the op,' said Fergus, kissing her neck. 'We'd probably have had triplets the next time.'

And she realised, at last, that it didn't matter where they lived, as long as she was with *this* man, and their children. Ashers was simply a house, after all. Her home would be wherever *they* were. The past could only hurt her if she let it. Look forward, not back. That would be her motto now.

She tried to stand up to leave, but he caught her round the waist and drew her back onto his lap.

'Next time you happen to be speaking to Remi, you could reinforce the idea that she should quit this permaculture lark now,' he said.

'She won't listen to me!'

'Then make her. It's for her own good, Belle. She wouldn't want the police nosing around to see what's buried there.'

'The *police*?'

He nodded.

'So it *is* diseased animals?'

Fergus nodded, but didn't look her in the eye. 'You could say that.'

'Och, what a fuss about nothing. I'll tell her though. I wonder what the farmers'll do then?'

'They'll have to find another solution, won't they? And Belle – no more vegetables from her place.'

'Why ever not? They're delicious. You said yourself you'd never tasted the likes of them.'

'Just because. Promise.'

'Only if you explain why.'

He kissed her neck. 'Because I say so.'

'You haven't said anything to her?'

'About what?'

'Your suspicions.'

'No, why?'

'She was talking the other day about moving to Portugal. Says it's a better climate for horticulture, and she'd be able to buy a lot more land there, with the price she'd get for the cottage.'

Fergus restrained himself from giving the air a victory punch. After all, the woman was Belle's friend. Hopefully 'was' would soon be the operative word, if this were true. 'Sounds like a plan.'

As soon as his wife had left the room, he fired up his laptop once more. He found the file where he had stored his research on Rose Mountjoy, and punched the delete key. This wasn't some intriguing case he was working on, or the plot for a novel. Briony had been right all along. Best leave it alone. This was Belle's business, not his, and if she was happy not to pursue it, that was her right.

He rose, hearing the sharp sound of the door-knocker striking its brass plate.

Fergus regarded Tom Ellis calmly, although he knew he had a twinkle in his eye. 'Me? No – why would you think that?'

'Well, *someone* sent me a note of where we'd start to find the trail of evidence. We'd never have found the place otherwise. The only person I can think of who's smart enough to have found it is one Fergus Learmonth.'

Fergus smiled grimly. 'Have you found your criminals then?'

Tom looked askance at him. 'I thought you might ask if we've found the missing persons?'

'I'm not at all sure you'll ever find them.'

'You know what's happened to them?'

'So do you, I imagine.'

'I suspect you know a lot more about it than you've told me. I suspect you have some idea of where they've been put.'

'Me? I know nothing, my friend. I drew a blank, same as you chaps, by the sound of it.'

'Did you get inside the building?'

Fergus assumed an expression of exaggerated innocence. 'Me? How could I have got inside? It was securely locked.'

Tom grinned. 'I could bring you in for questioning.'

'It wouldn't do you any good. I don't know any more than I've told you.'

The detective placed the carrier bag he was carrying beside Fergus's chair. 'Peace offering. And a way of saying thanks.'

The sight of the familiar green and black boxes brought a smile to Fergus's face. Fifteen-year-old Springbank. And two bottles! Very acceptable. His resolve not to spill any more beans evaporated.

'I'll tell you how I found that place. I simply took a wrong turning. I was looking for these stone arch sculptures,' he said. 'When I saw the building, I had a hunch, based on something I'd heard on the grapevine. I put two and two together and made five. You're the one who said my mind works differently from normal people's.'

'Sculptures!' said Tom. 'But they're miles away, nearer Moniaive. So tell me more about this grapevine. You must have got a tip-off. Who from?'

'You know I can't tell you that!' Fergus opened his wallet and drew out the press card he still carried. He waved it in front of Tom. 'And you know you can't make me. It wouldn't help you get any nearer the people you're looking for in any case. Surely you've found more than enough clues?'

Tom grimaced as he settled back against the soft cushions. 'We're following a couple of leads. Come on, Learmonth. Tell me where you reckon they were disposed of.'

'I can say hand on heart I don't *know*.'

'But you suspect?'

'That's a different thing entirely. Damn it, man, you must have a good idea of what was done there.'

Tom almost smiled. 'So you might give me a hand again, if I ran into another case involving a missing person?'

'I might. But don't you dare put the word around that I helped with this. I have my family to think of. Besides, I suspect we might be moving to Edinburgh soon.'

'Edinburgh isn't so far.'

'I suppose not.' Fergus rose and approached the sideboard. He took out the opened Springbank bottle. 'Dram?' he asked.

As he walked to his mother's house, Tom Ellis faced a painful realisation: it was *because* of Fergus Learmonth that Mabs was so radiant and contented. He hadn't been able to make her happy when they were in their twenties – well, only in one way – and he could not have made her happy now.

He knew there was just one thing to do: come to terms with that reality. Throw himself one hundred and ten per cent into his job, into tying up this case, and making a final stab at getting the promotion he'd dreamed of. That would have to suffice.

Meantime, once he got home he'd have another dram from the bottle of Springbank he'd bought for himself in Dumfries's only wine merchant's. They'd given him a special deal on the three.

He'd celebrate having reached the decision that work was the way out for him. *Better to light one candle than to curse the darkness*. Where had he read that?

TWENTY-FOUR

Galloway News 8th February, 2013

Dumfries and Galloway Police are seeking information on 58-year-old Charles Keddie of Kirtlemuir, who has been reported missing from his home.

'We have concerns for Mr Keddie's safety,' said DS Rachel Field. 'He does not appear to have driven anywhere, since his car is parked at his residence. Nor do we have any record of his having travelled by public transport. I would urge anyone who believes they may have seen Mr Keddie in the past two days to contact the police hotline on 0800 333 999.'

Locals say Mr Keddie has lived in the area for around three years. They believe he moved up from England. He lived alone, and helped with the local cub group.

The Herald 13th February 2013

Police have arrested two men close to an abandoned abattoir building near Penreith in Dumfriesshire.

The men, believed to be brothers, were driving a van that was found to have a body, wrapped in plastic, in the back.

'As a result of a lengthy surveillance exercise, at 2300 hours yesterday, 12th February, officers from Dumfries and Galloway police apprehended two men driving a vehicle which contained the body of a male. Paramedics were called, but life was pronounced extinct at the scene,' said DI Tom Ellis of the local force – due to become part of the new Police Scotland in just over two weeks' time.

DI Ellis refused to comment on local speculation that the body was that of Charles Keddie (58) of Kirtlemuir, who was reported missing from his home several days ago.

The Herald 18th February 2013

Police have charged two Hamilton brothers with the murder of Charles Keddie (58) of Kirtlemuir, who had been reported missing earlier this month.

Peter Gunn (50) and his brother Alfred (52) appeared in court in Dumfries and were remanded in custody. Police say they will make no further statement at this time.

The Herald 23rd March 2013

Police Scotland have revealed there is reason to believe that three people missing from Dumfries and Galloway for several months may be dead.

'We are now treating this as a murder enquiry,' Detective Inspector Tom Ellis of Police Scotland told a press conference in Dumfries.

Angus McPhedrie (43) has been missing from his luxury chalet at Colvend since mid-December 2012. Winston Bisset (58) and his wife Carol (57) disappeared from their converted farmhouse near Thornhill around Christmas.

'We are still anxious to speak to anyone who saw Mr McPhedrie after 15th December, or Mr and Mrs Bisset after 25th December,' added DI Ellis.

He would not comment on whether the bodies of any of the missing persons have been found, or if the police are treating the cases as linked.

'Our enquiries are ongoing, and we are following several positive leads,' he said. He was willing to confirm that the police believe that all three met their deaths at the hands of third parties.

Asked whether it was true that police suspect the deaths may be linked to a triple murder in Warrington, Lancashire, in December 2012, DI Ellis would only say that this was one line of enquiry being actively pursued.

'We are working closely with police forces elsewhere in the UK, to ascertain if these cases are connected,' he added.

The three Warrington victims have been named as David Black (48), Philip Scott (50) and Hamid Shah (39). Local media have reported that the three men have been linked to a paedophile ring operating in the north-west of England.

Former footballer Angus McPhedrie, who played briefly for Liverpool City Football Club before moving to Plymouth United, is understood to have owned a property in Warrington.

The Bissets, both retired teachers, moved to Dumfriesshire

from Manchester in 2010.

DI Ellis refused to confirm rumours that the disappearances are being linked to brothers Peter and Alfred Gunn, who were charged last month with the murder of 58-year-old Charles Keddie of Kirtlemuir, Dumfriesshire.

Inverness Courier 12th July 2013

Police are asking the public's help in finding a retired priest who has been missing from his home in Culloden since May.

Father Jack Smart (70) was a parish priest in the east end of Glasgow for more than twenty years, before moving to a parish on Skye in 1999. He retired to Culloden in 2004.

Local searches have so far failed to find any trace of Father Smart, who was last seen on 15th May.

The police are appealing to anyone who has seen him since that date, or knows of his present whereabouts, to get in touch with them.

Bathgate Herald 13th September 2013

Police Scotland have launched a fresh appeal for information on the whereabouts of Alexander Goudie (68), who has been missing from his home in Bathgate since late August.

Despite extensive searches, no trace of the retired electrician, who also served as a scout-master for many years, has been found. It is understood that he lived alone, after being divorced in 2001.

'We are extremely concerned for Mr Goudie's safety,' said DI Angela Milne. 'I would ask any member of the public who has seen him since 28th August this year to contact us on 121.'

The Scotsman 10th December 2013

Chief Constable Robbie McKnight, head of Police Scotland, has refuted the claims made in a recent report, that the police are increasingly using self-styled 'Paedophile-hunters' to track down men and women accused of child abuse crimes.

'It is always extremely useful to have input from the public on the whereabouts of alleged sex offenders – or indeed any offenders – we are seeking to trace. Offenders of that type are often extremely adept at covering their tracks. However, there are no circumstances in which Police Scotland can condone vigilante behaviour. It is essential that those accused of crimes are given the opportunity to defend themselves, and the State to put its case. Due process of law must be allowed to take its course. It is not for the private citizen to attempt to take the law into his or her hands. Anyone found guilty of inflicting bodily harm on an alleged paedophile will be treated like any other violent criminal. We will not tolerate the law of the mob in this country,' stressed Mr McKnight. 'Nor do we condone the illicit use of entrapment. These vigilantes risk allowing the guilty to go free, by posting videos of alleged paedophiles online, before we can gather valid evidence to bring cases to court. They are compromising our work, and thus perverting the course of justice.

'I recognise that the police are not winning this argument, because of the biased reporting in the tabloid press and on social media. However, as keepers of the law, we have no option but to obey the law of the land, and its due process.'

The report – collated by Justice for All – alleges that use of semi-professional 'paedophile-hunters' by police forces throughout the UK has risen by fifty per cent in the last two years, in the wake of such high-profile cases as Jimmy Savile, and the Rochdale and Rotherham child abuse scandals.

Many of the paedophile-hunters set up false identities as children in chat rooms, and use these to lure alleged paedophiles to meetings in public places, where they film them.

The Herald 10th February 2014

Two men and a woman have been sentenced to life imprisonment at the High Court in Glasgow for the murder of Angus McPhedrie (43), Winston Bisset (58) and Carol Bissett (57), and Charles Keddie (58), in Dumfriesshire more than a year ago.

Peter Gunn (50), his brother Alfred Gunn (52), of Hamilton, and Petronella Wyse (29) of Penreith, Dumfriesshire, all pleaded guilty to the murders.

Calling themselves 'Housekeeping.net', the trio had earlier taunted Police Scotland by using Twitter to state that 'Housekeeping' had a duty to remove child abusers from society, since the police seemed incapable of catching paedophiles and the courts of sentencing them appropriately.

The Gunn brothers, who come from Hamilton, were apprehended in February, 2013, after a tip-off had led to a surveillance operation at a remote abandoned abattoir close to the village of Penreith, Dumfriesshire. The body of Mr Keddie was found in the van they were driving.

Wyse was arrested shortly afterwards at a friend's home in Dumfries.

Sources close to Police Scotland have already confirmed that all the victims had been involved in the same paedophile ring as the three men found dead in Warrington in December 2012.

McPhedrie, a retired footballer, had been involved in recent years in training junior footballers in his home town of Lymm, Cheshire. The Bissets had both been teachers in a school in Lancashire before being given early retirement some years ago.

Citing the *'Giving Victims a Voice'* report, published in January 2013, plus the high-profile child abuse scandals in Rochdale and Rotherham, a spokesman for the Gunn brothers told reporters outside the court that it was clear that the police were doing nothing to reduce the incidence of sexual abuse of children. 'It is obvious that well-organised paedophile rings are continuing to operate with impunity,' he said. 'The police and the courts – those with an official duty to protect children – appear to be powerless to track down and punish these people, particularly the ones who use high-profile positions in show business, sport, the church and the schools to abuse children. The police are failing our children, time after time.'

He added that the Gunns and Wyse did not regret the murders. 'They are proud of the fact that they have prevented four abusers from damaging more children,' he stated. 'Although their work cannot continue for the time being, the work of the Housekeeping network will continue. There are plenty of branches all over the country, staffed by volunteers ready and willing to remove paedophiles from our towns and villages. It'll be of little help to the police to study how the branches operating in SW Scotland, and the ones in Cheshire, carried out cleansing operations. Each and every branch of Housekeeping has its own personnel, its own targets and its own methods,' he said. 'The work will continue as long as these predators are walking our streets. The human trash Housekeeping disposes of are not victims. The children they have preyed upon are the victims.'

The Gunn brothers and Wyse were all raised in Smythson's Children's Home in Bury, Lancashire.

Also speaking outside the court, Detective Chief Inspector Tom Ellis, of Police Scotland, said, 'This case is unusual, in that the remains of three of the victims have not been recovered, although traces of their DNA were found in a vehicle registered to Peter Gunn. However, it is not without precedent that a murder charge should be brought successfully in the absence of a body.'

The three convicted killers have refused to reveal how and where they disposed of the bodies of Mr McPhedrie and the Bissets. Despite the use of specially-trained dogs and LIDAR ground-penetrating radar, the police admit that they are no closer to finding the remains of the victims.

'Police Scotland found ample evidence that the deceased had been moved to a derelict former agricultural building in rural Dumfriesshire,' confirmed DCI Ellis. 'Our enquiries are ongoing, and we are confident that we will eventually discover where the remains have been disposed of, so that we can bring closure to the families of the victims. I would urge any member of the public who has any information on this to come forward.

'The hardest part of our job is having to tell relatives we have not found their loved one,' continued DCI Ellis. 'We have not given up the search for the remains of these victims. That aspect of the case remains open.'

DCI Ellis confirmed that Police Scotland are co-operating with other forces all over the UK and also in Europe, to ascertain if there may be links to the disappearance of known sex offenders elsewhere, or to other cases of long-term missing persons.

Mr and Mrs Bisset's daughter, Mrs Ilona Boston, was in

court to hear sentence passed. She declined to make any comment to the media.

Belle Learmonth hurriedly finished brushing her hair, and headed for the stairs. If she didn't get a move on, she'd be late for work. She and Claire Cochran took it in turns to open their shop in Frederick Street, and today was her turn. Customers tended to arrive on the dot of ten since they'd opened the coffee nook, and it didn't do to let them down. She loved her walk to the shop; no need to go anywhere near the seething crowds on Princes Street. And their customers tended to be local people rather than tourists.

Going into partnership with Claire had changed her world, in more ways than one. They rarely differed over what they should stock, and since Claire was a mere three years her junior, it felt almost like having a younger sister. Once, near the start of their friendship, Belle had asked her if she'd known Serena. 'Yeees,' had been the guarded reply.

'Was she as beautiful as in the photos?'

Claire had been aghast. 'Fergus never showed you *photos* of her?'

'He didn't actually *show* me. But I've seen some.'

The younger woman pursed her lips. 'She wasn't beautiful at all. Too vain and self-important. She was always making eyes at Nick, and you know what men are: he'd not hear a word against her. I detested Serena. I wouldn't wish what happened to her on anyone, but I'll tell you the truth – when I heard she was dead, I felt relieved. Ask any of the women who knew her, I bet they'd say the same. A cold-hearted, calculating bitch. Poor

Fergus, ever getting involved with her. Everyone knew it was a mistake. He was never happy while he was with her, not for a single day. He looks twenty years younger since he met you, Belle. He looks *contented*, as well as happy.'

Belle paused briefly at the stair window, gazing lovingly down her long garden. *Rus in urbe* indeed. The countryside in the city. The best of both worlds.

Occasionally, she dreamed that she was back in Ashers, but when she wakened it was with a sense of relief, only slightly tinged with nostalgia. Because, in the end, it had never been *hers* in the way their Edinburgh home was. Since selling it, she had realised she'd always felt like an impostor, because she wasn't a Mountjoy. She was free of any obligation to hang onto the house.

She'd heard the click of the letter box, and she knew Fergus was expecting a letter from his publisher. The TV series of his second book was about to start filming, and he'd been bombarded with offers of PR engagements. Alan Jones, the literary agent who had taken over from Meera a year ago when she left to work in Mumbai, was much better at rationing those.

The anticipated letter wasn't there. Apart from a few circulars, the only mail was a postcard from Remi McGregor. Belle started to give a little shriek of surprise and pleasure, but clapped her hand over her mouth. Fergus was deep into editing, and the entire household had been padding around on silent feet; when he was in the zone, the least interruption could bring on an eruption of frustration.

When her friend had announced so precipitately more than two years ago that she was emigrating, Belle had been distressed. Fergus, on the other hand, had scarcely concealed his relief. 'So someone else can eat Mr McGregor's carrots,' he had chortled, and when she had asked him 'Why "Mr"?', and become quite angry over the fact he was back to the tired old theme of thinking Remi was a man, he had laughed even more loudly. Men! Inexplicable, the things they found funny.

She looked at the picture on the card; an attractive tiled wall in the city of Tomar, Central Portugal. 'The City of the Templars', read the caption. The message was brief. 'Weather still wonderful here. Over 30 C most days. I've had a great crop from the fruit trees, and will be able to press my own olive oil this year. Also almonds! You have no idea what they taste like, fresh from the tree. Come and visit SOON.'

Belle had a brief pang of regret, missing her friend. She propped the card on the kitchen mantelpiece, beside the photo of the twins in their smart new Edinburgh Academy uniforms. She'd remember to show it to Fergus later.

After checking that the cats and Archie had water in their bowls and were all accounted for, she rushed out, remembering to close the door quietly.

7th December, 2015, Edinburgh

'Fergus, come and see this!'

Belle's tone was so urgent that Fergus sprinted into the family room.

His wife was staring at the TV screen. 'See who that is?'

'Bloody hell – it's Ellis. What's he up to now.'

She punched some buttons on the remote control, finding pause and rewind. The news item started again.

Fergus read the subtitling and guffawed. '*Detective Superintendent Thomas Ellis, Greater Manchester Police Major Incident Team?* So he made it at last. That was a hell of a quick rise then. It can only be a couple of years since he made it to DCI, on the back of that case in Dumfriesshire. I'd have thought he'd be looking at retirement, not another step up the ladder?'

'I wonder if his wife moved down there with him?'

He looked at her sharply. 'I didn't think you knew his wife?'

'I don't. I know *of* her.'

'Miaow.'

'Tremendously glamorous and hard as nails. Not his type, I'd have thought, but there you are. They've been married nearly thirty years.'

'Why would she not have gone with him?'

'I don't think it's a text-book happy marriage.'

'Ellis poured out his troubles about his unhappy marriage to *you*?'

'Of course not. But people gossip. You know what it's like in a small place. And he admitted that's why he'd got stuck in his career, that she wouldn't move.'

'When did he tell you that? I don't remember us having a heart-to-heart with him about his wife.'

Belle busied herself with rearranging cushions. 'That day he came looking for you and he ended up playing football with Eddie. You took ages to come out and speak to him.'

'Oh well, I suppose he'll find Manchester a queer difference from rural Galloway! Some real crime there.'

Belle didn't reply.

4th August 2016

@Housekeep.net #uselesscops #paedos We're like the bristles on your chin: pluck one out and another three take its place. We're watching. Don't imagine you'll see us before we see you.

ABOUT THE AUTHOR

Fiona Cameron is a former lecturer and journalist. She was born in Glasgow, and now lives in Galloway, SW Scotland. All of her books are published by Flying Swan Press, and are available on Amazon and through booksellers.

If you enjoyed PERMACULTURE, and want to read about how Belle and Fergus met, you'll love A SENSIBLE WOMAN.

There's more of Serena and Fergus's story in WHITE CRANES DANCING, the first volume in the BALVAIG TRILOGY and THE SWAN WIDOW, the third volume.

Also by Fiona Cameron
CONTAINMENT (volume 2 of the BALVAIG TRILOGY)
BY HEART
A WAY OF KNOWING

Follow Fiona at www.fionacameronwriter.com,
or on Facebook at Fionacameronwriter
or on Twitter @fionacamwriter